ୱଡ଼୦ଵ The Traitors' Gate ୱଡ଼୦ଵ

Nineteenth-century Novels by Avi

———◄○►———

The Barn

Beyond the Western Sea
Book I: The Escape From Home
Book II: Lord Kirkle's Money

Emily Upham's Revenge: Or, How Deadwood Dick Saved
the Banker's Niece: A Massachusetts Adventure

History of Helpless Harry: To Which Is Added a Variety of
Amusing and Entertaining Adventures

The Man Who Was Poe

Punch With Judy

The True Confessions of Charlotte Doyle

———◄○►———

The Traitors' Gate

by

Avi

illustrated by Karina Raude

A RICHARD JACKSON BOOK

Atheneum Books for Young Readers

New York London Toronto Sydney

ॐ✄ॐ

For Nancy and Dick Jackson

———————◆———————

◈ ATHENEUM BOOKS FOR YOUNG READERS ◈ An imprint of Simon & Schuster Children's Publishing Division ◈ 1230 Avenue of the Americas, New York, New York 10020 ◈ This book is a work of fiction. Any references to historical events, real people, or real locales are used fictitiously. Other names, characters, places, and incidents are products of the author's imagination, and any resemblance to actual events or locales or persons, living or dead, is entirely coincidental. ◈ Text copyright © 2007 by Avi ◈ Illustrations copyright © 2007 by Karina Raude ◈ All rights reserved, including the right of reproduction in whole or in part in any form. ◈ ATHENEUM BOOKS FOR YOUNG READERS is a registered trademark of Simon & Schuster, Inc. ◈ For information about special discounts for bulk purchases, please contact Simon & Schuster Special Sales at 1-866-506-1949 or business@simonandschuster.com. ◈ The Simon & Schuster Speakers Bureau can bring authors to your live event. For more information or to book an event, contact the Simon & Schuster Speakers Bureau at 1-866-248-3049 or visit our website at www.simonspeakers.com. ◈ Also available in an Atheneum Books for Young Readers hardcover edition. ◈ Book design by Ann Bobco ◈ The text for this book is set in Adobe Caslon. ◈ The illustrations for this book are rendered in pen and ink. ◈ Manufactured in the United States of America ◈ 0810 OFF ◈ First Atheneum Books for Young Readers paperback edition September 2010 ◈ 10 9 8 7 6 5 4 3 2 1 ◈ The Library of Congress has cataloged the hardcover edition as follows: Avi, 1937– ◈ The Traitors' Gate / Avi ◈ p.   cm. ◈. "A Richard Jackson Book." ◈ Summary: When his father is arrested as a debtor in 1849 London, fourteen-year-old John Huffam must take on unexpected responsibilities, from asking a distant relative for help to determining why people are spying on him and his family. ◈ ISBN 978-0-689-85335-7 (hc) ◈ [1. Spies—Fiction. 2. Poverty—Fiction. 3. Family life—London (England)—Fiction. 4. London (England)—History—1800–1950—Fiction. 5. Great Britain—History—19th century—Fiction. 6. Mystery and detective stories.] I. Title. ◈ PZ7.A953Tqm 2007 ◈ [Fic]—dc22 2006008825 ◈ ISBN 978-0-689-85336-4 (pbk)

CONTENTS

The Traitors' Gate

LONDON,
ENGLAND;
AUGUST
1849

PROLOGUE

"Don't speak!"

"But—"

"I'm warning you, don't speak! Yer life may depend upon it!"

Midnight on the River Thames: A rowboat in which two men sit. Water stinking of dead fish, sewage, and brackish sea. Fog so clotted with coal dust that the men, though a few feet apart, cannot see each other, no more than they can see the stars in heaven or the gas lamps of London less than a quarter of a mile away.

A paddle wheeler passes by. The churning water causes the rowboat to dip and bob. The first speaker rests on his oars. But once the wheeler is gone, he leans over his oars and whispers, "River police."

"*How do you know?*"

"*It's my job to know, ain't it?*" *His voice is low and husky.*

"*Do they know we're here?*"

"*Maybe.*"

"*How could they?*"

"*Them Metropolitan Police 'ave detectives now.*"

"*A dumb lot they are, I suppose.*"

"*Think so? Then 'ere's some advice: Keep away from Chief Inspector Ratchet. You never know when 'e'll show up. All right, then, 'ow are things back where you come from?*"

"*Couldn't be worse.*"

"*And you're 'ere to even things up, right?*"

"*We're going to defend ourselves, that's all.*"

"*So you called on me for 'elp, did you?*"

"*Right.*"

"*'Ow you get my name?*"

"*A girl said you'd help me.*"

"*Then she done 'er job fine. Now listen 'ard. I'm about to provide that 'elp you want. Then I'll get you back on shore quick as winks.*"

"*Why did you bring me out here?*"

"*You paid me for information. And you're brand-new 'ere, ain't you? People won't know you. But me, I've been round this city some. So let me tell you, London 'as more eyes and ears than any city. If them Peelers see you with me, it's over. Lot safer out 'ere on the river.*"

"*What about that police boat?*"

"Just 'ope it's a coincidence."

"All right. Go on. I'm listening. What's your information?"

"It's this: There's this clerk, Wesley John Louis 'Uffam."

"Huffam?"

"If you like."

"Why, I know about him!"

"Do you? Who told you?"

"That's my business. Go on."

"If you know 'im, I guess you also know 'e works in the Naval Ordinance Office. 'E's seen the wery plans you want. And 'e's more than seen 'em. 'E's copied 'em."

"For whom?"

"Who do you think? The Royal Navy. 'Ere's the point: There's reason to think you can get the information from 'im."

"Is he willing?"

"That's the word. The man's either a fool or too clever by 'alf. But 'e's surely got what you're looking for—in 'is 'ead. The best military invention in a 'undred years. Changes everything. Better yet, 'e's let word slide that 'e's willing to sell it to the 'ighest bidder. Why? Cause 'e needs money. Needs it bad. All right, then: Apply the right squeeze and you should 'ave no trouble getting what you want out of 'im. 'E's an easy mark."

"How much time do I have?"

"What's it now, August? I'd say you got till November."

"I have someone close to the man."

"Who?"

"You have your business, I have mine."

"You talk like a real spy."

"If you're asking if I'm willing to take risks? Well, I am."

"A real gambler, ain't you?"

"A man has to survive someway, don't he?"

"Fine, but from this point on," says the rower, "you're on yer own. Understand? I don't want to see yer face, and I don't want you to see mine."

"Don't worry. The bloody fog is so thick, I can't see anything."

"Good."

"Anything else?"

"Just this: From the way this 'ere 'Uffam put out 'is word, I'll bet there's others trying to get what you want. You're not likely to be the only one in the game."

"Who else?"

"The usual mob. The French. The Russians, per'aps. Maybe the Prussians, Turks, or Spanish. Could be Americans for that matter. Take yer pick."

"No idea which?"

"It could be all. Or some. Or none. Best be on yer guard. Now I'll take you back to the riverbank. No more talk."

"One more question."

"Go on."

"What's your *interest?"*

The rower leans forward and, guided by the voice, manages to tap on the other man's chest as if to punch a mark on it. "I can 'ave my own busi-ness too, can't I?"

"Suit yourself," says the passenger, pushing the hand away with a walk-ing stick.

The rower leans back and begins to propel the rowboat with powerful strokes. All is quiet save for the splash of oars.

"Fog lifting," he says, shifting his head so that his oilskin cloak covers him up to the eyes.

"Where are we?"

The rower peers through the murk. "There's the Tower of London. You can just make out Traitors' Gate."

"I'd rather not land there," mutters the other.

"Fitting . . . in its way."

"If that's a joke, I don't like it. Just get me on shore."

The little boat scrapes the riverbank where a narrow city street—Cousin Lane—runs down to the water.

The passenger clambers out.

"Mind the muck!"

"I'm fine."

"Good luck."

"I assure you," the man calls back as he vanishes into the fog, "luck will have nothing to do with it."

"Maybe," murmurs the oarsman as he pushes back into the foggy river, "just maybe I should 'ave taken 'im straight to Traitors' Gate. Might 'ave saved time. Well, I guess I'll find out soon enough."

He rows right to Old Swan's Pier, where the police paddle wheeler is waiting for him. "All right, then," he announces as he climbs aboard. "Our pretty little fishing expedition 'as commenced. By November we'll see what our net brings in."

Among those who hear him is a girl. She puts a dirty hand over her mouth and does a little jig of delight to keep from laughing out loud.

NOVEMBER
1849

CHAPTER 1
I Introduce Myself

"By the end of this week," said my father, as if speaking of a change in weather, "there's a possibility I shall be sent to prison."

With those words, Father—Wesley John Louis Huffam, who liked to add "Esquire" to his name as befit a gentleman—informed us of his circumstance.

My mother—Leticia—responded by shrieking, sobbing, and scolding. Clarissa, my older sister, bemoaned her likely spinster fate, then retired into a corner to whimper softly if audibly. Our Irish servant, Brigit, hid her face in her apron and no doubt whispered prayers.

Father, having provoked this domestic thunderstorm, closed his ears to the din, kept his hands in his pockets, stared out one of the small dirty windows of our rooms, and whistled his favorite tune, "Money Is Your Friend."

As for me—christened John Horatio Huffam—I could hardly grasp the situation except to watch and listen. That night, however, my feelings of anxiety were so great, I slept very poorly. As a consequence, it took considerable effort to keep my eyes open next day at school.

The nature of this school—which Father had selected—can perhaps be best understood from the sign affixed over its entry.

MULDSPOON'S MILITANTLY MOTIVATED ACADEMY

STRICTEST DISCIPLINE! NO RETREAT BEFORE IGNORANCE!

GOD SAVE THE QUEEN!

SERGEANT ANTHONY MULDSPOON, RET.,

PROPRIETOR & HEADMASTER

The only teacher at the school was this same Sergeant Muldspoon. His sergeant's rank derived from his days as artillery soldier when, thirty-five years previous, he fought Emperor Napoleon at the battle of Waterloo under Wellington.

Sergeant Muldspoon—we students called him "Old Moldy"— was a tall, gaunt, gray-haired man. The two bits of color about him were his nose, a veritable strawberry in texture and hue, and his polished Waterloo medal, which he wore upon his chest every day. Otherwise, he was always dressed in black from head to his one toe. I say "one" toe because his left leg was a wooden peg. The real leg—as he oft related in ghastly detail—had been left behind on the glorious battlefield.

So great was Sergeant Muldspoon's absorption in military matters, he could be said to dwell in a constant state of war. His lessons were such that I could tell you to perfection how to load a musket or cannon, without ever touching one. I could salute my superiors (meaning Sergeant Muldspoon) with considerable dash and I could recite the command structure of the Royal British Army, though I never thought of enlisting.

Hardly a wonder, then, that during class Old Moldy could always be found standing, as if at attention, beside his high desk—what he referred to as his "place of command."

The school consisted of but one room—an absolute barrack. Dim light. No heat. Cold, clammy air. Forty-one boys—ages four to sixteen—arranged in ranks of long benches and deal desks before the teacher. Youngest students forward. Oldest students back. Boys dressed in trousers and canvas jackets. Some with shoes. Others without. No books. No paper. No writing—save when we carved our initials on the desks.

Days of attendance: six days a week. Hour of starting: Nine in the morning. No recess. Lunch at noon with a two-hour interval. Whether we ate or not was of no interest to our teacher. Nor did we care that he vanished daily. *We* were free. The best part of my day. Sometimes I read to my classmates from my favorite books, *The Tales of the Genii* or *Robinson Crusoe*. Other times we roamed the City streets. Then, when Sergeant Muldspoon returned—promptly at two o'clock—the afternoon session commenced and wore on till five.

Despite the length of the day, Sergeant Muldspoon stood ever straight, more rigid than any man I knew—as if his spine had been replaced with a bayonet. In his hand was a cane, only slightly more flexible, which he used to attack the gray teaching slate that stood by him upon an easel. He also used that cane to assault us. In truth, Old Moldy brought his military experience to bear upon his pupils much as an artillery soldier might lay siege to thick walls: lethal persistence with maximum force.

On the chilly afternoon when my great adventure began, a thick, dank, brownish fog had crept in, rendering the classroom even more dismal than usual. The whale-oil lamp that sat upon the sergeant's desk glowed but faintly through a glass globe—a soot-smudged metaphor for the school's incessant dullness.

Using white chalk, Old Moldy had inscribed on the slate the words WAR, RIFLE, GUN, DEAD, HURT, HARD. The sergeant's teaching method was to strike the easel with his cane, pointing to each word in sequence. Thus, when he banged WAR and slightly cocked his head to one side, it was his signal that he was waiting for us.

We knew exactly what to do. "W-A-R spells 'war'!" forty-one boys chanted in a jagged chorus.

For the whole day I had been trying to keep my eyes open and focused on our teacher. To do otherwise was a declaration of war to Old Moldy.

He assaulted the next word on the easel. *Bang!*

True, I often daydreamed—eyes open; but that time I had in fact fallen asleep—eyes closed.

"R-I-F-L-E spells 'rifle,'" came the answer. From all but one, that is. Me.

"Halt!" commanded Sergeant Muldspoon.

I woke with a start and sat, along with the other boys, at attention. Their eyes shifted uneasily, trying to discover who had failed discipline. I knew.

"Eyes front! Feet together! Hands clasped!" barked the teacher. *His* eyes, narrow beneath shaggy gray eyebrows, burned with anger like a fuse, providing the only heat in the room. We boys did as ordered, not one of us daring to express amusement, I least of all, since I was very aware that the teacher was glaring right at *me*, something he did frequently since he had discovered me furtively reading *The Tales of the Genii* during class. When he had complained to my father, Father referred to him—to his face—as a "mere soldier." From that point forward Old Moldy demonstrated an aversion toward me that could only be considered vengeful. Hardly a wonder, then, that I considered Sergeant Muldspoon—to use his own terms—my great enemy.

From his waistcoat the sergeant pulled forth a large red handkerchief. He flourished it and blew his nose into it with a buglelike bleat, a proclamation that he was going into battle. After that he cannoned a cough into it, which resounded like the opening salvo of a general barrage. Next he rammed the cloth back into his pocket as he might wadding into a smoothbore musket. Finally, like a general announcing an advance, he stood straight and tall and cried, "Master John Huffam! Atten-shun!"

I, seated in the back form, rose up slowly and approached.

How shall I describe myself? For fourteen, I was somewhat small, with a round, perhaps placid face—with sandy-colored and lank hair that habitually fell over my blue eyes no matter how often I pushed it back. "Our dreamy angel," Brigit had dubbed me, since I often took refuge in fanciful thoughts.

Normally, I wore striped trousers and a wool jacket with a rounded front collar. My white shirt was gray. Around my neck was an ineptly tied neckcloth. On my feet, scuffed brown leather shoes.

Despite my uneven garb, I was by far the best dressed of my youthful comrades, who, in most respects, were quite ragged. But then, Father liked me to appear to the world like the young gentleman he insisted we both were. At times I thought he chose that school solely *because* I could appear better than my fellow students.

At the moment—standing in class, pushing the hair out of my face, and blinking—I was surely *not* better.

"You," announced Sergeant Muldspoon, aiming his cane directly

at my heart. He spoke, moreover, in the grave tones a general might use when telling a soldier he was about to stand court-martial for desertion. "You were *sleeping* in the line of duty."

"Please, sir," I whispered, "I didn't mean to."

"Did we hear *that*, students?" cried our educator, his jaw jutting forward so that he looked like a field gun run up to the battlements. "Master John Huffam didn't *mean* to sleep." The cane in his hand twitched menacingly. "*Did* we hear it, school?" he cried, cocking his head to one side, signaling that the class was to respond.

"Yes, Sergeant Muldspoon," everyone—including me—chanted like a shrill glee club. "We heard it!"

"If you did not *mean* it, then why, Master John Huffam, did you *do* it?" asked the teacher. "Do you think, midst the battle against ignorance, one can *sleep*?"

"No, sir."

"Is not *your* education *your* great war against *your* mortal enemy, which is to say, *your* great ignorance?"

"I was . . . tired, sir."

"Did we hear *that*, school?" exclaimed the teacher with mock shock. "Master John Huffam says he was *tired*." The cane positively leaped about in his hand with anticipation. "*Did* we hear it, school?"

"Yes, Sergeant Muldspoon," we scholars returned. "We heard it!" Now that I was named offender, the others could relax.

"And *why*, Master John Huffam, considering that your father claims to be a gentleman and lords it above all, including yours truly, while he bombards the world with false airs and rude condescension, when he is no more than a mere *clerk*—whereas I, *I* shook the hand of His Grace the Duke of Wellington himself!—why, Master John Huffam, should *you* be tired?"

"Please, sir," I said, "matters are uneasy at home, sir. I didn't sleep very well last night."

"Did we hear *that*, students?" asked the teacher. "Master John

Huffam says he didn't sleep very well because of unease within his genteel home. *Did* we hear that, school?"

"Yes, Sergeant Muldspoon!" we shouted. "We heard that!"

"Master Huffam," Sergeant Muldspoon proclaimed, "your response is inappropriate. Home is home. School is school. They are *completely* separate fields of battle. That said, it is very clear that your sense of discipline must be acquired not from your father, not from your fantastical genii, but in school. From me! Very well: John Huffam, you shall find *this* Englishman always does *his* duty. Break ranks. Step forward. March!"

"But, sir . . ."

"John Huffam, I am not aware that foot soldiers have been given leave to debate tactics with their general in chief. *Advance!*"

Most reluctantly I marched to the front of the room to stand before Old Moldy. Once there, I saluted. Then I bowed my head and extended my hand, palm turned up—following a practice understood by all. Indeed, such maneuvers were normally the first lesson our teacher taught his new pupils.

"Do *not* retreat in your war against ignorance, Master John Huffam," snapped Sergeant Muldspoon. So saying, he brought the cane down hard upon my upturned hand.

I bit my lip to keep from crying out.

"Receive your punishment," said Old Moldy, "like an English soldier. Now then, return to your place, march!"

"Yes, sir." Eyes welling with tears, I retreated to the back row.

"Discipline, young men," cried the sergeant, pointing to his sign upon the wall, "*military* discipline means *never* retreat. That is the byword of the true Englishman in this bastion of education. For this school is a fortress standing firm against those who would degrade the English monarchy and bring mob rule. Make no mistake! War upon the rabble's ignorance is *your* patriotic duty! *Tired* will not do! Not in Queen Victoria's England. Not in Sergeant Muldspoon's Militantly Motivated Academy."

"Now then, class, continue." He smacked his cane against the easel. *Bang!*

"D-E-A-D spells 'dead'!" we boys cried out in unison.

The sergeant was just about to assault the next word when Brigit, our family servant, burst through the door. The white cap she wore was in partial disarray, as was her graying hair. Her ankle-length dress was rumpled, as was the white—if stained—apron she wore. Her face was raddled with distress.

"I beg your pardon," cried Sergeant Muldspoon, "whoever you are, you're interrupting."

"It's Master John Huffam, sir," said Brigit. "He must come home at once."

"His *gentleman's* home?" said the teacher.

Ignoring the tone of raillery, Brigit looked at me and made a frantic beckoning movement. "Did you not hear me, Master John?" she hissed. "You must come now! Something perfectly dreadful has occurred."

I could have sworn the sergeant *almost* smiled. All he said, however, was, "John Huffam! Atten-shun! Stand down! Dismissed! March!"

లు@జు

CHAPTER 2
I Return to My Family

Brigit and I hurried down Bishopsgate, she leading the way as fast as a woman could go while maintaining decorum. I, in order to keep up, fairly well had to skip along the street gutter because the walkway was so crowded.

Such was her urgency, no words could be exchanged between us. Even so, I was just about to try when a sudden eruption of church bells filled the air from all points on the City compass, as if hearing the hour announced but once—it was four p.m.—was insufficient for London's two million. Indeed, the bells rang on, from one church to another, until at peak performance a hundred bells caroled piously, only to dwindle to a last feeble strike, tickling the ear of what would have to be a very sleepy soul.

Of course, if one did not know the hour by the bells, one knew it by the darkness of the late November afternoon. (I have been informed that London, on average, has but three and a half hours of sunlight per day.) The regular dismal brown fog, known as a "London particular," further congealed the gloom. Indeed, the coal-gas lamplighters, ladders over shoulders and glowing punks in hand, were already going from lamppost to lamppost, illuminating globes of soft light.

Crowds filled the sidewalks, three out of ten citizens looking to be my age, as if the whole City was at school upon the streets.

Street vendors were crying their wares: "Who's for an eel pie?" "Buy my lucifers!" "Sharpen your knives!" "Latest *London Spectator*— thrupence." "'Ere's yer toys for girls an' boys!" Tattered girls were hawking wilted watercress. Mud being universal, street sweeper boys were calling for custom at every corner. Braying beggars—crippled beggars, starving beggars, diseased beggars—were everywhere.

Then too there was a sluggishly moving chaos of wagons, barouches, carts, omnibuses, barrows, hackneys, phaetons, and Hansoms, pulled by London's hundred thousand horses. No wonder the cobblestones fairly sank beneath a sea of dung. No wonder that every breathing thing, every rolling thing, every voice, every cry, call, laugh, and sob, every shoe, boot, and hoof made so much din as to produce a relentless rumble that drummed and thrummed into every living London ear—and dead ones, too, no doubt.

But as soon as the clanging bells ceased their tolling, I turned. "Please, Brigit," I called up to her—for she towered over me—"what's happened?"

"Oh, Master John, I can hardly begin to speak it."

"Has someone taken ill? Is someone hurt?"

"Nothing like, Master John."

"Has someone died?" I cried, coming to a sudden halt.

"No, no," she said, pulling me onward. "Very much worse, I fear."

Remembering, I came to another stop. "Has my father"—I could hardly speak it—"has my father gone to—?"

"Out of the way!" a voice screamed.

Startled, I looked about, just in time to avoid being run down by a horse and goods wagon rolling past. Street mud and filth splattered my trousers. Though Brigit's long skirt was also dirtied, she paid no mind.

"Please, you must tell me *something*," I pleaded.

Brigit shook her head.

"But—"

"Jesus, Mary, and Joseph, Master John! It's for your own father—not me—to tell you of his disgrace."

"Disgrace!"

"Hush now! We'll be there in moments, and you can learn the dreadful truth from his own lips."

My heart thudding, we hastened round the corner to the quieter, darker Widegate Street, made a right onto Sandys Row, went scurrying past narrow Frying Pan Alley, until at last we turned into Mills Court, where my family resided.

In the light cast by the sole gas lamp at the head of our court, I could just see our family house, a soot-darkened brick structure of three levels. For five years we had been living on the ground floor while the upper two floors were rented to another family. I was not, however, allowed to be friendly with them since they, in my father's ironic words, were "too low." In fact, the big-eared boy who resided above us was leaning out an upper-floor window, smirking at the scene below.

It was, moreover, a scene I shall never forget—no, not if I lived for five hundred years.

∽◌◌◌∾

CHAPTER 3
My Family's Fortunes Fall

Two men were hauling my parents' bed—bedclothes heaped upon it—from the house. My own bed was already on the pavement. As was my sister's. So too the painted box in which we stored our clothing. Our blue Venetian glass vase. Our table. Our chairs. Mother's heirloom silver teapot. Our five books, including my *Tales of the Genii* and *Robinson Crusoe*. Also: The precious, ornately framed painting of my father's grandfather, the baronet Augustus Huffam. Everything was being loaded onto a wagon. Hitched to that stood a large gray mare willing, and able, to haul our household away.

Many of our neighbors were watching, milling about the street's central water-spigot. Innumerable children were underfoot in various degrees of dress and dirtiness. Among the crowd were a few uniformed constables—"Peelers," we called them—with their steel-reinforced top hats; belted, brass-buttoned, blue greatcoats; and gas-fueled bull's-eye lamps on belts. They did not seem to be doing much of anything.

On the crowded steps that led to the house door, my family

huddled like shorn sheep, looking on with what appeared to be disbe-
lief as the last of our possessions were rudely heaved into the wagon.
Simultaneously, they, along with everyone else, listened to a man read
loudly from a large sheet of paper adorned with official seals, a paper
he held in his plump, dimpled hands as far from his eyes as his short
arms allowed.

This squat, round gentleman was someone I had never seen before.
He sported long gray side-whiskers of the kind called "Piccadilly
weepers," the very image of a hard-blowing north wind emerging from
storm clouds. That is to say, he was a perfect assemblage of puffiness:
Puffy face, puffy nose, puffy cheeks, puffy eyes, puffy mouth, and *very*
puffy belly. Perched on his round nose were old-fashioned round eyeglasses. Perched on his head was an old-fashioned cocked hat. Indeed,
he even wore an old-fashioned greatcoat of faded scarlet, along with
old-fashioned green knee britches, stockings, and high black boots.
Tucked under one arm was a long walking staff, which he apparently
carried not so much for stability as for the authority it signified.

My mother, clutching my father's right arm tightly, was pale-faced
and crying, her copious bosom heaving with emotion, her corkscrewed
ringlets of hair quite unscrewed. My sister, as rail thin as Mother was
barrel stout, was affixed to Father's *other* side. Tears trickled down her
sallow cheeks as she mewed and lamented like a distempered kitten.

For a moment I could do no more than stare. Then, recollecting
myself, I pulled free of Brigit, calling, "Father! Mother! What is it?
What's happening?"

At first they did not seem to grasp that I was even there. But the fat man with the cocked hat and side-whiskers did.

"Here now, boy," he cried as I tried to join my family. "Stand aside. Are you not aware that you are impeding the Queen's majestic law in its ... hmm ... stately progress?"

"But what *is* it?" I cried. "What's happening to our belongings?" By then virtually everything was in the wagon.

"Who is this meddlesome youth?" demanded the man. He pushed his eyeglasses up to his forehead, where they remained so that I had— as it were—four eyes glaring at me with reproach. "Does he know nothing of the dignity of the Queen's law?"

Releasing my mother and sister, Father drew himself up. He was a tall and slim man, some might say (certainly he could and would say it) a handsome man, suggesting the amateur actor and clever theater critic he fancied himself. His thinning hair was ginger in color, his complexion unmarked by pox, his eyes a gentle light blue. His nose had been considered (certainly he could and would say it) rather noble. His erect bearing gave him the look of—as many had said (certainly he could and would say this, too)—a gentleman. Only on closer examination might one see that his jacket and trousers were frayed at the edges, shoes broken, shirt barely white, hair uneven at the ears, neckcloth soiled, chin in need of a shave—but of a certainty he would not admit to any of *that*.

"He is my son and heir," my father informed the puffy man, speaking with the theatrical diction he often affected. "John," said he,

turning to me, "it's my honor to present you to Mr. Tobias Tuckum, our parish bailiff. John, be so good as to extend Mr. Tuckum your compliments as befits the son and heir of a gentleman."

"But what's this all about?" I cried again.

"Your feckless father," announced Mother in a voice as brash as that of any costermonger, "has gone bankrupt!" She pressed a small hand to her heaving heart, even as she gulped down what looked to be a sob as large as an Irish potato.

"Now, now," said the bailiff with a bow in my direction. "Your father is merely in debt." He lowered his glasses to the bridge of his nose, held up his paper, and read: " 'Wesley John Louis Huffam, you are hereby summoned, and in Her Majesty's name, strictly enjoined and commanded personally, to be and appear before the Insolvent Debtors' Court at Parliament Street, Palace Yard, on' . . . hmm . . . 'Thursday next before ten of the clock.'

"As you can hear," explained the bailiff to me, "a writ has been sworn against your father. His property has been seized as security. In three days' time the court shall pass judgment. If his debt be not paid in its entirety by then, he will soon be . . . hmm . . . languishing according to the Queen's sacred justice *in* the debtors' prison at Whitecross Street until such time as it *is* paid."

It was, I realized, just what my father had warned might happen: That is to say, a catastrophe had come down upon us, a catastrophe very much harsher than the blow Sergeant Muldspoon had brought down upon my hand.

CHAPTER 4
I Learn About a Sponging House

With a loud *cluck* from the wagon driver—one of the furniture removers—all our household goods were hauled away, the horse's iron-shod hooves clattering upon the cobblestones like (or so it seemed to me) the rattling of bones in a coffin.

We watched the cart go in silence, though my mother and sister wept noisily. Brigit, white cap askew, apron bunched in one fist, looked tense. I turned my eyes toward my father, who had delicately touched the corner of his right eye with the tip of a well-manicured finger so as to dab away—in the most gentlemanly fashion—a solitary tear. Then he put his hands in his pockets, pursed his lips, and softly whistled that tune of his, "Money Is Your Friend." This time the normally sprightly ditty sounded like a funeral dirge.

From the top-floor window of our house the smirking, big-eared neighbor boy—his name was Rufus Pendergast—jeered: "Debtors' prison! That's where you be goin'. Y'bankrupts! Y'nasty, stuck-up snobs!"

That insult uncorked raucous laughter from the crowd of onlookers, a sound that made my sister wince and Mother's face turn pale even as her nose turned up. As for the policemen, they nodded to one another, grinning, while Mr. Tuckum only frowned.

"Father?" I whispered as the wagon vanished into the night. "Where will they take our things?"

"That, young John," he said, "is a most reasonable question." He turned to the bailiff and touched him gently on his arm. "Begging your pardon, Mr. Tuckum," he said, "but where will our possessions go?"

"The holding pen, sir," returned the bailiff. "On Pudding Lane. Hard by the docks. They'll be kept for three days. As the law has it, if you don't pay your debt, it all gets sold outright, the money going to your creditor."

"Ah, yes, of course," my father said. "And—if I may be so bold—one further little point. Might you be willing to inform me as to the *name* of the gentleman who has brought this writ against me?"

Mr. Tuckum lowered his eyeglasses the better to examine the official text. "Yes, here it is. 'Dated this twenty-third day of November 1849. For the debt owing by you as stated in the margin ... To answer the demand of ... Mr. Finnegan O'Doul.'"

"O'Doul!" cried Father.

To my eyes, his face—even reckoning for the hour's darkness—turned quite ashen. "But ... but ... ," he stammered, "I don't owe that man so much as a ha'penny!"

"All I can say," replied Mr. Tuckum, "is that here"—he rattled the document as if to shake away any words that might have alighted by accident—"it says you *do*. All proper and legal, I can assure you of that, sir."

"But—"

"See here, Mr. Huffam," the bailiff interrupted, "I am nothing if not old-fashioned. Without being old-fashioned, I'd be reduced to rubble—like one of those new railway cuttings that are tumbling London. But being old-fashioned, sir, I respect the Queen's law for being the firm foundation upon which this great nation rests. If it's revolution you desire, sir, dispatch posthaste to Paris, to Rome, or to Berlin. In London, sir, you'll find sanity. Stability. No, sir: According to this writ—and this writ is naught if it is not legal in an old-fashioned way—it's considerably more than a ha'penny you owe, sir. It's ... ." He studied his paper anew: "Three hundred ... hmm ... pounds, four shillings, twopence."

"*Three hundred pounds!*" gasped my father.

"Plus four shillings and twopence," added the bailiff.

"Mr. Huffam," Mother cried, "have I heard correctly? That you owe three *hundred* pounds? God have mercy! You have positively destroyed us!"

"I shall never marry now," my sister sobbed. "*Never.*"

"But I assure you, Mrs. Huffam," said my father, "it's not true. Not a bit. I owe *that* man nothing."

"Owe nothing," interjected the bailiff, while vigorously nodding, "and *you* have *nothing* to worry about. By virtue of Her Majesty's even-handed law, pay your debt and the Insolvent Debtors' Court shall set you as free as any English sparrow. But for the moment, sir, this writ being entirely legal, you must come to me."

"Where?" demanded Mother.

"My house."

"*Your* house, sir?" said my father.

"I assure you, sir, and you, too, madam," said the bailiff, "it's the way of our forefathers, so I cannot presume to know better. As laid out by parliamentary law, I keep a *sponging* house. Now then, Mr. Huffam," he went on, "if you'll come this way, please. As for you, madam, you and your progeny are more than welcome to join your spouse, if so inclined. Quite welcome. Indeed, I shall consider myself honored to gain your esteemed company." That said, the bailiff, wielding his staff of authority like a baton, beckoned to the constables, who crowded round and eased us along the street with the skill of Yorkshire sheepherders.

My father, head held high, offered condescending half bows to his neighbors as if they were his audience, an audience whose applause consisted of jeers: "Bankrupt, bankrupt!" But, as if he were hearing *bravo* instead, he strolled off—hands in pockets—after Mr. Tuckum.

A moment's hesitation and my mother followed, arm in arm with my head-bowed sister, who was supported in turn by Brigit.

I came last, walking beside a constable. "Please, sir," I said in an undertone as we passed down the street, "what's . . . what's a . . . *sponging* house?"

"Where your father will have a brief residence. While there, 'e's got a few days to wipe clean 'is debt—to sponge that debt away, if you get the meaning. If 'e can't, it's to the Insolvent Debtors' Court 'e'll go. From there—though for your sake I 'ope not—to debtors' prison. Now, now, no need to fret so. Being charged with debt, brought to court, and tossed into the clink is right common. And the prison ain't 'alf bad. So be a good bloke—you seem right sensible—and step lively."

His words only increased my sense of mortification. But there being no choice, we had to go, and so we did.

∽✸∾

CHAPTER 5
We Arrive at the Halfmoon Inn

Mr. Tuckum, bearing his walking staff as though leading a band, marched our party into the maze of London streets, leaving Mills

Court, down Sandys Row, down Widegate Street, across Bishopsgate, and then onto Halfmoon Street. Along the way we met with assorted cheers and jeers, for a procession such as ours—as the constable had informed me truthfully—was hardly unique.

"Welcome," cried Mr. Tuckum as we approached the deepest reach of Halfmoon Alley, which led off the street, "to an Englishman's humble home, the Halfmoon Inn." The bailiff, bobbing as agreeably as a tethered balloon in a gentle wind, gallantly gestured with his staff toward a structure. It was made of timber and horsehair plaster, with a wide, ill-thatched roof that ran the width of the court, much like a wall—a wall, no doubt, to keep persons, and time, from advancing any farther.

The Halfmoon Inn had not so much as one straight line to it. The roof was crooked. The porch was crooked. The windows were crooked. The main doorway was crooked. Even the shadows that draped it were crooked. Dormer windows stuck out from the roof in three irregular places. This same roof hung, like an old horse's neck, atop a long balcony—upon which doors faced—that stretched the inn's full width. In sympathetic reversal, the balcony bore columns that held up the roof. This balcony was the width of the alley, thus protecting the inn's crooked ground-floor doorway, as well as some small crooked windows.

It was as if the entire ancient structure was on the verge of slipping off its foundation. *Half*moon, indeed—and still waning.

The bailiff, however, was nothing if not waxing with life. He stood by the lopsided doorway, hand with hat extended through the irregular doorframe, the very image of a welcoming host. "Step lively, my friends," he exclaimed. "Step lively! I intend to provide—in a

gentleman's moment of distress *and* duress—all the famous comforts of a ... hmm ... cozy English inn. Being old-fashioned, I can, and so I surely will!"

Mother held back. "Are we expected to pay for lodging *here*?" she demanded in a tone of voice that indicated she knew the answer.

"A fair question," replied the bailiff, bowing, "from a fair lady. I assure you, madam, I charge no more than any London inn might charge. Cozy room. Delicious food. Impeccable service. At generally ... hmm ... competitive rates. True, it's more than you will be charged in debtors' prison—four pence a day—but far greater ease is to be found here than there. Of that, madam, you may trust me."

My mother, turning to my father, said, "Mr. Huffam, have we any money at all?"

"Not a penny."

Mother, now turning to the bailiff, asked: "And if we have no money?"

The bailiff bowed. "According to the law, and I respect the law beyond all else—and so should all good Englishmen—madam, you *must* still pay."

We each—even Brigit—looked to my father.

"Well, yes, of course," said he, holding himself very properly and displaying not the least emotion as he gazed upon the decrepit inn. "You are most obliging, sir. A true friend."

Then he turned to Mother. "Dear Mrs. Huffam," he said, "what could be more refined or fitting for a gentleman such as me than such an old-fashioned inn? Our genial host is quite correct. It's the way a gentleman *should* accommodate himself. So, dearest Mrs. Huffam, devoted children, loyal Brigit, be so good as to enter."

I took note that Father did not say how he would pay.

Mother, in fishwife tones, snapped, "If only you *were* a gentleman,

Mr. Huffam. You, who have neither land nor title—you merely play at it like the inept actor you are. Need I remind you, sir," she added, as if this were the most grievous of sins, "you draw *wages*."

"Dearest beloved," my father returned, "you know perfectly well that I am a gentleman. I have the genealogy to prove it."

"What good is genealogy," she countered, "if you don't have pennies to emblazon it?"

"As I have said many a time, most cherished wife," my father said, "it's all in the performance. I, for one, *choose* to act like the gentlemen my ancestors were."

"Well said, Mr. Huffam," cried the bailiff. "Well said! And I beg to remind you: Just pay your debt, and the court will set you free."

"Piffle!" exclaimed Mother. "I ask you, sir, how is he going to pay off *three* hundred? He's nothing but a *clerk*—a *clerk* at the Naval Ordinance Office at one hundred pounds a year."

"Be that as it may," said the bailiff, who was beaming so, his Piccadilly weepers stood out like the rays of a benevolent sun in the dark, "I again welcome you to the Halfmoon Inn." That said, he rapped his staff upon the ground and bowed the company in.

I was last to enter. As I stepped forward, I saw the bailiff dismiss the constables with a wave. Then the little man waddled after us and shut the warped door with a resounding *slam* about which there was *nothing* wobbly.

It was, I thought, as if we were already in prison.

⟡⊙⟨ↄ

CHAPTER 6
Mr. Tuckum Speaks to Me Privately

The entryway of the Halfmoon Inn led into a large, drafty, and dis-
heartening room. There were no gas lamps, but a few candles, which,
once the bailiff lit them, provided at best insipid illumination that
barely revealed wood-paneled walls, some askew panels; a low, sag-
ging ceiling, streaked with black soot; gap-toothed wainscoting; a
floor made of wide, cracked, and wavy planks, which, when stepped
upon, squeaked like so many pigs brought to a Smithfield butcher.
Scattered about in haphazard fashion were lumpish oak tables and
mismatched chairs and benches, none of which offered any promise
of holding much weight. To one side lay a large, open stone fireplace,
and at its center were black encrusted logs embedded in white ash,
like some offering to the god of decay.

"Here we are," exclaimed Mr. Tuckum. "All the good cheer of old
England. The privy is out back. Let me assure you, Mrs. Huffam,
that many other gentlemen of high repute—like your illustrious
husband—have paused here to . . . hmm . . . restore themselves in
their journey through life."

"What distinguishes *my* husband," Mother retorted with a toss of
her head, "is that he is a fool going nowhere."

"Dear Mrs. Huffam," said Father, who was standing in the middle
of the room rubbing his hands as if gently washing them, the look

upon his face remarkably placid, "what could be more well bred than to be in such a noble London establishment?"

I gazed at my father, marveling, as I often did, at his mildness, his calm. It was as if he were playing his favorite role: Sir Algernon Kindly in Markham's romantic comedy *Gentle Hearts Aflutter.*

"By which you mean," returned my mother, "acting as if nothing was amiss."

My father turned to the bailiff. "Mr. Tuckum, my compliments. Be assured that *I*, at least, find all of this very gratifying. I am much in your debt."

"Well, yes and no," agreed the bailiff. "Of course you may remain standing exactly where you are and not avail yourself of the . . . hmm . . . comforts of food, drink, and bed. But if you *do* wish to partake, there *will* be a fee for everything."

"Is it not absurd," demanded Mother, who had not budged from the spot where *she* stood, "to agree to new debts when one is so undone by old ones?"

"Madam," said the bailiff, "*I* never argue with a lady."

"Dear Mrs. Huffam," my father said, "surely we must have *some* comfort in our hour of *dis*comfort."

My sister had been looking about in silent misery. Now she said, "It's an awful place, Pa. It truly is. Perfectly hateful. All mean and low with nothing fashionable at all about it. I shall have no suitors here. Not even Mr. Farquatt."

"Oh, tut," said Father. "My dear, Mr. Farquatt is *below* you."

"Don't *say* that, Pa!" cried my sister. "He is that near to offering marriage."

"You *shall* be married, Clarissa," said my father. "Of course you will. A young lady with such wit and charm as you possess shall be courted agreeably and successfully. I give you my word."

"Mama," sniffled my sister, her tears beginning to flow again, "tell Pa to stop saying such *brainless* things!"

"I assure you, Miss Clarissa," Mother said, "your father won't listen to *me*."

"Now, now," said the bailiff, smiling brightly and extending his short arms as if they could embrace us all. "Let's not quarrel, pray, but be a loving English family. May I show you to some rooms and then to an excellent dinner?"

"Splendid suggestion," agreed my father. "Mr. Tuckum, if you would be so kind . . ."

The bailiff, a lit tallow candle in each plump hand, and with many a kind and coaxing word, guided us from the ground floor up a narrow, twisting stairway to the first floor. There, upon reaching the outside balcony that ran the building's width and onto which faced multiple doors, he turned to my father. "Sir, how do you wish to be accommodated?"

"Perhaps," my father said, "if at all possible, the women should stay together at *that* end. Whereas my son and heir shall stay with me in another room at *this* end. Your best room, of course."

"Of course."

I did wonder—considering the circumstances—that once again Father did not inquire about the cost, but that was never his fashion.

The bailiff led my unhappy mother farther along the balcony and threw open a door. "Here you are, madam, a commodious room. Not, in any significant way, too drafty. Sufficient, I trust, for you, your daughter, and servant."

Mother, without a word, marched right in and was followed by the others.

"Will it do?" called Mr. Tuckum from the safety of the balcony.

The response was to have the door slammed in his face.

"Well, well," said the bailiff, "it merely proves that no one enjoys . . . hmm . . . change. Least of all, me. Surely old-fashioned ways *are* the best ways. I sympathize with Mrs. Huffam, sir, I truly do. Now, gentlemen, indulge me and I shall guide you to your room."

At the other end of the balcony the bailiff opened a second door. "If you would be so good, Mr. Huffam," he said to my father, offering what had become the small stub of a candle.

My father went into the room. I started to follow only to have Mr. Tuckum pluck on my sleeve to hold me back.

"Master John," he said, low voiced, "a momentary word with you." He bowed to me as if I were an adult.

"Yes, sir," I said, taken by surprise but waiting upon him nonetheless.

Mr. Tuckum partially shut the door so our conversation might be private. "Unless my eyes and ears deceive me," he began, "it's *you*, Master John—and you alone—who appears to be the sensible one in the Huffam establishment."

"Sir, I'm only fourteen—"

"Apologies are not necessary. I simply wish you to know that in our brief acquaintance I've become mindful of your character. Your *good* character. Did not someone say, 'Where there is silence, there is depth?' And you have been *very* silent, Master John. It bespeaks a precocious wisdom. I shall . . . hmm . . . humor your parents, but it is to *you* I shall confide, Master John, Englishman to Englishman."

"Sir—"

"The debt your father owes is a very great sum indeed. Three hundred *pounds*. Many a laborer or maid lives on *twenty* a year—often far, far less. Unless your father can find a way to pay this Mr. O'Doul during these next few days, his prospects for the future are, shall we say, quite without . . . hmm . . . luster.

"He spoke of you as his heir. Is there, perhaps, some extended family nearby? Some property? Some entailed wealth? Some reserve of worldly goods that might be secured? In short, some way—any way—to raise the . . . hmm . . . money?"

"I really don't know, sir."

"I feared as much!" said the bailiff, frowning.

"But . . . what . . . will happen?" I stammered, taken aback by both the solemnity of the bailiff's warning and the responsibility he had laid upon me.

"As previously stated," said Mr. Tuckum, "I fear that, for your father, it shall be debtors' prison. Or the poorhouse. Perhaps the treadmill. Or"—his voice lowered—"worse."

"Worse?"

"Transportation to a penal colony in ... Australia."

"Australia!"

"I assure you," said the bailiff in the most kindly fashion, "it's England's enlightened way."

"I suppose," I admitted, though in truth, such a ghastly fate seemed unimaginable for a Huffam.

"Good, lad," he said, patting me on the shoulder. "I thought you

would appreciate my confidence. How delighted I am that there is *somebody* in your family with clear perception! I've no doubt in *my* mind but *you* shall manage everything splendidly. If I can be of any service, Master John, *any,* Toby Tuckum is at your beck and call. Now then, if you will excuse me, I will see to your dinner."

He bowed again and stepped away.

I could only look after him, but as to which I felt more, astonishment or misery, I could hardly say.

⁂

CHAPTER 7

Father Makes a Request of Me

The small room I entered—as revealed by that meager stump of a burning candle—was plain enough. It consisted of a large bed, four-posted, with a mattress as thin as a postage stamp plus one blanket. A single grimy window. A small, much-scarred table. A chest for storing clothing in which a family of mice had recently stored itself. A small and tattered rug upon a floor so stained, it seemed unwise to uncover what it considered worth concealing. On the wall a faded Hogarth print titled *The Distressed Poet.* Finally, an empty fireplace, offering nothing to modify the room's damp, moldy, and chilly air.

Nevertheless, my father stood looking into the fireplace. Since there was nothing to observe there, I had no idea what he was pondering, though now and again he whistled that tune of his, "Money Is Your Friend."

I sat on the bed and waited. All I learned was that the bed was hard.

At length my father—his back to me—said, "My dear John, I wish to tell you, upon my honor as a gentleman *and* your devoted father, I owe *no* such debt to this O'Doul fellow."

"Yes, Father, I'm sure."

Something in my voice caused him to look about and consider me with his clear blue eyes. "You *don't* believe me, do you?"

"Yes, sir, I do," I replied, for as God as my witness, I truly *wanted* to believe him.

"I am, of course, not without . . . some *small* debts, due the next quarter." He waved a hand in the air as if brushing away cobwebs. "Trifling. My pay at the Naval Ordinance Office is more than enough to cover them. Of course, dearest boy, debt is perfectly common. Part of a gentleman's life. Indeed, society *expects* it of a gentleman. As for this O'Doul fellow . . . no." He shook his head with an air of bewilderment. "No truth to it. Not a jot. I owe him nothing of the kind. I swear. Truthfully, I would hardly know the man if we were face-to-face and proper introductions had been made."

I stared at my shoes, wishing he would stop referring to "truth." It rang in my ears too much the opposite. "Then who is he?" I asked.

"A man . . . whom I do not like. No one likes him. A foreigner."

I lifted my eyes and gazed at him. "But, Father—do you, then, know him well enough to *not* like him?"

My question brought a slight flush to his cheeks. "Very slightly," he said, turning from me.

"Sir," I asked after a few moments of silence, "how could this have happened?"

He shifted about, put his hands in his pockets, and pursed his lips as if to whistle but instead replied, "I . . . really don't know how to

explain." There was such frank simplicity in the statement, I found it hard not to believe him. "As for this O'Doul business," he insisted anew, "I repeat, it's a *deep* mystery to me."

I said nothing.

"Of course," he said momentarily, "that said, I shall make certain he removes this writ against me. I'll do so immediately. Well, tomorrow. In fact, I'm considering bringing a claim upon *him* for false arrest."

"But, Father . . . if you don't know him, how shall you find him?"

"I . . . I shall make it my business to."

"And you'll really do so right away?" I urged as much as asked.

"John, a father's word is . . ." His voice faded.

"If you don't," I felt obliged to say, "you'll be in prison. We'll be ruined. Mr. Tuckum spoke of . . . Australia."

"Aus—! Nonsense! Such a thing can't—won't—happen."

But, as if to make a point, our candle remnant flickered, then guttered away. I felt very much in the dark—in more ways than one.

"John," I heard my father say in the gloom, "as you know, I gain great pleasure from acting on the stage in amateur theatricals."

That much was true: I had seen his performances and enjoyed them. Being someone else seemed to give him energy.

"Was it not the great Shakespeare who spoke of us as being merely players on the stage of life?"

"If you say so, Father."

"Well then, in this matter I am . . . merely a player. Though a fair critic, too, John. For there is always . . . judgment."

Having nothing to add to that, we sat for a while in the shadowy chill until he said, "John, I fear I must call upon you for some . . . small assistance."

His hesitation made me tense. "Of what kind, Father?"

"Perhaps you have heard me speak from time to time of Lady Euphemia Huffam."

"Your grandfather's younger sister."

"Exactly. The very one. My great-aunt. Your great-great-aunt."

"The one who inherited all your family wealth."

"And wrongly so! John, heed me: It is as immoral for family money to go to a woman as it is to a child."

"You've often said so."

"*I* would never . . . !" exclaimed my father, as if he were in a position to act upon his words. Then, perhaps realizing he could not act upon them, he dropped into another silent space.

I waited, uncomfortably aware he was leading someplace distasteful.

"Young John," he finally resumed, "this difficulty in which we find ourselves . . . most unfortunate. A mere misunderstanding . . . very cruel for your good mother. And sister. And me, of course. . . . But you and I, being gentlemen . . . Still, the short of it is, dear boy, the honor of the family is at stake and . . ." He paused, and I heard him take a deep breath. "John," he said at last, "I need you to go to Lady Euphemia Huffam and apply for a loan."

"Me?" I cried.

"Better you than me."

"But why?"

"Some time ago my great-aunt and I quarreled. A small matter really. Incited by another. Truly. It would be so much better if *you* went."

"But I have never even met the lady!"

"Precisely why you are the one to speak to her. She can, at least, harbor no prejudice toward *you*."

"Must I?"

"As you love me, John. Besides, as Mr. . . ."

"Tuckum."

"Exactly. As Mr. Tuckum said, I'm not allowed to leave this place."

I sighed. "What shall I ask of her?"

"A short-term loan merely. And you must say it's only a *loan*. Upon my honor as a gentleman."

"For how much?"

"Oh . . . say . . . three hundred pounds."

"Three hundred pounds!" I cried.

"I assure you, John, it will be *nothing* to her," my father said in haste. "She's a very wealthy woman. Immensely so. Mind, she used *my* inheritance to invest in these new railroads that are all the rage . . . or so I have been reliably informed."

"Who informed you?"

"Her solicitor, Mr. Nottingham," to which he added, "a man who delights in tormenting me."

"Why should he?"

"Oh, I wrote some trifling critique of his acting abilities. He took it ill. A man should be willing to learn from his failings."

Not wishing to engage in that topic, I said, "What is your great-aunt like?"

"Of middling height, rather stout, a pale complexion—"

"I mean, is she kind? Is she pleasant?"

"Well, actually, I haven't seen her for a year. As for being pleasant, I should certainly think so—to *you* in any case. Does not everyone dote on you, John? Does not Mr. Tuckum favor you? Forgive me. I heard what he said to you.

"Rumor has it that my great-aunt is mostly bedridden. Considering her age, I imagine she might expire any day now. It would be a terrible waste if . . ." He did not complete his thought out loud.

How I wished I could have seen my father's face! But there was just his melancholy voice.

"Father, where does she reside?"

"Great Winchester Street. I shall give you the number presently. I have it somewhere." I heard—but I could not see—him pat his pockets. "Will you go?" His voice was soft, pleading.

"Do you truly think she will listen to me?"

"How could she refuse such a smart, upstanding, earnest young fellow as yourself? What has our Brigit dubbed you? 'Our dreamy angel.' Dear John, Lady Euphemia will *want* to help you. You *are* the last of the Huffams. The best! I don't doubt it. That should count for *something*. She will *beg* you to take her money. She will *throw* money at you! So you will go, old fellow, won't you? It's . . . necessary."

"Yes, Father, I will."

"Good. Excellent. Well done! Only one bit of advice, John: If that lawyer, Mr. Nottingham, is there, best avoid him. A most unpleasant man *and* a bad actor.

"But I've not the slightest doubt," he continued, "that you shall be successful with my aunt. Between my dealing with Mr. O'Doul and your speaking to her—depend on it—this vexing financial difficulty shall be ancient history in . . . hours."

There was a knock on the door.

"Enter!"

Mr. Tuckum put his head in. "Oh my, it's quite dark, isn't it? Never mind! With compliments," he said, "dinner is on the table."

My father, seemingly glad of an excuse to depart, left the room immediately.

I remained behind for a few moments, sitting in the shadows. Perhaps it was best that I had not seen Father's face. I suspected I would have observed only embarrassment. I was glad we'd been spared that.

In any case, I followed him to dinner with but one thought: Was it in any way believable he did not know this Mr. O'Doul?

Oh, sad truth that lets a son discover his father is not an honest man!

❧❧❧

CHAPTER 8
I Receive More Requests

A small roast chicken, cold to the bone, had been set upon the table— by whom, I never knew—along with stale bread, pallid potatoes, limp leeks, and some wine to drink. (Since the recent outbreak of cholera, no one with any sense touched London water.) The size of the chicken left much to the imagination and little to assuage hunger. But then, as it turned out, it was just my father, the bailiff, and I at the table for dinner. My mother and sister refused to partake, or so I was informed.

"May I bring them some food?" I asked.

"What a good, old-fashioned fellow your son is!" exclaimed Mr. Tuckum, beaming at me while reaching over and chucking me under the chin with a greasy hand. "As kind as he is sensible. Food for the ladies. Egad, sir," he said to my father, "he does you great honor!" The bailiff proceeded to tear off a chicken wing and a leg from the carcass and set them, along with some bread, on a chipped platter.

I carried the meager meal up the steps and to the room where the rest of my family was lodged. I knocked. When Brigit let me in, I glanced about. Mother lay prostrate on the bed, a cloth over her eyes.

"Is that you, John?" she whispered.

"Yes, Mother. I've brought some food."

"I couldn't possibly eat," she whispered. "Give it to the others."

No sooner said than my sister, like a starved hound, fell upon the plate and ate rapaciously in a corner. I do not know what Brigit consumed—if anything.

"John," my mother called weakly, beckoning. "Come here."

I approached as if she were on her deathbed. "Yes, Mother."

"John, heed me." She did not remove the cloth from her eyes.

"I am listening, Mother."

"Your father is a fool. An incompetent wastrel. You are the only one with any sense in this family. I do believe he thinks he's performing a play with a happy ending. I must leave it to you to work out this matter."

"But, Mother, I'm only—"

"John," she murmured, "do your best. For my sake." She waved me away with some feeble finger movements.

There was nothing for it but to leave. Brigit came out of the room with me.

"Master John," she said as she closed the door behind her, "a word with you."

Though weary of these private conversations, I prepared myself to listen.

"It surely pains me to be saying so, Master John," she began in an undertone, "but your mother spoke the truth. It's you and only you who can save this family from destruction."

"Brigit," I said, "I am but *fourteen* years of age."

"Now, Master John, you know the years I've been with the Huffams. You've become my family. Your sister and you, are you not like my own children? As for your father and mother, whom I surely and dearly love, they are perhaps—despite *their* years—somewhat ... imprudent. No, Master John, only you can save us."

"But how?" I asked.

"You must insist your father solve his problem."

"I already have."

"What did he say?"

"He asked me to visit—tomorrow—his great-aunt, Lady Euphemia."

Brigit seemed taken aback. "I was sure his great-aunt broke off all connection."

"Brigit, I don't know anything about that except he's asked me to go to her and beg a loan of the three hundred pounds. I don't want to go."

"Will you?"

"Do you think it wrong?" I asked.

"Master John," she said, "do you know what's happening in Ireland?"

The question took me by surprise. "No. Should I?"

"There's a terrible famine there. People—like my family—are dying by the thousands. The thousands."

In truth, I knew Brigit had come from Ireland, but when and under what circumstance, I had no notion. Apparently, then, she did have family: mother, father, sisters, brothers. It was the first I'd ever heard of them. As for the famine, to my young ears, there were always problems in Ireland.

"I'm sorry," I offered. "I didn't know you had other family."

She fixed me with eyes that I thought uncommon fierce. "I do, Master John, and to live, a people will do whatever they need to do."

"I'm sure," I said, hardly knowing what else to say.

"You must insist your father raise the money as best he may. That alone will be the saving of us all," she said. *"All of us,"* she repeated. Abruptly, she reached out and hugged me only to push me away and run back into the room. She clearly was as upset as my mother.

My appetite roaring, I returned to the dinner table just in time to see the last of the chicken being consumed, a little heap of bones serving as an alabaster memorial.

Mr. Tuckum lifted a glass to my father, and my father, putting aside the bone he was sucking on, returned the compliment. The bailiff made a toast: "To your prosperity, sir, your abundant prosperity—may it come apace."

My father turned toward me and smiled weakly.

In that smile I could read his regrets. My thought was: *A father's regrets are his son's shame.*

After dining on a slice of bread and leeks, I again slept poorly.

At one point I was sure I heard someone walking along the balcony. There were voices, too, muffled and indistinct.

Though I wished to see what was afoot, I was sorely in need of sleep. And I was dreading the next day.

༒

CHAPTER 9
I Go Out at Dawn

Next morning I woke quite early but remained abed alongside my sleeping father. I could not help but be weighted down by the fact that he, my mother, Brigit, and even Mr. Tuckum were all convinced that only I could keep Father out of debtors' prison and thereby protect the family's name and fortunes, such as they were.

Why—I asked myself—could they not have asked my sister, Clarissa? She was seventeen, three years older than I. Of course, just to think of Clarissa was to contemplate an unhappy mix of great anxiety, like my mother, added to an inability to do much about anything, like my father.

In short, though convinced I must fail, I accepted that there was no help for it: *I* must at least try to solve our problems.

Sighing at the realization, I slipped out from beneath the blanket onto the cold floor, pulled on my shoes, and went outside to the balcony. It was barely dawn on a raw, blustery day, with a wind that shook the Halfmoon Inn as if to wake it from its antique slumbers.

Briefly, I recalled the voices I'd heard the night before. Presumably, they had come from this very spot. Needless to say, at the moment no one was about, neither on the balcony nor in the courtyard below. I dismissed my concerns as the product of uneasy dreams. Or people going to the privy.

I made my way down to the main room. There, in the cheerless light, I found the table strewn with dirty dishes, walnut shells, half tumblers of sherry, and crumbs of food, as well as congealed puddles of spent candle wax. It was all one with the inn's air of dingy decay.

A scattered deck of cards suggested that after I had gone to bed, my father and Mr. Tuckum had been up late. (My father had taught me a few games, explaining that a gentleman *must* know such amusements.) I wondered what they had played, consoling myself with the thought that—since my father, by his own admission, had no money—he had at least *not* gambled. Hungry—for I'd eaten little the previous night—I picked at stale bread crumbs. But when I saw a rat deftly ascend a table leg for *his* breakfast, I decided to go out and take some air.

Halfmoon Alley was murky with the morning's cold, clammy fog. It made me hesitate at the door, fearing my jacket, though wool, would fail to keep me warm, it being short at the wrists. Then I reminded myself that in all likelihood I would not have to go to school and deal with Sergeant Muldspoon. That thought provided enough warm cheer to get me moving. Pushing the hair out of my eyes, I set off.

As it happened, I had taken just a few steps down the court when, out of the shadows right before me, a girl leaped up, ran straight away from me, then out onto Halfmoon Street. Such was my surprise, I could do little more than take in a vague impression of a raggedy-looking girl dressed in a long skirt and a boy's cap too large for her head.

My first thought was that my appearance had caused her flight. Then I chided myself on the absurdity of such a notion. No doubt the girl was late for work or school. Our near collision at that moment was only a coincidence. Besides, if one took note of all the ragged girls in London, the day would never end. I had been taught to ignore them.

Putting the urchin out of mind, I continued down the alley, passing the curiously named Green Dragon Yard, where, I confess, I looked but saw no monsters. I pressed on—mindful that I must not lose my way in the labyrinth of unfamiliar streets.

Though it was yet early, a fair number of people were abroad. Still, I hardly expected to see anyone I knew, for I was far from my regular neighborhood. But as I rambled along the street, not to any great purpose other than to keep warm and use up time before I could wake Father, I suddenly recognized someone I did know: It was none other than my sister's particular suitor, Mr. Farquatt.

Mr. Farquatt was a most persnickety man and, to my young eyes, could have been anywhere between the age of twenty to forty years.

I always felt there was something of the child about his person. That is, his face was very smooth, with eyebrows fair to the point of invisibility. He dressed like a jack-a-dandy, with a brushed top hat that seemed to be held up by his ears, so that I rather thought of him as a small candle wearing its own snuffer. He had small, childlike hands, their fingertips stained with ink like a schoolboy's. But then, he was an accountant in the city at a French commercial establishment called the Credit Bordeaux, or so he had informed my sister, and she, making much of it, had told me.

Mr. Farquatt had been courting Clarissa since last summer. How he had met her, I didn't know. He had just appeared. When he visited—which he often did—the two inevitably sat together in a far corner. It was a puzzle to me what they spoke about, for when they chatted in such whispery voices, it sounded like twittering sparrows. Mr. Farquatt liked to engage with my father, too, though Father was not so inclined.

In the event, as I spied Mr. Farquatt, he saw me and came forward with small, hurried steps, actually lifting his top hat as if greeting another adult. Hadn't Mr. Tuckum done the same?

"Ah, Master John," he said to me in his careful voice with just a trace of foreign accent (French, I vaguely assumed), "I am so *very* delighted to meet with you."

He offered me his ink-stained fingers, which I shook, finding his hand as limp as an old apple peel.

"Yes, sir," I returned, not knowing what to say to him regarding the state of our family affairs.

"You will wonder," he said, "that I am on the streets at such an early hour."

Having no reason not to be polite, I said, "Not at all."

"I went to your home last evening so as to call upon Mademoiselle Huffam. Alas, she was not there."

I said nothing.

"I was informed," Mr. Farquatt hastened on, "that the family was—how shall I say?—removed."

"Yes, sir."

Though no one was close, he lowered his voice: "That your father . . . is in some deep difficulty . . . and has gone . . . to a . . . sponging house."

"Yes, sir," I said.

"I'm afraid," he continued, "your neighbors were only too pleased to tell me what happened. You are—am I correct?—currently residing at the old Halfmoon Inn."

"I fear it's true, sir."

"I thought," he said, "before attending to my accounting work, I would acquaint myself as to the precise location of this inn. So I am very pleased to have met you."

"Yes, sir."

"Did your mother accompany your father?"

"Yes, sir."

"And . . . your esteemed sister? Mademoiselle Huffam, is *she* there too?"

"Yes, sir."

"I see."

Not knowing what else to say, I stared at him.

"I believe"—he gazed at me from under his pale eyebrows—"it would be unkind to wait upon her in such an establishment. Perhaps even embarrassing. So then, Master John, since it's my very good fortune to meet you, I wonder if I might impose . . . Could you deliver a message to her from me?"

"Yes, sir. I'd be happy to."

"Give Mademoiselle Huffam my warmest compliments and tell her . . . if you would be so kind . . . that Mr. Farquatt would be pleased to meet her at three o'clock this afternoon at . . . the park behind St. Botolph's Church. It's not too far from the Halfmoon Inn. Do you think you could tell her that?"

"Three o'clock. Behind St. Botolph's."

"Exactly," he said. "And, please . . ." He grew flustered. "Please tell her I have a . . . proposal to make to her."

"I'll do so."

"And, though I hesitate to say it . . . I beg you to inform your esteemed father that if his difficulty is such that *I* might ease it, he need only request assistance—of me. But he should do so before I leave."

"Leave?"

"Alas, a business trip to France. Can you pass on those *two* messages?"

"Yes, sir."

Mr. Farquatt slipped a few copper pennies into my hand before turning about and scurrying off on his little feet.

Not wanting him to think I would follow him, I turned and went back past Halfmoon Alley and on toward Bishopsgate, where the shutters on shops were just being taken down. Here, people were on the street in great numbers. There were many vendors, too. With one of the pennies I'd just been given, I purchased a hot pork pie for

myself, as well as one for Clarissa and one for Brigit. Gobbling my share, I returned to the Halfmoon Inn.

As I entered the court, I saw—or thought I saw—the very same girl I'd startled when I'd come out of the inn at dawn. She had *not* gone to work—or anywhere else for that matter. But anxious to get back to my family, I set her presence aside as yet another coincidence and went into the inn.

None of my family was up. But Brigit was attending to the table.

"Ah, there you are, Master John," she said upon seeing me. "You are up early."

"I could not sleep," I explained.

She said, "Your father woke me last night—before he went to bed—and told me where you might find your great-aunt, Lady Euphemia Huffam."

That explained the voices I'd heard during the night.

"Am I to go now?" I asked, my stomach instantly tense.

"Master John," she said severely, "not only would it be the wisest thing for you to do, it's the *only* thing for you to do. Did you tell your father what I said, that he had best solve his problem himself?"

"I tried," I said, puzzled that she should be so insistent on this obvious point.

"Very well, then: Your father says Lady Huffam is to be found at Forty-five Great Winchester Street. I think you should go now."

I hesitated. "Brigit, do you think I shall be successful?"

"I fear not," she said. "But, Master John, surely it would not be so very bad if Mr. Huffam understood he *won't* have help from her."

"Why?"

"It would force him to solve the matter on his own."

Puzzled by her attitude, I nonetheless presented the meat pies I'd purchased and started out.

"Oh, Master John," Brigit called after me. "I forgot to tell you another thing."

I stopped.

"Mr. Huffam also requests that—after you visit with Lady Euphemia—you stop round to the Naval Ordinance Office and tell them that he's indisposed and won't be reporting for work today."

I had completely forgotten my father's employment. I did know— for Mother complained about it often—that as a clerk he made only one hundred pounds a year, which she considered a paltry sum. I now wondered what would happen if he *were* put into prison. Would he lose his position? His salary? And if he did . . .

"Can he not write a letter?" I asked. "The Penny Post makes six deliveries a day."

"Master John, I'm only repeating his asking."

"But, Brigit," I protested, "he's asking me to lie."

She drew herself up. "Master John," she said, her eyes quite severe, "I should think you're old enough to know that for things held dear to the heart, all kinds of sacrifices must be made."

With that reproof stinging my ears, I slunk away.

·ⵍⵣⵏⵓ·

CHAPTER 10
I Set Off to Visit Lady Euphemia

Great Winchester Street, off Broad Street, was not that far from the Halfmoon Inn. Nevertheless, I walked slowly, all but wishing I were behind my desk at Muldspoon's Militantly Motivated Academy. The next moment I wondered if I would ever return to its ranks or see Old Moldy again.

That being all too much for my head, I turned my eyes to the street. Happily, the day was now firmly in tow and there was much to distract me. Stalls were being filled. Shops were doing a brisk trade. The street was swarming with laborers, clerks, costermongers, businessmen, and vendors whose great number and variety always fascinated me. That morning I saw a peppermint-water seller, children selling necklaces of red berries, a packman selling shawls, an organ-grinder boy, and a long-song seller. Also a muffin and crumpet peddler, a rag vendor, and a blind Irish piper. I would have stopped for the last, for I liked music—and I was thinking about Brigit's unhappy Ireland—but feeling the pressure to complete my missions, I walked on.

Even so, at one corner I paused to watch a man and his boy erect a Punch-and-Judy booth. I always loved the puppets and had secretly wished to be such a boy assistant. Even as I looked on, he beat his drum to announce the start of the performance. But as I glanced about, I saw in the gathering crowd *that* girl again—the one with an overlarge boy's cap. Seeing her gave me such a jolt, I quit the place in haste.

In just one morning I'd seen this ragged girl three times. It could *not* be a coincidence. She must be following me! *Why* she should pursue me—I had never seen her before—was an uncomfortable mystery.

As I hurried away, I kept looking back over my shoulder but did not see her. Instead, I tried to focus my energy upon the importance of what lay before me. And in such a fashion I soon arrived at Great Winchester Street.

At some time there must have been fine houses there. That morning they appeared drab, more like storage vaults than places for the living. Number Forty-five Great Winchester was on a corner, set back within a shallow flagstone courtyard. The brick house had a half basement, plus two stories with large windows. A wide, funnel-shaped flight of seven stone steps—the broad end of the funnel fronting the pavement—crossed bridgelike over the basement ditch and led to double doors with a large knocker in the shape of a lion's head. A gas lamp with a pinky point of flame flickered over the doorway.

Checking to see if I had been followed—the idea that the girl was stalking me kept creeping into my mind—I climbed the steps slowly until, breathless with nervousness, I stood before the fierce lion's face.

The doors had seemed large when I first saw them. Standing right before them, they seemed immense. Anxious, I glanced over my shoulder to make sure I had an escape route. This time a tall gentleman was passing, who, upon seeing me, abruptly stopped and scrutinized me, as if surprised, before bolting round the corner.

Brushing the hair out of my eyes, I took a deep breath and, using the heavy knocker—the lion's lower jaw—rapped upon the door. I felt as if I were Daniel asking permission to enter the lion's den.

There being no response, I knocked again. One of the doors opened, and a man dressed entirely in black looked down at me. There was something perfectly skeletal about him. That is to say, he was more bone than flesh, with a hollow, ashen-cheeked face. He was shiny bald, too, with such a small nose that it was almost as if he had none. Very more distinct were deep-set, dark eyes—eyes that glared at me with what could only be perceived as disapproval. His funereal appearance made me wonder if he was in fact an undertaker, if, as my father had feared, his great-aunt had indeed passed beyond his desperate reach.

"Yes?" said the man, drawing out the word while simultaneously frowning and lifting his thin left eyebrow, thus managing to convey disappointment, disgust, and dismissal all at once.

"Please, sir," I said, "I should very much like to speak to Lady Euphemia."

"*Who* are you?"

"Please, sir, I am John Horatio Huffam. Wesley Huffam's son. Lady Euphemia is his great-aunt. My great-great-aunt."

"Oh?" he said, making it less a question than a response of disgust. For this time his lifted left eyebrow communicated mockery. "Why," he intoned, "are you here?"

"My father . . . sent me."

"Your father *sent* you? Is madam *expecting* you?"

"No, sir." By now I was sure the man was a butler. "But it . . . it's very important I see her."

He looked beyond me, on to the street, perhaps to determine if I was with anyone else.

"I'm here alone," I hastened to say.

"*How* important is this?" he asked.

"Life and death," I suggested.

A softening. "Is your father ill?"

"No, sir. Not at all."

A stiffening. "Then what is it?"

Fetching up some pluck, I said, "Please, sir, the matter is only for Lady Euphemia's ears."

He contemplated me anew with his deep, dark eyes. This time I thought the lifted eyebrow suggested curiosity. "Step in," he said.

I did, and he shut the door behind me noiselessly. "You may sit in that chair. Do *not* move," he admonished, and ascended the stairs at the end of a long, gloomy hallway.

He had directed me to a small chair with a hard, faded red, and threadbare cushion. I had barely sat down when, from the same direction the butler had gone, a gray-haired woman appeared. Dressed in black, with a white lace cap and an apron, she clearly was a servant. She drew no closer to me but stood in place, hands clasped, staring at me as if at some oddity. I was quite certain she was there to ensure that I did not steal anything. Nonetheless, I did steal some looks about.

The hallway had a few doorways—all shut—which led, perhaps, to drawing rooms. Opposite where I sat was a small table and a salver onto which one might lay visiting cards. No cards waited, but a booklet rested there, a pamphlet with a light blue wrapper covered with many small illustrations.

The walls appeared to be covered with purple silk patterned with bunches of flowers, all quite faded. The threadbare rug bore a pattern of flowers too. A few portraits of dour men in old-fashioned dress looked down on it. In their dim and dusty faces I saw a vague resemblance to my father.

There was also a standing clock, which ticked loudly and had a minute hand that moved with slow jerks, as if it required constant yanking—like a reluctant dog on a leash—to keep pace with the present time. But then, between the dull light and the ticking, the house made me think of a fading garden in perpetual twilight.

How long I sat there, I don't know. Under the watchful—if unmoving—eyes of the servant woman, it felt forever. Once, I shifted toward her and attempted a smile, even lifting a hand to make a timid wave with my fingerstips. She offered no response.

Tired—I *had* woken quite early—I believe I actually nodded off until, quite unexpectedly, a door opened and a tall man crossed in haste from one side of the hall to the other, paused momentarily to snatch up the blue pamphlet, then vanished through another door. For the briefest moment I imagined him to be the *same* man who had observed me as I stood before the doors of Lady Euphemia's house. But before I could gather my woolly wits, he was gone. I was quite sure, however, the man *had* considered me with some suspicion. It was as if a regiment of guards surrounded my great-great-aunt.

Trying to put the man out of mind, I returned to waiting, making a church of my hands and peopling it with my dirty fingers. At length the butler returned, coming down the steps and walking toward me in grave silence.

I stood up.

He stopped and considered me, as if unsure whether to speak. "Lady Euphemia will see you—briefly," he finally said even as the communicative left eyebrow rose and signaled disapproval.

"Thank you, sir."

A flicking motion of his skeletal hand dismissed the servant. To me he said, "You will deliver your message, and then you will leave. She has an appointment with her solicitor. Indeed, he has already arrived. By the servants' door," he added, as if to remind me that I had *not* used it.

I recalled my father's warning regarding one Mr. Nottingham. "Yes, sir," I said, only too willing to be done quickly. "I understand."

"You will *not* sneeze. My lady catches illness easily. She will be furious if you bring contagion."

"Yes, sir."

"And you will speak softly. She does not approve of loud noises."

"Yes, sir."

"Your speech must be slow. She does not like to be rushed."

"Yes, sir."

"You will be respectful. She does not like children."

"Yes, sir."

"Now then, follow me." He turned and led the way up the steps. I followed a few paces behind.

Upon reaching the first floor, I looked about. There was much in the way of heavy furniture, tables, chairs, mirrors, and curtains. Everywhere, objects were patterned with flowers as wilted above as below.

"This way," said the butler. He knocked softly on a door, put his ear to it, presumably received permission to enter, and pushed the way open.

A full sense of what I was about to do—what I had to do— overcame me. My heart thudded. I felt weak to the point of dizziness. I tried to remember the rules: Speak slowly. No sneezing. No loud noises. No diseases. But by then I was already being ushered into the presence of Lady Euphemia herself.

⠏⠙⠑

CHAPTER 11
I Meet Lady Euphemia

A large bedroom. Two windows, curtains partially drawn, the light diminished. More silk wallpaper with more faded flowers. A tall armoire against one wall. Two chairs against another. A fireplace with a fire screen. To one side of the room, a chaise lounge. A corner wash-stand table upon which sat a great variety of pillboxes, bowls, cups, and apothecary jars. The room reeking of the medicinal smell of car-bolic acid such as used for general disinfectant.

But it was a large four-poster bed that dominated the room. In turn, the bed was dominated by a woman beneath sea green blankets, which did nothing to hide her great bulk, which made a mountain of her bedclothes. In truth, I had never seen such a large woman (or man!), though all I could see of her were shoulders and head, propped up by at least five plump pillows.

Her eyes, nose, and mouth were all but drowned by folds of flesh: pendulant cheeks, multiple chins, beetled brows—the skin being the pallor of unbaked bread, and just as unappetizing.

From what I could see, she was dressed in a gray sleeping gown, with a profusion of white lace and a high collar round her many-layered neck. Her head was crowned by an ill-fitting sleeping bonnet, which allowed thick strands of gingery hair—not unlike my father's in color—to hang about her face like slack snakes. Her hands—assuming she had them—were beneath the sea green blankets.

As she lay there, I was reminded of a landed whale depicted in the *Illustrated London News*: immense and helpless.

Standing to one side of the bed was a servant woman, dressed very much like the woman I had seen below. In one hand she held a little brown bottle.

The butler guided me to the foot of the bed, where I stood, my hands clutching each other, overwhelmed by the sight of this prostrate figure.

The woman on the bed—who I assumed was my father's great-aunt Euphemia Huffam—shifted her head slightly that she might

scrutinize me. Her eyes, sunk within her bulging face, were cold blue and glared at me with an icy severity.

"My Lady Euphemia," the butler announced in a whisper, "may I present Master John Horatio Huffam."

Some long moments passed while the woman—breathing deeply, all but wheezing—appraised me. Slowly, she withdrew a hand—flipperlike—from under the blankets. It was a very fat hand with many a jeweled finger, the jewels throwing sparkling light about the otherwise dull room.

Ponderously, she reached toward the servant woman. The servant, in response, handed her the bottle she was holding. My great-great-aunt put the bottle to each nostril in turn, inhaled, and shuddered—twice. I could have sworn the blankets—like the surface of the sea—trembled at the disturbance.

She returned the bottle, settled herself, and only then spoke. "Boy," she said in a voice that startled me—for it was deep and breathy, as if echoing from deep within. "Boy, are you *diseased* to any degree?"

Hardly able to find my own voice, I answered, "No, my lady."

"Touched by dyscrasia, dysentery, or dyspepsia?"

"No, my lady."

"Are you *prone* to any disease?"

"No, my lady."

"I'm prone to the 'dys,'" she said. "And the medical men find more of them each passing day."

"I wish you better health, my lady."

"I should hope you do. I suffer much. And constantly. Far more than most. My doctors inform me that in all probability I shall, at some point, *die*."

"I'm sure I should be very much grieved to hear it."

"I appreciate your sympathy. There is so little compassion in the modern age. Generally, I must buy it." The thought seemed to remind her. She turned toward the butler. "You may go, William," she said.

"Yes, madam," said the man. He withdrew in silence.

Aunt Euphemia focused her deep, cold eyes on me. "I have been reliably informed," she said at last, her voice all but rumbling, "that you are the son of Wesley Huffam. Are you his *youngest* son?"

"His only son, my lady."

"Then *you* must be the *last* Huffam."

"I have a sister."

"She does not signify. You are the last male Huffam, the bearer of the name."

"I suppose I am," I murmured.

The room was filled with the sound of her heavy breathing.

"You look very much like a Huffam. Repeat your name."

"John. John Horatio Huffam."

"Named after my brother. Your father's great-uncle. Christened, I presume, to insinuate you into *my* good graces."

"I don't know that, my lady."

"I do," she said, breathing noisily and staring at me with what I took to be such disgust that it was all I could do not to bolt from her presence. "Your father," she intoned, "is singularly improvident."

Not knowing the word—save that it sounded like an insult—I said nothing.

"A wastrel," she chose to inform me. "A spendthrift. A squanderer. In short, a knave." Her face quivered with such indignation, my cheeks burned.

I hung my head.

"Your shame speaks well of you," she said.

"Yes, my lady," I returned, hardly knowing what else to say.

"Was it *he* who sent you to *me*?"

"Yes, my lady."

"Why did he not come himself?"

"He ... he is ... indisposed."

"*Ill?*" she cried in alarm. "With what disease?" The jeweled hand reached toward the servant.

"Not ... physically," I hastened to say.

"Ah! That's to the good." She returned her hand beneath the blankets. "Then I presume he's indisposed with *embarrassment.*"

"I can't say, my lady."

"I have no doubt," she went on, "he sent you because he desires *something* of me."

My mortification growing, I could only nod.

"Now then, if your father sent you to me, he must be in exceedingly difficult straits. He knows I hold him in unrelentingly low esteem. Tell me what he wants."

I hardly knew where to begin.

"Young man," she prompted, "you would be wise to speak the truth about your father. And quickly, too. Since I am so often ill and likely to die at *any* moment, I'm compelled to speak *only* the truth. Now, tell me what has happened."

"My lady," I began hesitantly. "My lady, my father is . . . in debt. If he does not pay what he owes, he will go to debtors' prison."

Her lips puckered as if she had just sucked upon a lemon. "I have no doubt he *deserves* to be there," she said. "Where is he now?"

"At the Halfmoon Inn. It's a . . . sponging house."

"A Huffam . . . in a *sponging* house! When does he go to court?"

"In two days' time."

"I had been informed," she said, "that he was employed and drawing . . . wages." She uttered the last with distaste. "Is that correct?"

"He works," I said, "at the Naval Ordinance Office."

"To whom does he owe the money?"

"A Mr. O'Doul."

"An *Irishman?*"

I shrugged.

"Who is he?"

"I don't know."

"So your father—in this acute difficulty—sends *you* to plead his case. How old are you?"

"Fourteen."

"Are *you* employed?"

I shook my head.

"Do you go to school?"

"Yes, my lady."

"Where?"

"Muldspoon's Militantly Motivated Academy."

"It sounds as if your father should attend. And the rest of your family? Aside from your sister. Who might they be?"

"My mother."

"Yet, it is *you* who have been sent to me."

"Yes, my lady."

"Why?"

"The . . . family . . . seems to think it best."

"Which is to say, *you* are the best of a sorry lot."

Though it was all I could do to keep from bursting into tears, I managed to whisper, "I don't know that."

"I do."

I said nothing.

"So far," she pressed on, "we have avoided the most distasteful question of all." She breathed deeply. "How much money does your father wish me to give him?"

I lifted my head with effort. "My lady, he said to tell you it would only be a loan."

"A subterfuge. A trick. He will never repay it. Not in my life. Still, tell me, how much has he asked you to request?"

Unable to speak, I was acutely aware that the only sound in the room was her labored breathing. Then came a slight noise at the door. As if someone was listening. The butler, I decided. The thought magnified my shame. Knowing I had to speak, I took a deep breath and replied, "Three hundred pounds."

"Three *hundred*!" Like a whale leaping from the sea—breaching— Lady Euphemia sat up and fairly lunged toward the servant woman, who again handed her the bottle. She put the bottle to her nose, inhaled at each nostril, gave the bottle back, and then sank again beneath her ocean of blankets, visibly shuddering.

"It is a joke," she rasped between deep breaths. "A *monstrous* presumption. Master John, your father is a greater idiot than even *I* had imagined."

Though my eyes were brimming with tears, I made myself look at her. "He is . . . my father, my lady."

She stared at me. The eyes seemed to harden. "Do you love him?"

Unable to speak, I nodded.

"Your loyalty is commendable," she said. "Your judgment is not."

I could not bear it any longer. "Please, my lady," I whispered in a choked voice, "I must . . . excuse myself."

"Why?"

"You are . . . insulting my father."

"But I have yet to give my answer."

"I . . . I think I know what it will be."

"Do you?"

I nodded.

"*Never* presume to know what *I* might think," she declared in her rumbling voice. "Where will you go now?"

"To the Naval Ordinance Office."

"Why?"

"To say my father cannot report for work."

She stared at me. "Since you are a Huffam," she rumbled, "the last of a noble breed, I wish you to return . . . tomorrow," she said. For the first time she spoke to the servant woman. "Peggy, what time will my doctors be arriving?"

"Doctor Fitzwillow at nine. Young Doctor Watson at ten. Doctor Ferguson at eleven."

"You shall come tomorrow at twelve thirty," she said to me. "Promptly. Any later and I shall be exhausted. Of course, if, in the interval, you fall ill, do *not* return. And, if I should die before your return, do *not* expect one penny. Now go. I have an appointment with Mr. Nottingham, my solicitor. He is already waiting. Since I usually defer to his judgment, I shall consult with him as to what to do about you." That said, she closed her eyes and seemed to sink even deeper into her bed.

I didn't know how to react, until the woman servant touched my shoulder. "This way," she whispered into my ear, and led me—eyes foggy with welling tears—out of the room.

Just outside the door there was, I thought, the same tall man I'd seen in the downstairs hall. Presuming it was Lady Euphemia's solicitor, I hastily averted my clouded eyes—for I could not bear to have anyone look at me—and allowed myself to be guided to the head of the steps. I went down alone.

The butler was waiting for me at the foot. Assuming it was he who had been listening at the door, I wondered how much he had heard. He said nothing, though he did lift his eyebrow as if to say, *I told you so.*

When he finally closed the door behind me, I ran down the steps and round the corner of the court. There, leaning against a brick wall, I burst into tears.

∾ৎ৶৫৶

CHAPTER 12
I Gaze Upon the Traitors' Gate

I required considerable time to recover from the misery and shame brought on by my visit to Lady Euphemia. It was not her great bulk that had so belittled me: It was her harsh words about Father. I hated them. Found them to be cruel. Was certain they were wrong. Yet (I could hear myself say), what if they *were* true? The possibility burned my heart. But then, can a son desire anything more than that his father be *better* than other people say?

As I stood there, miserable, I chanced to look up. To my surprise, I saw blue sky and a clear sun, rare sights for late November in London. Not only did I take much pleasure in it, I wanted to believe it was an omen of good things to come. I reminded myself that, after all, Lady Euphemia had *not* said no. To the contrary: She had asked me to come back tomorrow. Perhaps I would then receive good tidings—and she *would* provide the money my father needed—so our calamity could be over. Oh, how I wanted to believe that!

Bolstered in my spirits, I dried my eyes and took a deep breath. I had one more chore to accomplish—to report Father's absence from his work. Certain it would not be nearly so painful a business as I had just survived, I started off.

The Admiralty, where most of the naval affairs of our nation are conducted and where the First Lord of the Admiralty resides, is near the new Parliament building, in Whitehall. My father once took me there to show me the spot where England's great hero, Lord Admiral Horatio Nelson, had lain in state. He had told me my middle name was to honor this man who sacrificed his life to defend us from the French, our old enemy.

But Father, though he worked *for* the Admiralty, worked *in* the Naval Ordinance Office, a different place altogether. For, as my father once informed me with considerable pride, his office had secret business to conduct and it was thought best to give it a separate location. Just what secret business that might be, he never had divulged.

On my way there I used Mr. Farquatt's last penny to purchase a baked potato from a vendor with an oven cart. I ate it slowly, letting its warmth fill me with a makeshift sense of well-being. Then off I went—a long walk.

My father's place of work was to be found in Black Swan Court, close behind the Church of All Hallows, very near the Tower of London. In fact, as I drew close to my destination, I could not help but catch glimpses of the Tower itself.

I knew some of its menacing history. Built by King William to overawe Londoners after he conquered England in 1066, the central Tower had ever since served as a royal castle. It filled many a purpose, but I knew it best, as did most Englishmen, as the spot where numerous highborn traitors or falsely accused subjects had been put in jail—passing through the Traitors' Gate—to await beheading.

Some claimed the place was haunted by a few of those poor souls, so that whenever I saw the Tower, I had the shivers. I sometimes thought my reaction explained *why* the Naval Ordinance Office was situated so close by. If, as my father told me, there were state secrets to be found there, a view of the forbidding Tower must give pause to would-be traitors or spies.

Yet, since the office was also close to All Hallows Church, that proximity, I presumed, served as a reminder of all that religion called morally right. It was as if the choice between right and wrong—and their consequences—were *both* close to hand.

Restless, yet not quite settled enough to go to my father's office, I crossed the open space between the church and the Tower's outer walls. I peered down. The moat had been drained for some time, the space currently being used for military exercises. None were going on.

I continued downhill, passing the outer, middle tower, where people, for a few pennies, were allowed to enter the Tower precincts and walk about. Some years back there had been a fire within, and not all had been restored. Still, a few soldiers lived there, as well as the guards who protected the Crown jewels. A lone Beefeater, as the Tower's red-coated guards are called, stood in position, musket in hand, before the entryway.

From the wharf, which fronted the Tower complex, the smell of the river was quite foul. Any number of ships, mostly sailing ships but a few small steamers, were anchored or tethered here.

Farther on, I found myself looking down upon the infamous Traitors' Gate. I say "down" because it is an arched entryway to the Tower at water level, strongly gated so no one can enter. There was, however, another archway built through the wharf upon which I had stopped. This provided access to the gate, since the only way one could reach it was by water, and then only at high tide. But I did see a wooden ladder, which might allow one to go down from the wharf to water level, presumably to a small boat.

It was all fascinating to me, bringing to mind the tales I knew of famous and infamous people who had passed in and out of the Traitors' Gate. I would have stayed and let my imagination roam, but I reminded myself of my errand and went on.

Besides, I thought, what had *I* to do with traitors?

I was soon to learn.

 cههو

CHAPTER 13

I Go to the Naval Ordinance Office

The Naval Ordinance Office was a modest three-story stone building with little to distinguish it from the adjacent structures—merely a small brass plaque next to its blue door.

When I approached the building that morning, however, there was a difference. Standing next to the door, as if on guard, was a blue-coated constable. I immediately recognized him as one of those in attendance when we were removed from our home to the sponging house. He was, in fact, the very one who had informed me as to what a sponging house was.

I hesitated. I was not so dull-witted as to believe his presence was happenstance—any more than were the sudden but regular appearances of the ragged girl with the large cap. That is to say, it was impossible for me not to consider that this constable was connected to my father's affairs. But how? And why?

Though I was determined to do my errand, I did so with a feeling of dread, wondering if, when the Peeler saw me, he would summon other police.

I started for the door. Sure enough, the constable looked up, saw me, and called out, "'Ere there, lad!"

I stopped on the instant, my stomach churning.

"Fancy meetin' you again so soon," he said in a pleasant enough voice. "And where might you be goin'?"

"To the naval office."

"And *why* might you be goin' there?"

"I have to deliver a message for my father."

"And 'e is . . . ?"

"Wesley Huffam."

"Ah, yes, 'im. I 'ad forgotten the name. And what kind of message might 'e 'ave asked you to bring 'ere?"

I considered. While I thought the questions reasonable in themselves, I could not imagine why the constable might ask them at all.

"It's because my father works in the naval office. A clerk. As you know, he's . . . he's indisposed. He asked me to report his absence."

The policeman grinned. "I figure 'e *is* indisposed, ain't 'e? But don't you worry none, lad. I'm duty bound to keep yer secret—and 'is. But would you like to know why I'm 'ere?"

"Yes, sir. If you'd be so kind."

" 'Appy to oblige," he said, touching his hat with a finger in an easy salute. "When a man is sent to a sponging 'ouse, the law says— ask Mr. Tuckum—'e's expected to stay put. Knowing this 'ere is yer father's place of employment, I was asked to make sure 'e didn't come."

"Yes, sir."

"You're not about to take anything *from* 'is office, are you?"

"Oh, no, sir."

"Then, seeing you're 'ere—not yer father—and learning of yer errand, *I* need not be 'ere no more." With that, he touched a finger to his hat again and said, "Go on in, then."

He was surely agreeable. Yet, I kept feeling that something in all this was very odd. I wanted to ask him who had requested this guard duty—or what he thought I could possibly take from the office—but feared to. Instead, I went up to the door, turned the handle, and since it was very heavy, had to push my way in with two hands.

I entered upon a long hallway with shiny marble floors and bright white walls on which hung many paintings of great ships in full sail. Some were in furious battle, with blazing cannons blasting away at close quarters. I could almost smell the smoke.

In the middle of the hallway was a high desk, which faced the door. Perched behind this desk sat a naval clerk dressed in the dark blue uniform of a junior officer. Junior in rank perhaps, but senior in age, with white hair and many a ratlinelike wrinkle on his face. He had a black patch over one eye and, moreover, a scar across his left cheek, as if he'd been cut by a sword. It was easy for me to imagine him in one of the pitched battles depicted in the paintings.

He must have been sitting on a high stool, for he was able to look down at me from what felt like a lofty height, as if from a yardarm.

"Yes, mate, what can I do for you?" he asked.

"I wish to report for my father, Wesley Huffam. He's a clerk here."

"What's his ranking?" he said, opening a large ledger book.

"I'm not sure."

"Huffam, you say." He turned the pages. "Hayman. Hochman. Huffam! Here it is! Wesley Huffam. Copy Department." He looked down at me. "For your information, he copies ordinance specifications for the cannon manufacturers."

"I didn't know that, sir."

He considered me with his one good and severe eye. "Lad, the more a sailor knows about his captain," he said, "the more he'll know how he'll weather the gales. You'd best remember that," he said, wagging a bent finger at me as if wielding a curved saber.

"Yes, sir."

He studied his ledger book momentarily before returning to me.

"Are you aware that your father has missed a fair number of work-days?"

I felt my cheeks grow hot. "No, sir, I am not."

"If I were you, I might inform him that there are those in the First Lord of the Admiralty's quarters, so to speak, who might take exception to his shirking his watch. They just might."

"Yes, sir."

"All right, then, end of fo'castle preaching. Now, what about him?" He picked up a steel-pointed pen, dipped the nib into an ornate bottle of ink, and readied himself to make a note in his book while awaiting my answer.

I said, "He bid me to say he would not be coming to work today. He . . . he's not well."

"What's his ailment, then?"

This not being a question I had expected, I could feel my face grow hotter. Fortunately, I remembered a word from Lady Euphemia's list. "Dyspepsia," I blurted out.

The old sailor looked down at me, rather sternly, as if he doubted my word, but then he wrote, I presume, what I had said. "All right, then, mate. Dyspepsia. I've marked it in the log." He aimed his finger at me. "Now then, some advice: Sail back to your home port. Convey the message to *your* captain that the Lord High Admiral trusts that every man will do his duty at his appointed watch on the morrow."

I didn't have the heart—or stomach—to say such an event would be unlikely. I said only, "I'll tell him, sir."

As I turned to go, the clerk's words—*The more a sailor knows about his captain, the more he'll know how he'll weather the gales*—made me think what I'd not thought of before: To wit: I knew my father well enough at home. But of his life *outside* home, other than his theatrical interests, I knew very little. It had never troubled me before. It made me uneasy now. For surely we were sailing in a fierce storm.

Regardless, I was relieved to have accomplished all Father had told me to do. So it was with a somewhat lighter heart that I pushed open the door and stepped out into Black Swan Court. There, standing before me, was a man I had never seen before. Nonetheless, he was staring at me in such a direct, aggressive way that I could have but little doubt he was waiting for me.

✿◕◕✿

CHAPTER 14

I Meet a Mysterious Man

The man was rather tall and skinny, with a long and, from what I could see of it, narrow head. Not only was he heavily bearded, his features were further concealed by a large brimmed hat in the American style. He wore a common black frock coat, buttoned high to his neck. In his hand was an umbrella, which he held before him like a rapier.

The more I considered him—and we stood there staring at each other for a goodly time—the more I sensed something *false* about him. Which is to say, I became uncomfortably convinced he was

wearing an ill-fitting *disguise,* that his beard was not real. I truly had
to curb an impulse to leap forward and yank it away. Of course, I
dared not. For while he stood there looking most peculiar, there *was,*
notwithstanding, something menacing about him, for his eyes gazed
upon me with ill-concealed hostility.

I glanced about, very aware of the fact that the constable I'd previously chatted with was nowhere in sight. Other than this man and
myself, no one was in Black Swan Court.

"S-S-Sir . . . ," I stammered, "were you . . . were you waiting to speak
to me?"

By way of answering, the man tucked his umbrella under an arm,
took a little gray book from a pocket, and began to leaf through it
rapidly, touching finger to lips to aid him in turning each page.

"What . . . what do you want?" I demanded.

"Father," he fairly barked, reading from his book, "Wesley John Louis Huffam. Father's employment: Naval Ordinance Office. Present circumstance: In debt three hundred pounds. Owed to: Mr. O'Doul. Current residence: Halfmoon Inn, a sponging house. You, John Horatio Huffam, his son, went to Forty-five Great Winchester Street. Why?"

He snapped a page over. "Because you called upon your father's great-aunt, Lady Euphemia Huffam. For what purpose? To beg money. Next: Came to the Naval Ordinance Office. Next: Met me." He lowered his little book and stared at me. "Dare you," he demanded, "deny any item?"

"How do you know all that?" I cried, dumbfounded.

"An informant," he said, rather smugly, I thought.

On the instant I recalled the ragged girl with the cap, the one who had been stalking me, and made the quick guess that it was she who provided this man with all this information.

Now, I could have escaped with ease. But where would I go? For, even as I contemplated fleeing—wanted to go—I realized that this man had already revealed that he knew where my family was staying. That meant, since I fully intended to return to my family, I would not be able to escape him.

"Who are you?" I asked. "Why should you care about me?"

He made a stiff, jerky bow. "Inspector Copperfield. Scotland Yard."

Having never heard of such a person *or* of Scotland Yard, I replied, "What do you inspect?"

"Crime! Misdeeds! Frauds! Which is to say, thieves, burglars, robbers, cheats, housebreakers, embezzlers, blackmailers, pickpockets, swell mobsmen, shoplifters, assassins, muggers, and"—he glanced in the direction of the Tower of London—"traitors."

"Do you think *I* have committed a crime?" I gasped, now feeling very alone and quite afraid.

He pointed his umbrella right at me. "You look just like your father, and I have little doubt *he* is one of those criminals."

"Please, sir," I said with all my heart, "I don't think so. I truly don't."

"Think again," he returned.

"But . . . when you *inspect* criminals," I managed to say, "what do you *do* to them?"

"Jail them. Set them to the treadmill. Put them in the hulks. Transport them. If necessary, hang them. Now then, explain what you have been doing."

"I've . . . I've been running errands for my father."

"Errands?"

"It's the truth, sir! It really is."

"Your father is," he repeated, "*is* Wesley John Louis Huffam?"

"Yes, sir. That's his name. Does he know you? Do you know him?"

"I know a great deal *about* him," he replied. "What do *you* know?"

"Why, he is . . . as you just said, my father, sir." Then I recalled what the clerk at the naval office had told me. So I added, "He copies ordinance specifications for cannon manufacturers. What else, I'm not sure."

"You need to know more. Consider this a warning."

"A warning? A warning about what?"

"Your father," he said. "It's your *business* to know more. When and if you do learn more, remember, I am Inspector Copperfield of Scotland Yard."

"But . . . how can I find you?"

"You can't, but I can find you. Good day." That said, he again pointed his umbrella at me—as if to mark me—pulled the brim of his hat lower, then spun about and strode from the courtyard, leaving me in a state of astonishment and fright. Indeed, I was shaking.

Trying to steady myself, I left the courtyard and went along Tower Street until I reached Trinity Square, the little oval park overlooking the Tower. There, I found an iron bench, upon which I sat to calm down.

Though I gazed again at the ancient White Tower with its fluttering royal flags, that time I barely saw it. Instead, I tried to make some sense of the things this Inspector Copperfield had told me. Gradually, I realized something: It was one thing for him to have known about what I did that morning—my *public* movements. They were there for anyone to see, and presumably, that raggedy girl had noted them. But how did he know about Great-Aunt Euphemia? Or that I had requested a loan from her? Even the amount! Yet he spoke nothing of my meeting Mr. Farquatt. In short, he did *not* know everything I had done that morning.

As to *why* he wished to know these things, he more than implied a crime was involved. And . . . my father was in some way implicated.

Did he mean the crime of being in debt?

I almost hoped so. That is to say, I hoped there was nothing *more*. Among the other crimes he had mentioned—perhaps because we were adjacent to the Tower—treason loomed large. But then, I didn't even know what made one a "swell mobsman."

Quite agitated, I decided to return home as quickly as possible, report on what I had done, and then beg my father to explain more than he had previously. I suspected that if he wished to do so, he could.

My head filled with the questions I was determined to put to him. The primary ones were: What *was* Scotland Yard? Secondly, why was the inspector from that place interested in my father?

Deeply troubled but resolved, I headed toward the Halfmoon Inn. I walked as fast as I could—occasionally, for such was my anxiety, even breaking into a run. But no sooner did I turn, quite breathlessly, onto Halfmoon Alley, than someone leaped up before me, bringing me to a sudden halt.

I gasped: It was none other than the ragged girl with the large cap, the one who had been following me, the one, I was sure, who had provided Inspector Copperfield with all that information about me. And this time she was not running away. On the contrary: She was blocking my way.

CHAPTER 15
I Am Confronted by the Ragged Girl

Small, slight, and wiry, she had snarled, dirty brown hair that hung below her neck in disarray. While her face was positively filthy, it yet offered up the broadest grin of crooked teeth I'd ever seen, along with eyes positively bright with merriment.

She wore what appeared to be a man's jacket—much too big for her and thoroughly ragged—so that I had little doubt if I had pulled upon it, it might tear apart in any number of places. As it was, the sleeve cuffs were tied round her wrists with bits of string to keep out the chill. As for the baggy skirt she wore, it, too, was torn and patched in more than a few places. Her overlarge shoes were old and did not match, giving her a clownlike look. As for that hat, I had never seen such on a *girl*. It positively flopped upon her head like an oversized and cockeyed muffin cap.

Moreover, she stood before me arms akimbo, shockingly brash, with something fierce and determined about her, as if enjoying my discomfort. Indeed, her whole appearance suggested nothing so much as a belligerent and scruffy bug, one capable of quick, darting movements and the ability to give a sharp sting.

"I knows all 'bout you," she proclaimed loudly, as if daring me to contradict her.

"Because you've been following me."

"I guess I 'ave."

"And you told Inspector Copperfield where I went."

"Inspector Copperfield? Can't say I knew that. But then, in me line of work a surprise is like a bright shillin'. Course, I don't much like the Peelers, but they are some of me best customers."

"Customers?"

"Don't they pays me to sneak 'bout to follow types like you? They do indeed! Who's goin' to notice a shabby mite of a girl like me? An' since they pays me, shouldn't I do what's asked? It's not easy findin' work—respectable work—for a girl these days. Sellin' flowers on a curb ain't me style, no more than sittin' in a sewin' shop for fifty, sixty 'ours a week for three shillings or less."

"Are you suggesting that minding *my* business is respectable work?" I said.

She only grinned. "Matter o' fact, I *do* call it just that, when you consider mindin' other people's business *is* me business. So I guess that's all right, ain't it?"

"How did you know my great-great-aunt's name was Euphemia?"

"Don't know that I did," she said. "But since you've just tossed me 'er name—Eup'emia, great-great-aunt—I'll keep it up 'ere." She lifted her ridiculous cap. "See, what I am is a *sneak*, a street sweeper o' bits o' information. Got more bits in me 'ead than most dogs 'ave fleas. I don't forgets nothin'. See, there's money to be 'ad for bits o' information. Good as the Queen's coins. Sooner or later, I'll sell that bit—Great-Great-Aunt Eup'emia—see if I don't."

"You can do what you like with it," I said, quite sure she was mocking me. "I have to get on."

"I've no wantin' to stop you, mate, though I'd guess you're goin' back to the 'Alfmoon Inn to be with yer family."

"Are you going to tell him that, too?"

"I've done me work for the day, thank you. Been paid for what's been sneaked, an' no more sneakin' till more coins cover the palm."

"Then what do you want of me?"

"Well now, as it 'appens, Master John 'Uffam—see, I knows yer name, don't I?—sometimes when I finishes a job followin' a fella, like I done this mornin' o' you, then, when I'm done, the fella I've been followin' pays me to follow the one who 'ad 'im followed, if you can follow that."

"And a girl, too," I said with indignation. "You should be ashamed of yourself!"

The smile vanished. "What's wrong with a girl doin' what I do? I've never 'ad a look inside me insides, except I'm guessin' a girl 'as a stomach like a boy, don't she? And it needs food too, don't it?"

"At any rate, I have no need for you," I said, not wishing to answer her question.

"Not *now* maybe. But maybe. I'm just offerin'. Keeps everythin' even'anded. I may be a sneak, thank you, it suits me, but I'm proud to say I'm an even'anded sneak."

"I'll get on very well without you, thank you," I said, and walked past her.

"Mind," she called after me, "if ever you change yer notion, just come 'long to the Rookery of St. Giles. Ask for Sary the Sneak. Full name Sarah, but Sary works fine. People there know where to find me. Get that, Sary the Sneak!"

I shook my head in annoyance. I had never met a girl like her and sincerely desired I'd never meet her again.

 భాేஂ

CHAPTER 16

I Wonder About Father

Putting the girl out of mind, I made my way to the Halfmoon Inn. When I got there, Mr. Tuckum was sitting on one of the benches, intently reading a light blue pamphlet covered with many illustrations. I recognized it as the same as I'd seen in Lady Euphemia's hallway.

"Ah, good morning to you, Master John," he said, glancing my way as he pushed his eyeglasses up onto his forehead. "You've been out and abroad early like the good old-fashioned boy you are."

"I had some errands to do for my father."

"Did you now? Then let me be so bold as to hope that they were fruitful. He's a fine gentleman, your father is, and I hate to see him mired in these . . . hmm . . . troubles. I do enjoy his company. And he plays a fair game of all fours," he added.

I recalled seeing the cards on the table when I'd come down that morning.

"Unfortunately," continued the bailiff, "the cards were not falling his way. Still, he took his losses like the old-fashioned gentleman he is. 'Put it on the bill,' says he, laughing. 'I can do that,' says I."

"Has he come down?" I asked, for as I looked around, I saw no one.

"Not him nor any of your excellent family. But your servant girl—Brigit, is that her name?—was about asking for you and brought up some tea. Have you had any yourself?"

"I had some of the leavings from last night, thank you."

He lay down his pamphlet, sat back against the bench, and considered me in a speculative fashion. "Well then, my lad, might I ask—in a purely professional, old-fashioned way—have you *had* any success?"

I stood there, but my feelings of shame and embarrassment kept me from answering his question.

"Ah, well," he said with a sigh, "perhaps it's too early to say. Can I fetch you something to eat? To drink?"

"No, sir. I should see my father." I started for the steps but paused. "Please, sir, might you know what Scotland Yard is?"

"Scotland Yard!" cried the bailiff. "What makes you ask about that?"

"I . . . I heard it spoken of and wondered what it is."

"It's the offices of the Metropolitan Police, where the constables are all headquartered. In old-fashioned times ambassadors from Scotland resided there."

"Would . . . would someone called an 'inspector' come from that place?"

He nodded. "The *top* constables do. The ones who investigate the most serious crimes. The best is Chief Inspector Ratchet. Reports right to the superintendent, he does, who then reports directly to the home secretary."

"Do you know one named Inspector Copperfield?"

"Copperfield?" He held up the pamphlet he'd been reading. "That's the name of this serialized story everyone's been following. *David Copperfield.* By that author, Mr. Dickens. Wonderful story. Wonderful writer. Is that truly this inspector's name: Copperfield?"

"He said so."

"I never heard of him. Perhaps a new man on the force."

"Would they wear disguises?"

"Disguises? Well, yes, from time to time. They surely aren't in uniforms."

"And what's a 'swell mobsman'?"

He considered me thoughtfully. "He's a clever confidence man. A cheat. What makes you ask all this?"

"Just curious," I said, and started off.

"Master John!" he called, and held out a small book. "I acquired this for your father. Bring it to him with my compliments. Not entertaining like *Copperfield*, but, given his circumstances, practical."

I took the book, noting the title: *The Prisoner's Guide; or, Every Debtor His Own Lawyer.*

"And, Master John, do remind him," said the bailiff, "he must not leave the premises."

I ran up the steps before he could say more.

Happily, my father was not in bed, as I feared he might be. Instead, he was fully dressed, working upon his neckcloth, folding it with great exactitude.

"Ah, there you are," he said when I came in. "Wondered where you'd gone. At school, perhaps."

"Father," I said, frustrated that he should have forgotten, "I went to do the errands you asked of me."

"Did you? Ah, yes." He turned and continued to work on his neckcloth, his back toward me, as if unwilling to look me in the eye.

"And how, young sir," he asked, "is the weather today? Chilly? Damp? I heard some wind rattling the shutters. But, of course, this is an ancient place and—"

"The bailiff wanted me to give you this book." I held it out to him.

He took it, barely glancing at the title before tossing it on the bed as if it had nothing to do with him.

"He also asked me to remind you," I said, "that you're not allowed to leave the inn." When Father made no comment, I said, "Don't you want to hear what happened?"

"*Did* something happen?"

"You asked me to visit your great-aunt Euphemia."

"Do you know, I'm quite sure she should be called 'Lady.'" He still refused to look at me. "She *is* the daughter of a baronet. My great-grandfather. I'm assuming she must hold land somewhere.

But there are strict rules regarding what you call someone, very strict rules."

"Please, Father, I want to tell you what happened. If you're interested."

"Of course I'm interested! How did you find her?" he said with a final fussing over the neckcloth. "Was she friendly? Chatty? Full of family gossip? Did she offer you a substantial breakfast? Were other people calling?"

Gazing at him, I realized he was trembling.

"Father," I said, "she didn't say no."

He swung right around, eyes upon me. "Oh, excellent! What did she say exactly?"

"That I should return for her answer. Tomorrow."

"Well done, John!" he cried. The trembling gone, he clapped a firm hand upon my shoulder. "I'm absolutely sure our little difficulties will soon be resolved. Of that we can be quite confident."

"But, Father—listen to me—I'm not sure she *will* say yes. She . . . she said some very unpleasant things about you."

"She or her solicitor, Mr. Nottingham?"

"There was a man there. I don't know if it was him. But when Lady Euphemia spoke of you—disparagingly—I . . . I defended you."

"Good lad! With excellent reason too. Am I not your father? John, buck up. Pay no attention to her. Or that Nottingham cad. The most unpleasant of people, both of them. She thinks herself wise. He considers himself a good actor. Wrong, both. As you know, it's really *my* money she has," he babbled on. "I'm glad I've little to do with her. What of her health?"

"She said her doctors told her she will die."

"Did she really? Well, so must we all. So must we all. But it's good to know she will provide the help we need."

Ignoring his last remark, I said, "Then I went to the Naval Ordinance Office."

"Much pleasanter, I'm sure."

"I was asked to remind you that you have missed many days of work."

"Were you? I'm not so sure I would believe *that* if I were you. Come, let's have some breakfast." Full of energy, he opened the door to the room.

"And when I came out of the naval office," I went on, "I was met by an inspector from Scotland Yard."

That stopped him. For a moment he neither spoke nor moved, but then he slowly turned back to me. "Were you?"

I nodded. "Do you know about Scotland Yard?"

He shut the door behind him and drew close. "I suppose I do. Who was this inspector?" he said, his voice low. "What did he want?"

"He ... Inspector Copperfield ... said I should consider his words to me a warning."

It was as if I'd struck him. Panic suffused his face. "Copperfield? A *warning*? What exactly did he tell you?"

"Not very much. Except that . . . warning." I watched Father carefully. "Father, what does it all mean?"

His fright subsided. "Oh, goodness, John," he said in his plummy actor's voice. "What a question to ask of *me*! You just said it was *you* he warned. I have not the *slightest* idea what that man was talking about. The impertinence. If he has business with me, he should have addressed his remarks to me, not you."

That said, he turned in haste toward the door. "You'll excuse me. I'm quite famished. Oh, please don't mention that incident to anyone." He fled.

I looked after him, hearing anew Inspector Copperfield's words. I thought over that roster of criminals the inspector had listed: thieves, burglars, robbers, cheats, housebreakers, embezzlers, blackmailers, pickpockets, swell mobsmen, shoplifters, assassins, muggers, traitors.

Which one, I wondered, might apply to my own father?

છે૭૭૭

CHAPTER 17

I Hear an Odd Story

When I finally reached the main room, I discovered my family assembled around the table. Mr. Tuckum was nowhere in sight—perhaps he'd gone off to continue his reading. It was Brigit who was serving the breakfast.

Halfway down the steps I saw that my mother and sister were in far better spirits than the night before. And I heard my father saying: "So you see, Mrs. Huffam, just as I promised you, Great-Aunt Euphemia will be providing the necessary money. In a few days all this unpleasantness will be over. All will be restored to normal."

I stopped—two steps from the bottom—not sure I was hearing correctly.

"But, Pa," Clarissa said, "how did you ever persuade the old biddy to give you so much money?"

"As for that," said my father, glancing over toward me and giving me a private wink, "she was only too happy to oblige. Of course, she's perfectly aware that I'm the *rightful* heir to Grandfather's fortune, not her. All but admitted it. No doubt she has an awkward conscience. She certainly should. In any case, she's willing to share."

"Does that mean," asked Mother with ill-disguised eagerness, "that when she dies—which, considering her age, surely can't be far off—the entire Huffam estate will come to you?"

"Indeed," said my father. "Best to be cautious about such matters, my dear. Aunt Euphemia did not say yes to *that*, not *exactly*. Though she did hint strongly at it. Mind, *only* a hint. But a hint nonetheless."

"And Mr. Nottingham, that lawyer who fills her ears with false allegations about you, does *he* agree to such?"

"Oh, him," my father said blandly. "No doubt he must if *she* says so."

"Ever since you foolishly published a critique of his acting," continued my mother, "he has poisoned her thoughts about you. When we move into the mansion, that man shall have no entry."

"Absolutely none," agreed my father. "But, of course, we can't move into her mansion tomorrow. Not quite. But—Ah, John," he said, extending an open hand to me as if he had only just then seen me, "you lazy dog. Up at last, are you? Do join us for breakfast or at least partake in the good news."

I could hardly believe what he'd been saying about Aunt Euphemia and about what she said and that I was just getting up, for not a word of it was true.

"Tell us," Clarissa asked Father. "What is her house like?"

"Very grand, you may be sure," he replied. "All in the latest fashion."

I stood there, unable to say a word, marveling at my father's—to put it kindly—playacting.

"Can we visit?" said Clarissa. "Pay our respects?"

"I should certainly think we should," agreed Mother, "if only to express our gratitude."

"As for that," my father said, "I fear my dear great-aunt is not well enough to have callers."

"But at least we should leave visiting cards," said Clarissa.

"All in good time, all in good time," said Father, rising from the table in haste and turning to me. "Not eating, John? Oh well, then, come take a stroll with me. I've a mind for some fresh air. My dear Mrs. Huffam, Clarissa," he said, bowing toward them. "Come along, John." He tugged at my arm as he headed out.

I did not move.

"John," cried Mother, "for heaven's sake, go with your father. After sleeping so late, some fresh air will do you good."

"Clarissa," I said, "I need to speak to you privately."

"John," she said with a toss of her head, "you have no secrets I'd be interested in."

"I think I might."

"John," shrilled Mother, "don't keep your father waiting!"

"After Clarissa," I insisted.

My sister, with a roll of her eyes to make sure I understood she was merely condescending, came to me.

"What is it?" she demanded.

I led her off into a corner. Whispering, I said, "I met Mr. Farquatt this morning."

"You didn't!" she cried, suddenly interested. "Where? When?"

"I went out early."

"Father said you just woke up."

"He was . . . mistaken."

"Did you . . . speak with Mr. Farquatt?"

"He sends his compliments and asked me to bring you a message."

"Did he?"

"That he would be happy to meet you at three o'clock this afternoon at the park behind St. Botolph's Church."

Her cheeks glowed. "John, did he truly say that?"

"He did and that he had a proposal to make to you."

Clarissa turned pinker yet. "Are you sure?" she whispered, her normally dull eyes shining with excitement.

"His words."

"I . . . I shall have to get Brigit to come with me," she murmured.

When I shrugged, she remained silent a moment, as if making a decision. "But, John," she said, though she might have been speaking to herself, "if we're to be taken up by Great-Aunt Euphemia with all her riches, I'm not so sure I should bestow any thought upon Mr. Farquatt."

I hardly had the courage, not then, to tell her the truth—that Father had lied about all that. All I could say was, "Clarissa, be careful. Don't assume too much."

"*You*, dear brother," she said with sudden anger, "who will be the last male Huffam, will inherit *all* from Father. A girl must look out for herself. Little boys never need to think of such things."

Not wishing to argue, I said, "Mr. Farquatt also said he'll be going to France shortly."

"He did? Why?"

"He did not say." In haste I added, "Clarissa, Father is waiting." With that, I hurried out of the inn, remembering that Mr. Farquatt had a message for Father, too.

Father was in the courtyard, pacing up and down in a casual fashion, whistling that tune of his. Hearing me approach, he stopped and took me by the arm. "Did you contradict me?"

"No, sir."

"The best of lads! Now come along. We must talk."

"Father," I said, "I don't think you're allowed to go anywhere."

"Don't be silly. That kind of rule doesn't apply to gentlemen like us." Whistling, he began to stroll away.

I watched him, then decided it would be better if I went along.

"Father," I asked, when I caught up to him, "what is it about that song that you like so much?"

"A catchy air. But it's the words I like most. You could learn something from them:

Of friendship I have heard much talk
But you'll find in the end,
That if distressed at any time,
Then money is your friend.

If you are sick and like to die,
And for the doctor send,
To him you must advance a fee,
Then money is your friend.

If you should have a suit of law,
On which you must depend,
And must pay your lawyer for a brief,
Then money is your friend.

Then let me have but a store of gold,
From ills it will defend:
In every emergency of life,
Dear money is your friend.

"Do you like it?" he asked.

I said, "At church I once heard Dr. Grantly say, 'Money is the root of all evil.'"

"John, John, I thought you were too old to believe such twaddle. Like it or not, money *is* your friend. That's the modern view. One must do the necessary to have it. You're just bothered that I told the family that it was I—not you—who went to Lady Euphemia."

"I'm not, sir."

"My dear boy, you know how *down* they all are on me. A gentleman like me—head of the family and all that it pertains—wants *some* support, don't you think? You might have sympathy."

"I told you," I insisted, "I don't care about what you said. You can claim it was you. It's just that Lady Euphemia did *not* say she'll give you the money. Only that I was to come back tomorrow."

"Phoo! It amounts to the same thing."

"Father, I don't think so."

"Anyway," he said, brushing away my objections with a wave of his hand, "I'm off to see if I can sort things out on my own."

"With that Mr. Finnegan O'Doul?"

He came to an abrupt halt. "How do you know that name?"

"His name was on the writ. And you and I talked about him last night."

"John, must I repeat, I don't know the man." That said—as though he were rebuking me—he started off, faster, trying now to get away from me.

"One other thing," I called after him. "As I was going to Great-Aunt Euphemia, I met Mr. Farquatt."

That held him. "Did you?"

"He said that if your difficulty is such that you require assistance, you need only request it of him."

My father grew thoughtful, as if turning something over in his mind. "Were those his exact words?"

"Close enough. Is there something wrong in his saying so?" I asked.

"No, no," said my father. "I'm much obliged, I'm sure. Now, John, I must be off." Making clear he did not want my company, he turned and strode away.

I watched him, wondering where was he going in such sudden haste, when, after all, he was not supposed—by Mr. Tuckum's decree—to be on the streets at all.

Then the thought came: If I could be followed—as that Sary the Sneak had done to me—I could do some following too. *Learn more about your father,* the inspector had said. So had the clerk in the naval office.

Keeping a discreet distance, I went after Father.

∽⊙∾

CHAPTER 18

I Enter the Den of the Red Lion

The streets were filled with pedestrians, vendors, costermongers, hawkers, and newspaper callers. But then, it was midday and all of London had become an endless market. I could not help but think of my school, since noon till two had been the best time of the day for me: Sergeant Muldspoon went off we knew not where, while we boys had two free, blissful hours. Released from military discipline, we often just wandered aimlessly. Or I might regale my schoolmates with the latest stories I'd read in *The Tales of the Genii.* As I followed Father that noon, however, school, Ali Baba, and Old Moldy seemed but memories of the distant past.

Despite the crowds, my father was not hard to follow. No doubt thinking he had freed himself from me, he appeared to be in no great hurry. Rather, he ambled along, as if the world's problems fell exclusively to the Queen's first ministers.

So it was that after many turns he made his way to Crispin Street near the Spitalfields Market—the old French silk weavers' quarter. Once there, he turned into a public house, which bore the image of a red lion rampant and thereby made itself known by that name.

HOT ELDER WINE read the placard in the window. Men and boys were going in and out, mostly laborers, but a fair number of businessmen, clerks, shop tenders, and gentlemen of my father's class. The few women entering were all escorted. There seemed nothing in the least unrespectable about the Red Lion.

Still, I stood by the main door, not sure what I should do. It was only after catching glimpses of the inviting interior beyond the swinging door that I went inside.

Glowing gas lamps hung from the ceiling from many places, providing bright light directly or by reflection from the many mirrors and cut-glass panels that dotted the walls. But there were pools of darkness, too, in corners, where one might be enfolded by shadow and thus go unnoticed.

I went in and first passed a booth enclosed by glass. Inside sat a great mustached fellow at a high table, back to the wall, a tumbler before him. I assumed he was the publican keeping a watchful eye upon his establishment.

Within was a long, polished wood counter upon which bowls of shucked oysters had been placed, nets of lemons, and baskets of bread. A young woman dispensed drinks from brown bottles or beer pulls. Walls were covered with paintings of racehorses, of soldiers, of Queen Victoria and her consort, Prince Albert—for I suppose even *she* would need an escort there. In one corner a cheerful fire blazed in a large stone fireplace.

The large room was crowded, rumbling with constant babble and chat, the air ripe with smells of gin, beer, brandy, and pipe and cigar smoke whose swirling reek ebbed and flowed.

As I pushed my way through the throng in search of my father, I realized there was another room to the right, a place set out with tables and booths. Lunch was being served by scurrying waiters. My father was not there. To the left, however, was yet another room, where men were playing cards. At a corner table, along with two other men, sat my father. One of the men was a workingman, the second a clerk, perhaps a businessman. These two had half-filled glasses before them. My father did not. The trio concentrated solely on the cards before them. In the middle of the table was a pile of coins to which they added or from which they subtracted as the game progressed.

I could see by the ongoing action that they were engaged in a game known as commerce. Its play was simple: Three cards were dealt, facedown. The players peeked at them, kept some, discarded others, then received new ones as they tried to get the strongest combination of three, the highest winning. In short, it was a gambling game.

I watched as Father reached into his pocket and produced a fistful of coins, which he dumped upon the table. From time to time he won. More often than not he lost. What most amazed me was not his losses, but my clear memory of him saying he had "not a penny."

I held back, trying to make sense of the scene before me. Father's ease at playing the game—the three played in almost complete silence—suggested considerable experience with it, an aspect of his life previously unknown by me.

As I stood there watching from across the room—no one paid me the slightest attention—I noticed another man seated apart and alone. I had no idea who he was, but I was struck by the intensity of his gaze, which appeared to be focused solely upon my father.

He wore a fine black frock coat like a man of business, a top hat, white neckcloth, and a maroon vest. His smooth face showed little emotion.

He stood up—a walking stick was in his hand—and made his way to the cardplayers' table and stood just behind the man playing opposite my father—as if he desired to be noticed. As it happened, it wasn't long before Father chanced to glance up. When he saw this man, he started.

The man responded with a quick nod. My father returned the same brief gesture. Even so, he finished his hand, losing all the coins he'd set down, then threw down his cards—whether disgusted or frustrated, I could not tell—and left the table. Then he and the man withdrew into a shadowy corner, where they engaged in earnest conversation that clearly was not meant to be heard by others. I certainly heard none of it. But it was perfectly obvious that these two men knew each other, speaking to each other as they did with considerable familiarity.

Indeed, it appeared to be a most serious discussion—perhaps an argument—with much nodding and shaking of heads. At one point the man with the walking stick used it to tap my father on the chest. I saw it as a gesture of contempt and command. My father's face grew redder. Which is to say, I was seeing something I rarely experienced in my father: anger.

At length the two stepped apart—without shaking hands. My father turned toward the door. His face was flushed, serious, unusually grave. So deep was he in his thoughts that he actually passed close to me without noticing. I watched as he quickly left the Red Lion.

I was about to follow but chose to glance back at the man with whom he had argued. That gentleman had gone to the table where my father had been, seated himself, picked up the discarded cards, and played. He won hand after hand, until the other men left, fuming. The man I'd been watching simply sat at the table, as if waiting for others to join him.

I tapped the arm of the man closest to me.

He turned. "Yes, boy. What do you want?"

"Excuse me, sir, but that man over there," I whispered, pointing to the man with whom my father had spoken. "Do you know his name?"

The man glanced over, then gave a short snort of a laugh. "Course I do. 'E's become well-known round 'ere."

"Who is he, then?"

"Showed up last summer," he said. "Some say from America. Some say Ireland.'E's become one of the best gamblers in the City. Finnegan O'Doul."

O'Doul! The man to whom my father owed the three hundred pounds.

I stared at Mr. O'Doul. As I did, another man approached him, standing as straight as a rod, saluting in military fashion, and then bringing down his wooden leg sharply upon the floor—*bang!*

It was none other than Sergeant Muldspoon.

CHAPTER 19
I Seek Advice

Are not teachers human? Are they not, really, people just like us? Do we not realize that they—like ourselves—have lives beyond school? Then, why, when we *do* see them in places *other* than in the schools we share, does it seem so strange?

My primary thought was not how remarkable it was that O'Doul and Muldspoon should meet, but that Old Moldy would catch me, and cane me, for not being in school. This despite the fact that there was no law requiring any British child to *be* in school—Old Moldy's or any other. Still, I felt compelled to flee, to leave the Red Lion as quickly as I could.

Even when I managed my escape—nothing hard—I did not stop for breath, but hurried off as though pursued. In my head I could almost hear the clump of the sergeant's wooden peg leg following me.

When, after a few blocks, I finally slowed, I looked back to make sure Sergeant Muldspoon was *not* following. Only then did I allow myself a pause to consider what I had observed. Here was something ominous: The two men who were causing me and my family the most misery, *together.*

Beyond that I had to consider:

First: Not only had I seen my father gambling, I had seen him losing money—money that he'd claimed he did *not* have.

Second: My father, despite saying he did *not* know Mr. Finnegan O'Doul, was approached by this very man. Then he spoke to him at some length—with familiarity, albeit with anger.

Third: Mr. O'Doul had a reputation as a sharp gambler.

Fourth: Sergeant Muldspoon, the one adult in the world who might be called *my* enemy, approached that same Mr. O'Doul on the most familiar terms. What possible connection could they have?

Fifth: I could not help but sense that something very unsavory was swirling about my father, not merely debt, but something grossly illegal. Inspector Copperfield's words more than suggested that.

Even when I considered all these points, I could make little sense of them, save one major thing. It was what I'd suspected but now knew for a certainty: To wit: I could not trust my father to tell the truth.

The more I absorbed this awful fact, the deeper grew my fright. I had known the threat of debtors' prison loomed before us. Yet, seeing my father in the very *act* of double-dealing—seeing him engaged in a secret life—was truly shocking.

Only gradually did I realize I was panting with the press of my emotions, as if I had run a very long way. In a sense I had: That is, I had come a distance toward a fuller understanding of our awful predicament. What I had fully grasped was this: My world was crumbling.

Yet, as I looked about at the passing parade of people, none of them so much as glanced in my direction. The world cared nothing for me—a mere boy. I felt adrift, alone, in the very midst of London's millions. That said, I felt compelled to do *something*. I had absolutely no idea, however, *what* that something might be.

Gradually, an idea formed. It was not so much a thing to do. Rather, it was the urgent need to speak to *someone* and seek advice. But whom?

No longer willing to trust Father, I did not wish to confide in him. Nor could I speak to my mother or my sister. Their response would be too angry, too self-absorbed.

I considered Mr. Tuckum. Though he appeared kind, he was a stranger. Moreover, he was the law. I could hardly tell him my father was not committed to the truth.

Lady Euphemia? Out of the question.

One of my schoolmates? It wouldn't do.

In the end, the only person I could think of was Brigit.

In truth, I really did not know much about Brigit, the person. For example, I did not even know her last name. It was never referred to or used. I had to wonder if even my parents knew it. Brigit was simply "Brigit, our servant." Of course, this was in no way different from how most servants were spoken of. Had not Great-Aunt Euphemia referred to her butler as merely William, whereas her doctors had last names? Clarissa once told me of a house where successive servants were always called "Alice," so as to save the mistress the painful exertion of learning new names.

All I knew of Brigit was that she had been a faithful servant in our household for most of my life. She had raised me more than my mother had. Dressed and fed me. Taught me my letters. In that sense, as far as I knew, our lives were her life. By the same token, her life was our life. Had she not, just yesterday, told me *we* were her family, that my sister and I were *her* children?

It was only natural, then, that I should turn to her. And that is exactly what I made up my mind to do.

So resolved, I hurried down the street, looking into shop windows until I found one with a clock on display. It was almost three o'clock—

just what I had hoped: the hour Clarissa was to meet her suitor, Mr. Farquatt, in the park behind St. Botolph's Church. While my sister had more than hinted that she now saw scant reason to consider the little man's attentions, I had no doubt that her vanity would bring her to the meeting. Moreover, if she went, Brigit must, as a discreet chaperone, accompany her. Clarissa was nothing if not proper. So it was that I turned in the direction of St. Botolph's.

As I strode along, I realized there was another reason to reach the park quickly. I *must* inform Clarissa—and convince her—that the likelihood of support from Great-Aunt Euphemia was nil and that she should know that when she made her reckoning in regard to Mr. Farquatt.

I soon stood opposite St. Botolph's Church. Looking across Bishopsgate, I realized that just next to it, on the far side of a narrow lane, was a police station. Police stations had been of little consequence to me . . . previously. Given my new world of worries, including my talk with Inspector Copperfield, the sight made me uneasy. It was almost as if, even as I looked at it, *it* was looking at *me*—and with none too favorable an eye.

As I stood there, the church bells began tolling the hour, which made me recall the urgency of my mission. All the same, when I crossed over the street, dodging the flow of cabs, carts, omnibuses, and horses, I made a point of approaching the park from the *far* side of the church, thereby avoiding any nearness to the police station.

The park in question was small. In older days it had been a cemetery, so a few melancholy gravestones still stood. They looked like exhausted sentinels, guarding a past that had already fled, their eroded words unreadable by those who never came to read them.

Around the edge of the green was an ill-kept flagstone walk, lined with benches. As I came round the rear of the church, I spied Brigit on one bench. On another, across the green, I saw Clarissa. Seated next to her was Mr. Farquatt.

"Brigit!" I called in a low voice.

She actually jumped and looked about. "Oh, Master John!" she cried, hand to throat. "I had no idea—"

"I must speak with you," I said.

"But your sister . . ." She glanced across the grass.

"Brigit, it's urgent," I pressed, coming up to her. "And it concerns Clarissa."

"Master John," said Brigit, lowering her voice, "I think Mr. Farquatt is about to request your sister's hand in marriage."

"Now?"

"I believe so," she said, her voice full of emotion. "But, John, I truly haven't the knowing if she should accept him or no. Either way I must stay to protect her."

Again I glanced across the park. My sister and her suitor were certainly in deep conversation, though it appeared—for I could not hear their words—that Mr. Farquatt was doing most of the talking. Clarissa was listening intently, a look of perplexity on her face.

I sat down next to Brigit and said, "Brigit, I have to tell you what I've discovered."

"Master John," she whispered, "surely your news can wait."

"Brigit," I blurted out, "my father was not telling the truth."

"About what?"

"Anything."

"Jesus, Mary, and Joseph!" Brigit suddenly exclaimed. "Mr. Farquatt is going down on his knees!"

"My father *is* in debt to that Mr. O'Doul," I went on, barely attending to what was happening across the way. "I'm sure of it."

Brigit, even as she put hands to her ears to keep from hearing me, whispered, "Master John, I beg you, don't talk of that matter."

"And though Father said otherwise," I continued, "I'm sure he *does* know this Mr. O'Doul. What's more, Mr. O'Doul is a gambler. And, Brigit, I saw Father gambling."

"She's listening to him, Master John. She's listening!"

"That's not all," I persisted. "There's no way Father can get relief from that debt from his great-aunt. It will not happen."

"Oh, my dear, dear Clarissa . . ."

"Which means he will surely go to debtors' prison."

"Sweet Jesus," cried Brigit, coming to her feet and pressing her two hands before her chest in a gesture of anguish. "I think . . . I think . . . she's refusing him!"

"And, Brigit," I hurried on, "I myself have received warnings from a police inspector."

Brigit turned sharply. "What did you say?"

"Father seems to be mixed in with something . . . very odd. I don't know what it is precisely. But it . . . may be a *crime*."

She stared at me. "What kind of inspector did you say?"

"A police inspector. From Scotland Yard."

She stared at me. But then, as if recalling what was happening across the way, she abruptly turned to look back across the green. "Great heavens," she cried. "Mr. Farquatt is going. Clarissa has sent him off."

"Brigit, listen to me!" I cried. "If what I say is true, we are truly ruined! We shall all be on the streets—or worse!"

Brigit swung around toward me, her eyes glistening with tears, gazing at me through a torrent of emotions. "Master John," she whispered, "it's only Clarissa I can be thinking of!" She jumped up and ran across the park toward my sister.

A moment later I went after her.

⁓◈◈⁓

CHAPTER 20

I Learn of Mr. Farquatt's Proposal

By the time I caught up with Brigit and Clarissa, the two were embracing each other. There were many tears.

"But why did you refuse him?" Brigit was asking.

"Brigit," my sister struggled to say between gulping sobs, "when Great-Aunt Euphemia bequeaths her wealth to Father, we shall ascend to a new station in life. There shall be no end of wonderful suitors to choose from then—gentlemen of wealth and position. Mr. Farquatt will be beneath me."

"Clarissa," said Brigit, "you must follow your heart."

"Dear Great-Aunt Euphemia told Father it would happen. He told us."

"Clarissa," I cried, unable to hold back any longer, "she said nothing of the kind."

Clarissa turned and looked down upon me. "What are you doing here? And what would you know about the matter?" she said. "You're just a little boy."

"Clarissa," I said, "Father *didn't* go to Great-Aunt. He asked *me* to go. Which I did. And she *didn't* say she would give him *anything*. She only said she would *think* about it."

A flicker of unease furrowed my sister's brow. She looked to Brigit and then back to me. "What are you talking about?" she said in a choked voice. "How could that be?"

"Clarissa, Father wasn't telling the truth."

"Pa . . . not telling the truth?" she echoed faintly. "Why?"

"I don't know why. But he's still in debt. And it's a debt he can't pay. I'm sure Great-Aunt won't give him the money he needs. Which means he *will* go to debtors' prison."

Clarissa stared at me. As she absorbed my words, her face seemed to crumple. Tears began to flow anew. She turned to Brigit, as if Brigit must provide verification. "Brigit . . . ?"

Brigit seemed at a loss for what to say.

Clarissa's fist went to her mouth, and she spun about to look in the direction Mr. Farquatt had gone. "But . . . but . . ." The next moment she threw herself back into Brigit's arms. "But what am I to do?" she cried.

We started back to the Halfmoon Inn—my sister gasping and gulping, eyes swollen and red, supported by Brigit, who had an arm around her waist.

Even I pitied her.

"Brigit," Clarissa managed to cough out after a while, "Mr. Farquatt *pleaded* with me to marry him. He offered to settle me in France. I said it was not . . . possible. My new life made it . . . undesirable. And he . . . he . . . even offered to pay Pa's debt."

"He did what?" cried Brigit, coming to an abrupt stop.

"I met him this morning, and he asked that I tell Father so," I said.

"Mr. Farquatt truly said that?" Brigit demanded of us both.

Clarissa nodded. "So you must go after him, Brigit," she pleaded. "Tell him I forgive him. That I *will* accept him. Then everything can be happy."

Brigit, suggesting she hardly knew what to advise, bit her lip. Then she finally said, "Clarissa, I'm thinking it's not the womanly thing to do."

"But you must!" said Clarissa with a stamp of her foot. "That way all our problems will be solved."

I said, "Do you know where he resides?"

Clarissa thought hard, only to have confusion fill her face. "I have no idea. Just his place of work. It's called . . ."

"You told me the Credit Bordeaux," I reminded her.

"Then go there," she cried. "Or I will!"

"You mustn't," Brigit said firmly. "I'm telling you, pursuing him would be the most unwomanly thing. The best we can do is hope that his heart is strong and that he will return."

"But, Brigit," Clarissa said again, all but wailing, "I told him . . . he must never see me again. *Never!* I shall be a spinster. I know I will!" She broke again into sobs.

As she and Brigit, with much moaning and weeping, made their way back to the Halfmoon Inn, Brigit said no more. I crept behind the two women, dreading our return because I would have to inform Mother of all I had learned.

Happily, when we arrived, Mother was not there. Neither was Father. But Mr. Tuckum was. The moment we walked in, he accosted me.

"Where is your father?" he demanded. "Has he fled?"

The truth was, I had no idea.

CHAPTER 21

I Sit in Darkness

"He's not allowed to leave this establishment," Mr. Tuckum scolded. "It's the Queen's law. When he goes out—if he goes out—a deputy or I must be in his company. The entire intent of his being here is that he not flee. Has he?" His severity took me aback.

"I . . . I don't think so," I said, though even as the bailiff spoke, I wondered if he had.

My sister, meanwhile, fled up to her room, Brigit with her.

"Your father claims he is a gentleman," said the bailiff, his voice touching anger, "and I wish to treat him accordingly. But now . . . Have you truly no idea where he went?"

There it was: The great horror of having a liar in the family. Was I to tell the truth and betray my own father? Or was I to protect him with a lie and therefore tarnish my own character?

"Come, come," snapped Mr. Tuckum, "your looks suggest you do know something."

"Please, sir," I said, my eyes welling with tears, "I do know where he went from here, though I don't know where he is now. I can only ask you to forgive me, for I don't know how to reply without doing him injury. I beg you to consider he is my father."

"Do you expect him to return?"

"I . . . think so," was the best I could offer.

Mr. Tuckum's glowering looks softened. "I understand your predicament, and your answer does you honor. You're an old-fashioned boy, and I'm old-fashioned enough to follow my instincts and trust *you*. As to whether I can trust anyone else in your family, I shall consult my superiors."

"Thank you, sir," I whispered, and retreated to my room.

In fact, I was much upset by the bailiff's anger. Not only was it unexpected, but, knowing my father, it hardly seemed warranted. Not for a debtor. Unless—once again Inspector Copperfield's ominous words came to my head—it was much more.

As the evening drew close, I increasingly wondered if Father *would* return. When he did not, my tension grew.

It had also occurred to me that if my sister could not go to Mr. Farquatt, I should. But that would have to wait for the next day.

My mother returned. I heard her as she passed along the balcony and went into her room at the far end. She returned at a much faster pace and threw open my door.

"What has happened?" she demanded, holding up a candle in such fashion that the shadows beneath her eyes gave her the look of a tragic mask. "Your sister informs me that it was *not* your father who went to Great-Aunt Euphemia, but you!"

"Yes, ma'am."

"And that Euphemia did *not* promise *any* of those things your father claimed she had."

"Yes, ma'am."

"It is *not* to be endured!" she cried. "I spent the entire afternoon making arrangements to purchase a new wardrobe. No, I will *not* endure it!"

"I'm afraid it's true, Mother."

"Then if *you* went to his great-aunt, *you* must tell me what she said."

"That I was to return tomorrow."

"Is that *all*?"

Not having the heart to repeat my aunt's condemnation of my father, I simply hung my head.

"Where is your father now?"

"I don't know," I replied.

"Do you understand what this means?" she cried. It was virtually an accusation.

"Yes, ma'am."

"Our possessions, gone. Our liberty, gone. Our lives—me, your sister, and you—all prospects, blasted!"

For a few moments she stood before me, her rage visibly boiling. As for myself, I feared that she would push me as to where my father had gone and that I would be forced to reveal what I'd seen regarding gambling and Mr. O'Doul. Luckily, she did not. All the same, I felt ashamed.

Abruptly, she turned and hurried out of the room, slamming the door behind her. Her angry steps crossed to the far end. Another door slammed. After which, blessed silence.

I don't know how much time passed—the room grew completely dark—but at length Father did return. I heard his voice below. I heard Mr. Tuckum. My anxiety eased.

But Mother must have heard him too. Her steps thundered along the balcony.

My parents argued, fiercely. What they said, I don't know. I had no desire to listen. Alas, I doubted my father told the truth.

Then came the sound of my mother returning—with irate stumps—along the balcony. She was followed by new sounds: my father's slow steps.

I dreaded his arrival.

The door opened. He entered the room. Lit candle in hand, he stood at the threshold for a moment and gazed at me.

"You are sitting in the dark," he said wearily.

"I didn't wish any other companionship," I returned.

"Mr. Tuckum has dinner—"

I said, "Clarissa refused Mr. Farquatt's offer of marriage because she thought Great-Aunt Euphemia was going to bestow a fortune on us, as you suggested she would."

He smiled, faintly. "Two things, John," he said. "Firstly: By your own account my great-aunt may yet give us something. Secondly: Miss Clarissa can do far better than Mr. Farquatt."

"She sent him away."

"If she chooses, she can call him back."

"She doesn't know where he lives."

"Ah."

"Do you?" I asked.

"No. But I have reason to think he'll be back."

Ignoring that wishful notion, I asked, "Where have *you* been?" and hoped he would tell the truth.

"Trying to raise the money."

It was not, I was willing to believe, a complete lie. Perhaps he thought his gambling would bring in enough to pay the debt.

"How?" I asked.

He shrugged. "Different ways."

"Father," I said, my voice trembling with emotion, "in two days you will be in the Insolvent Debtors' Court."

"Well then," he said with unexpected mildness, "so be it. I came to fetch you for dinner. It was meant as a kindness. I, at least, am hungry. I, at least, should enjoy *your* company." He moved to go.

"Father . . ."

He halted.

"I followed you to the Red Lion. I saw you at your gambling. I saw you talking to Mr. Finnegan O'Doul. Your conversation suggested familiarity. He is a well-known gambler."

Though the light was dim, I could see his face flush with embarrassment.

"Spying on your father . . . ," he murmured.

"Father," I pressed, "please tell me what it all means! What is happening? In what are you entangled?"

His eyes were upon me, but whether he was actually looking at me, I was uncertain. To my surprise, he pointed to his head: "In here," he said, "sits a great fortune. For the moment that is all I shall—or can— say. Now I am going down for dinner. The pleasure of your company is requested." With that, he turned about and left, like an actor making a grand exit.

By so doing, he plunged the room into more than one kind of darkness.

CHAPTER 22

I Overhear a Private Meeting

The thought of sharing a table with my unhappy family was something I could not bear. Believing the scene would be too acrimonious, I chose to deny my hunger and remain in the dark room. It fit my mood. And at some point I fell asleep.

When I awoke, it was abruptly. What roused me, I had no idea, nor could I guess the time. My father was on the other side of the bed, snoring, so it had to be late, or early morning. I lay there for a while, increasingly aware that having barely eaten the day before, I was famished. Just thinking about food caused my stomach to rumble.

Church bells announced the time: two in the morning.

Assuming that there would be—as there had been the previous night—food left on the table, I got up. Clumsily, I felt my way to the door and stepped out onto the balcony.

Raw, foggy air swirled about me, causing my skin to prickle with chill. But since it also cleared my mind, I remained there, pondering my father's claim, that "a great fortune" sat in his head. I tried to guess what he could possibly mean, but here my imagination failed me.

As I thought about it, I leaned against the balcony rail and gazed out along Halfmoon Alley. The omnipresent fog made the gas lamp by the main street indistinct, hardly more than a glowworm of illumination, giving me the sensation that night itself was brooding on discouraging matters. But there was some light seeping from the inn, enough so that I gradually realized a black Hansom cab was parked in the courtyard right below me. The dark horse was in its traces, one foot lifted, indicating its sleepy state. I made out the driver, too, seated high at the rear of the cab, in greatcoat and hat, arms crossed over chest, head bowed upon his chest—presumably, he, too, slept.

From the Hansom's position, I could only assume it had delivered someone to the inn and was waiting to take that same person away.

As I considered the cab, it came to me that—considering the hour—this was no ordinary call. The guest could not be my father's: He lay asleep in our room. Could Mr. Tuckum be having a visitor at such an hour? Then I recalled his saying he needed to consult his superiors. Was one of them his guest?

Just as I was considering slipping down the steps to investigate, light sliced onto the court: The door to the inn had opened. The driver, roused from his sleep, sat up, straightened his hat, and climbed down to light the cab's two side lamps. The light revealed he was no common driver: He was, in fact, a policeman.

I squatted behind the balcony railings so as not to be seen. Within moments, I heard voices.

"Then am I to understand," came a voice that I immediately recognized as Mr. Tuckum's, "that no choice will be extended to him? That he will stand before the Insolvent Debtors' Court at Queen's Bench?"

I instantly grasped that he was talking about my father.

"That appears to be our best chance," came another voice, low and husky.

"I must confess," said the bailiff, "I can't tell if he's a complete fool or not."

"Or a traitor," said the other, causing me to gasp. "Certainly, 'e's playing a deep game, and with a nasty crew."

"Can he manage it?"

"I've 'eard say 'e's a credible actor."

Two men sauntered toward the Hansom. The shorter of the two—I could see now—was indeed Mr. Tuckum. The other was someone I had never seen before. Considerably taller than the bailiff, he was broad-chested, rather burly, and wearing, if my eyes saw properly, an oilskin cloak against the damp, cold weather.

"And," Mr. Tuckum said, "you have no idea who this Inspector Copperfield might be?"

"Without question, an imposter," said the other. "Very troubling. But no doubt 'e's one of the spies."

Spies! I could hardly breathe.

"But you trust the 'Uffam boy, you say?" the newcomer went on.

"Young as he is," said Mr. Tuckum, "John Huffam is as right as English roses. The only one in the family with any . . . hmm . . . sense."

"Fine," said the other. "Then we must make sure to use 'im."

"I agree."

The big man reached out and tapped the bailiff on the chest with his forefinger. "Mr. Tuckum, sir, just know there are 'igher-ups—very 'igher-ups—watching and waiting. The nets are all set. If all goes well, we'll make a good catch, so the affair could be good for you."

"And for you, too, sir."

"For me," said the big man, "it's all in a day's work. The thing of it is, Mr. Tuckum, I never makes it personal." He held out his hand.

Mr. Tuckum shook it. "Always a pleasure to work with you, Inspector Ratchet, sir."

"And mine," said the big man as he got into the Hansom, drew the gate closed, and settled himself.

Mr. Tuckum returned to the inn. The door shut.

"Scotland Yard!" the inspector called out to the driver.

"Yes, sir," said the constable, who had returned to his post at the back of the cab. With a flick of the reins, the horse trotted out of the court and vanished into the fog, leaving only the diminishing sound of hooves clattering on the cobblestones.

I remained on the balcony, trying to make sense of what I'd heard. *Traitors! Spies! Scotland Yard!* All connected to my father! So much more than gambling. Or debt. Was *that* the great idea Father had in his head? And for what were the "higher-ups" watching and waiting? What "nets" were set out? Perhaps it was only because I'd seen it earlier in the day, but my head filled with the image of the Tower of London and the Traitors' Gate. I am not ashamed to say I shuddered. Indeed, I was truly frightened.

This Inspector Ratchet—was *he* real, whereas Inspector Copperfield was not? Or the other way around? As for Mr. Tuckum's agreeing to make "use" of me, it put me on sharp notice that I'd best be very cautious in my dealings with him.

All that understood, I was not beyond hunger. Accordingly, I crept down the steps into the dining room, where, as I'd hoped, some food scraps remained on the table. Mr. Tuckum was there too, sitting near the low fire, a glass of something in hand, reading his serial story.

As I came into the room, the bailiff looked round at me. "Well now, lad, you're up very late."

"Yes, sir. I'm afraid I missed dinner and woke hungry."

"Do sit down, boy, and make yourself comfortable. I'm old-fashioned enough to always be happy for company. There's more than enough," he said, gesturing to the leftovers. But then he so closely scrutinized me that I wondered if he knew I'd been aware of his visitor. In any case, he said, "I had a friend here."

"Yes, sir."

He gazed at me for a moment and then held up his reading. "Can you read?"

"Yes, sir."

"Do consider this story. A brilliant thing. I've saved all the installments. It's about a boy, you know. Not like you, but how a boy grows to understand the world as it is."

I had no desire to read, but I drew up a chair and helped myself to some bread and cheese. I was aware the bailiff was still observing me intently.

At length he said, "Master John, does your father confide in you?"

"No, sir," I answered truthfully, though not without some regret. "He does not."

"Is there any hope that he might raise the money . . . on his own?"

"I . . . I don't think so, sir."

"None at all?"

That time I remained mum, and he stayed silent too, as if to wait me out. Feeling compelled to speak, I finally said, "I shall visit my great-aunt again, in the morning."

"A wealthy woman?"

"Yes, sir."

"'Hope'—to quote an old-fashioned poet—'springs eternal,'" he said.

I focused on my food.

"See here, Master John," the bailiff said, "you *can* trust me, you know. You truly can. You're a smart lad. I can see that. And you don't want to go hurting your family or yourself. So if there's something about your father's ... hmm ... situation that might be helpful for me to know, I'm your man. I have ... hmm ... connections," he added.

Wanting no part of his offer, I pushed myself away from the table. "Thank you, sir. I'm sure I appreciate it. Good night, sir."

That said, I returned to our room, where I spent the rest of the night in fretful sleep.

ఌఌఠౄ

CHAPTER 23
I Return to Lady Euphemia

I slept late into the morning, but not so late that there was any danger of missing my day's appointment with Great-Aunt Euphemia.

I got up, doused my face in a bowl of cold water, used the outdoor privy, and then made my way to the main room. Father was seated before the fire. Brigit was sweeping the floor. I had no idea where my sister or mother was. Nor Mr. Tuckum.

"Good morning, Master John," said Brigit. "Shall I fetch you some breakfast?"

"Yes, please," I returned. I was watching my father, who had not even acknowledged my presence. I went up to him. "Good morning, Father," I said.

He turned a sad, weary look upon me. I wanted so much to ask him questions, but in truth, I was afraid of the answers he might give—for now I assumed they would be false.

In a low voice he said, "Shall you go to my great-aunt today?"

"She requested I do so. But I'll go only if you wish me to."

He reached out and held my arm. "If I'm to stay out of prison, it's our only chance," he said.

I gazed at him. Something had happened to make him realize his true plight. Was it his talk with Mr. O'Doul? My words? Had Mr. Tuckum related the inspector's words, that he would go to court?

"I'll go," I said.

He sighed. "And, perhaps, if you don't succeed, it might be just as well."

"What do you mean?"

"I shall be safe in prison."

"Safe?" I cried. "Safe from what?"

When he didn't answer, I shifted uneasily and noted that Brigit was watching and listening to our conversation. It suddenly occurred to me that she might have the answers I needed. Not only was she an adult, but perhaps she was aware of things in the family I was not. My sister confided in her. I assumed my mother did as well.

I turned back to Father. He was not going to answer my question. "Your office?" I asked. "Do I need to go and tell them what has happened?"

"Mr. Tuckum has made it abundantly clear that I must not leave this place," he said. "In that regard I am already a prisoner. So, going to my office, I should say . . . no." He offered up a dry smile. "As long as the Naval Ordinance Office is not aware of my situation, I might yet collect my salary."

In the ensuing silence I said, "Where's Mother? Clarissa?"

"Sulking, I suppose," said Father. He reached out and gently pushed the hair out of my face. "Young John, do take some nourishment. Make yourself presentable and then trot off to my great-aunt's. We shall hope all will go well."

I looked around for Brigit. She had left the room. Had she heard? Did she agree?

The church bells rang for noon as I walked along Broad Street toward Great Winchester Street. With November's raw chill penetrating deep, my father insisted I wear his greatcoat, which was too large for me. I was reminded of that girl, Sary, in her tattered, oversized jacket, but to no useful purpose.

A gray drizzle filled the air. It made all seem dull and smudged. Every edge, every crevice was indistinct, each separate thing becoming part of each other thing. It was, I thought, altogether fitting—a visible representation of my father's muddled affairs and my jumbled understanding of them.

I was thinking so hard, I paid but little mind to the street vendors: eel pie men, ribbon sellers, bird sellers, secondhand clothing sellers, and early beggars. But when I did look about, I caught a glimpse of Sary the Sneak. She was still spying on me. For Inspector

Copperfield, I had no doubt. But now, recalling Inspector Ratchet's words, I believed this "Copperfield" was a spy. What did that make the girl?

Yet, such was my mood of discouragement, I did not really care one way or the other that she was stalking me.

Then I had a thought: Perhaps I might accost the girl and *insist* she tell me who Inspector Copperfield was. She had spoken as if she didn't know the man's name. I was not prepared to believe her, any more than I was ready to believe *anyone.* Yet, so befuddled was I—so desperate—that recalling the girl's offer to sneak about for *me,* I also contemplated the notion that maybe I should employ her to find Mr. Farquatt. At least my sister might be made happy.

But when I looked around again, the girl had disappeared.

There were moments—such as that one—when I could not tell if I was at the edge of all the mystery . . . or at its very center.

It was as close to twelve thirty as I could make it when I—feeling the weight of the hopelessness of my mission—banged the lion knocker upon the door of Forty-five Great Winchester Street.

William, the butler, opened the door. He looked down at me and lifted an eyebrow disapprovingly.

"Yes?" he said, as if I were a perfect stranger.

I would have as soon kicked the man's shins and run off. But that would hardly do. Instead, I said, "Do you not remember me, sir? I'm Wesley Huffam's son, John. Lady Euphemia asked that I call at this hour."

"Ah, yes," the butler said, as if he had just recalled, though his raised eyebrow more than suggested that my visit was a waste of everybody's time.

All the same, he opened the door, and I stepped into the same drab, dead garden of a vestibule.

This time he said, "Follow me."

We went up the dim flight of steps. At the top he knocked

gently on Lady Euphemia's door, again pressed his ear to it to hear her response, swung the door open, and all but shoved me in.

It was the same bedroom, though there may have been more medical supplies about. I recalled her three doctors had already visited.

As for Lady Euphemia, she lay beneath her coverlets, her shoulders and head propped up by her five pillows, this day her sleeping gown and lacy bonnet pale blue in color.

By her side stood the same servant woman, the bottle of smelling salts in hand at the ready.

As I stood at the foot of Lady Euphemia's bed—the butler hovering behind me—the woman studied me with her small eyes, breathing loudly, working her mouth in such a fashion as to again remind me of a great fish gasping for air.

"John Horatio Huffam," she said finally, "I hope you are well."

"I am, my lady. As I trust you are too."

"I am *never* well," she informed me.

There was a touch of pride in her declaration. All the same, I said, "I'm sorry to hear that."

"I'm glad for your sympathy," she returned as she had on the day previous. She paused and then said, "Master John, you are the last of a distinguished line of Huffams. What does that mean to you?"

"I . . . I should . . . like to honor the name," I stammered.

"The correct answer."

I stood there, not sure what else to say while she continued to gaze at me. After some time had passed, I finally said, "My lady, you requested I come to see you."

"So I did," she allowed. "In the matter of your profligate father. I trust you know the word."

"No, my lady."

"Profligate: A man who has given way to a life of calumny and dissipation."

I wasn't sure what those words meant either, but they sounded dreadful and I was in no mood to ask for further explanations.

"Do you work? Earn any income?"

"I told you: I go to school."

"What good will school do you if your father is in prison?"

"I can only hope he will not be," I said, hanging my head.

"I assure you," she said, "he will. What's more, I've no doubt he *deserves* to be. I rather suspect he shall remain there for a long time. Perhaps he shall be transported. To Australia."

"I pray not, my lady," I said, feeling my anger rise.

"My knowledge of him is far better than yours. Three hundred pounds is a vast sum of money to owe."

It was too much for me. I looked up. "Is that why you asked me to come? To insult my father and humiliate me further?"

"See here, young man—"

"You're a beastly, mean-spirited woman," I cried. "I don't want to be here." I turned toward the door.

"Stop him!" she cried.

The butler stepped between the door and me. His skeletal face showed both ferocity and surprise.

"Let me pass!" I cried.

"If you go," shouted Lady Euphemia, "you will receive no assistance from me. *None!*"

"You weren't going to give me any," I said.

"I was!"

I could not run from that. "In what fashion?" I asked.

"I assure you, it has nothing to do with your—"

"If you say one more cruel thing about my father, I shall leave and never return!" I shouted as all my frustrations pressed in on me. "I think you're a bully!"

"A *what*?" she gasped, one hand reaching for the smelling salts.

"A bully!" I fairly screamed, my hands balled into fists.

The butler gripped my arms.

"Let him be!" cried Great-Aunt Euphemia. She was breathing—or at least gulping—heavily. The butler backed off—willingly, I thought.

"Very well," she said. "I won't speak of your . . . father. In any case, it's not him, but *you* I wish to help. I admire your . . . fortitude. Your courage. Most people are frightened of me."

"I refuse to be!" I shouted, my heart hammering.

"In fact, you remind me of *my* father, Augustus Huffam," she said between breaths. "He, too, was a hothead."

Struggling for breath, trying to keep from bursting into tears, I said nothing.

"I am searching," she said after a moment, "for a suitable position for you."

Taken by surprise, I said, "You mean, employment?"

"Exactly. In hopes you will be able to support yourself and thereby rise honorably in the world."

"But . . . what about the loan?"

"Out of the question. Entirely. I am interested only in you. The *last* Huffam."

I didn't know what to say.

"My trusted solicitor, Mr. Nottingham, will inform you about this position once it has been determined."

"When shall that be?"

"In two days' time, at seven thirty in the morning, you will return *here*."

"What ... what kind of position will it be?"

"I have no idea. I have instructed Mr. Nottingham to find something suitable. I have faith he'll do so. Now you may go," she said with a dismissive wave of her jeweled hand.

I stood there for a moment and forced myself to say, "Thank ... you," after which I left the room with the butler.

⚜

CHAPTER 24
I Have a Curious Encounter

Following William, I walked away from my great-aunt's bedroom and down the steps, hardly knowing what I felt. Should I be disappointed that the money, which I never thought would be offered, was not to be forthcoming? Or should I be pleased that I had received something I had not expected: employment?

As we went along the hallway, we passed a gentleman sitting by the small table. Head down, he was engrossed in a blue-covered pamphlet, which I recognized as an episode of *David Copperfield*. He was the same man I had seen in the hallway the day before.

When I went by, he paid me no mind. Indeed, he averted his face. After I'd gone by, I glanced back over my shoulder and saw him—or his back, anyway—ascending the steps. The thought crossed my mind: Was *that* Mr. Nottingham?

At the front door William broke into my thoughts: "Young sir, you are a brave fellow." He did not speak in his normal funereal fashion, but with some real warmth. I took note too of the "sir."

I looked up into the man's gaunt, ashen face.

"If Wilkie can be of service to you, then call on William," he intoned.

"I . . . I don't understand," I stammered.

"Madam prefers to call me William," he said. "She has *always* called all her menservants William. My Christian name, however, bestowed upon me by my late mother, is Wilkie. So, I repeat," he said, lifting one eyebrow, and this time managing to convey conspiracy, empathy, and friendship in one look, "if Wilkie can be of service, then I beg of you to call on William." To my surprise, he held out a bony hand. I shook it as if making a bargain. His grip was surprisingly strong.

"Just be advised, Master John, my lady's attorney, Mr. Nottingham, has even less fondness for your father than she."

"Why?"

"It may seem trifling to you, but . . . Mr. Nottingham, having a great love of the theater, was a serious amateur actor. His Christian name is Connop. Well then, your father authored a critique of one of Mr. Nottingham's performances for *Fraser's Magazine.* 'Mr. Nottingham,' your father wrote, 'while attempting to play the part of Romeo, only succeeded in being a noncompoop, which is to say, he was more *ham than not.*' The pun 'noncompoop' and the phrase 'more ham than not' were joyfully bandied about in theatrical circles and prevented Mr. Nottingham from finding further engagements. Mr. Nottingham has neither forgotten nor forgiven. He's now obliged to create his own roles."

"Then why should he help me?" I asked.

"He will *not* help you, sir," continued William/Wilkie. "But insofar as he is employed by Lady Huffam, he must—in his fashion—do what she requests. You are, after all, the last of the Huffams. That means much to her."

"Was that Mr. Nottingham just now—in the hallway?"

"I believe it was, sir," he said, making me wish I'd taken a better look.

I walked out of my aunt's house into a sodden mist thick enough to claim the name of rain. Heading for the Halfmoon Inn, the air was positively souplike, a recipe of garbage, coal dust, and dung.

As I approached a turn in the road, I was drawn—perhaps wishing I were an innocent infant again—to look into a shop window crowded with children's toys. As I gazed at the playthings behind the glass, I caught sight of a reflected image of Sary the Sneak. She was not far behind. Seeing her gave me a jolt of anger. Perhaps it was

because she was a girl, and slight, that I thought I could deal with her—not one of the exasperating adults with whom I had been dealing, who were all so frustrating.

While trying to decide what to do—because I very much wanted to do something—I pretended to continue looking into the toy shop window. As I stood there, such was my pent-up aggravation that I determined I *would* challenge her and find out something about Inspector Copperfield.

That intent in mind, I backed away from the toy store and moved on, walking slowly so she would keep following. But when I reached the next corner, I made a quick darting turn and stepped into a recessed doorway. Heart pounding, I waited.

Sure enough, the girl came sneaking round the corner, quite unsuspecting, her attention focused farther along the street, where she must have assumed I'd gone. The moment she took a step past me, I leaped out and flung my arms about her. My assault came with such surprise that she tumbled to the ground, me atop.

"'Ere, what's this?" she cried. "What you doin'?" She lay upon the wet pavement, facedown, attempting to twist her head round to see who had accosted her. I took advantage of my position by snatching up her cap and slapping her repeatedly on the head.

"Why are you following me?" I cried.

"Oh, it's only *you*, is it?" she said, bursting into galling laughter. "Well, I guess you did me up one, didn't you? I give you that fair an' square. An' no 'ard feelin's."

"Why are you still following me?" I repeated.

"Not to worry, mate," she said. "Nothin' personal. I told you, if yous was to pay me, I'd be sneakin' round whoever *you* wanted."

"But it's none of your business what I do."

"Never said it was me business. But it is me business. You can do what you like. I'm not goin' to interfere in no way. I just reports what you do. Think o' me as a newspaper with legs. It's 'armless."

"I want to know," I said, "who wants all this information."

"Oh, *that*," she said. "Why don't you get off me back, an' we can talk to faces."

There was something altogether cheerful about Sary, so even as I was angry with her, I could not help but ease off, stand, and back away.

"Last time we talked," I said, "you suggested you were finished with me."

"Yup," she said, brushing off her ragged clothing. "Thought I was too. But when I made me report, this 'ere client o' mine says I need to keep on yer 'eels. Don't know why. Never asks. I like the coins they pay. Told you, it's me eatin' 'abit."

"Don't your mother and father give you food?"

Her face clouded. "Don't have none o' them," she said.

"What happened?"

"Last summer me ma got sick with the cholera an' died."

"I'm sorry," I said.

"Before that—a year ago—the old man got transported to Australia."

"Why?"

"For nothin'," she said with great fierceness. The next moment the anger seemed to melt. "Still," she said, "it's the same for others I could mention. The good thing is, in six years Pa will be back. 'E will too, don't doubt it. Course, 'e 'as to pay 'is own way 'ome, so I've been puttin' aside some to 'elp. Or just maybe," she added with a saucy wink, "I'll get to 'im first."

Not wishing to be put off by her chatter, I said, "Tell me about Inspector Copperfield—the one who paid you to follow me."

"I told you, I never 'eard o' no Inspector Copperfield."

"Then who was it?" I demanded. "I must know."

She looked at me and grinned. "I guess I do owe you one," she said. "Considerin' 'ow you fooled me so. I'll 'ave to think you're smarter than I thought so as not to let you do that again."

"Girls are not expected to be smart," I said.

She laughed. "That proves how dumb *you* are," she said.

"Do you intend to follow me further?"

"Long as I get paid."

"Then," I demanded, "I must know who's paying you."

"All right. I'll give you a name 'cause you caught me fair an' square," she said. " 'Ow's that?"

"Fine!" I cried.

She thought for a moment. Then she said, "It's O'Doul. Do that mean somethin'?"

Mr. Finnegan O'Doul! Of course! It made perfect sense. I tried to think of the man I had seen at the Red Lion and then the man with the false beard who had accosted me outside the Naval Ordinance Office. It could very well be one and the same.

"And he's the one paying you to watch me?" I said.

"You asked a name, so I gives you one," returned Sary. "You can do what you want with it. Even that's bendin' me rules some." That said, she began to move off. "Just remember," she called, "if you need me to sneak someone for you, come after me at the St. Giles Rookery. I'll give you a special price. I like you enough."

"There is someone I need to find," I called.

She halted. "Who's that?"

"Mr. Farquatt."

"Farquit? Who's 'e?"

"A family acquaintance."

"What do you wants to know about 'im?"

"I need to speak to the man. I'd go to his place of employment if I knew where it was."

"It got a name?"

"Credit Bordeaux."

"Cred Board-o. 'E a Frenchy?"

"I think."

"Farquit. Cred Board-o. Right. I don't forget nothin'. I'll see what I can find," she said, backing away. When she reached a safe distance—that is, beyond my reach—she grinned and suddenly cried out: "That O'Doul! Don't be so sure 'e's a man!" With that, Sary the Sneak raced away.

ঙ৯৩৩

CHAPTER 25

I Hear Father Proclaim His Fate

I took one step after Sary, prepared to fight, but she ran off, laughing loudly. Gone though she was, I had little doubt she would circle back around and start sneaking after me again. All I could do was shrug.

Besides, if she managed to find Mr. Farquatt, she might be worth something to me.

Annoying as Sary was, she'd helped solve a few of the mysteries that troubled me. To begin, I had no doubt that it was Mr. O'Doul—hiding behind a beard—who was calling himself "Inspector Copperfield." With that understanding, his "warning" to me was easily explained: He wanted my father to pay his debt, and if Father did not, he was reminding me of the prison consequence.

It further followed that it was Mr. O'Doul who was paying Sary to follow me. As to *why*, I imagined he had somehow learned about me—perhaps by way of Sergeant Muldspoon, since *they* seemed to be associated—and wished to see if I was engaged in finding the money he was owed.

As for Inspector Ratchet referring to him—in the person of Inspector Copperfield—as a spy, that, I will admit, I did not understand.

Regarding Sary's last words—*Don't be so sure 'e's a man!*—I easily dismissed the notion as the girl's makeshift attempt to confuse me, revenge for my surprising her. But I was not so dim-witted as to be taken in.

More importantly, while there were some rough stitches holding this garment of speculation together, the explanations satisfied me. All in all, then, I had to consider it a productive morning.

The mood at the Halfmoon Inn, however, was not nearly so positive. When I returned, I found Father, hands in pockets, pacing restlessly about the main room. Mother sat in a corner, look-ing angry. Not far from her Clarissa huddled, forlorn and weepy. Brigit, who was flitting among them, trying to soothe each in turn, appeared equally tense. As for Mr. Tuckum, he was seated next to the fire, absorbed—or so it appeared—in his reading of *David Copperfield.*

When I entered, all turned to look at me.

"Well?" cried Mother with her customary impatience. "What did Great-Aunt Euphemia *say?*"

"As for the loan . . . ," I began, crossing the room to stand by the fire.

"For goodness' sake, John!" cried my father in a rare display of emo-tion. "Will she give us the money or not?"

"She said . . . no," I replied.

"Lord have mercy on us!" shrieked Mother. "What a despicable relation! How *cruel* that woman is. To abandon one's own nephew! Mr. Huffam, we are ruined. *Utterly* ruined!"

"I shall never, *ever* marry," sobbed my sister, pressing a hand to her forehead in the most dramatic of poses, as if she had made a study of Father's theatrical skills. "Oh, dear Mr. Farquatt," she cried, "where *are* you?"

Brigit stared at me for a moment in silence before turning to com-fort my sister.

For his part, Mr. Tuckum shook his head, which, with his Piccadilly weepers, appeared like nothing so much as a dust mop.

I glanced sidelong at Father, for, after all, it was *he* who was the one most directly concerned. He contemplated me, turned ruddy in the face, and then hurriedly examined his hands. Discovering them to be as empty as his prospects, he leaned on the mantel and simply stared into the fire. Did I hear him whistle—very softly—that dismaying "Money Is Your Friend"?

"But there *was* something else," I said into the ensuing silence.

They all turned back to me.

"Aunt Euphemia offered to find me a position."

I.hardly thought the news would bring cheers, but in fact it was greeted by an even deeper silence.

"What . . . kind of position, John?" Father asked at last.

"I . . . I don't really know," I admitted. "She said I should come to her house the day after tomorrow at seven thirty in the morning and meet with Mr. Nottingham."

"Nottingham!" my father exclaimed. "That detestable man! What does he have to do with it?"

"She's asking him to find me a place. Something elevating."

"It was," said my mother, "Mr. Nottingham who turned Great-Aunt Euphemia against your father. Who made sure your father received nothing of his rightful inheritance."

"Anyway," said my sister, "your having a position is of no use to *me.*"

"Now, now," put in Mr. Tuckum delicately. "Perhaps something good *shall* come of this. Decent employment might be quite remunerative. It could perhaps make your stay in prison, Mr. Huffam . . . hmm . . . tolerable. You will recall that you will need to pay for your comforts. Master John, might this position be in some . . . City establishment? A trade apprenticeship, perhaps?"

"No son of mine shall go into trade," announced Mother.

"I'm sorry, sir," I told Mr. Tuckum. "I know only as much as I've said."

Silence and gloom filled the room as thick as any London particular.

"Well," said Father at length, gently rubbing his hands together, "at the moment, then, there is *nothing* to look forward to beyond the court."

Mr. Tuckum cleared his throat. "Yes. Tomorrow morning. At ten o'clock."

"Then," said my father, "there it is," to no general purpose that I could see. "There—it—is!" That said, he pursed his lips and—this time I had no doubt—did whistle his annoying tune.

CHAPTER 26
I Attend the Queen's Bench Court

Next morning we went to Parliament Street, Palace Yard, where the Insolvent Debtors' Court functioned as part of the Queen's Bench Court. It was called Queen's Bench, explained Mr. Tuckum, because it was as if the Queen herself "in full majesty sat in judgment there, by way of *her* law. Of course, if we had a king," he confided, as if it might be a state secret, "it would be the *King's* Bench."

Mother, too distressed to witness the fearful proceedings, had remained abed at the Halfmoon Inn, a shawl over her eyes. My sister stayed with her. While Clarissa insisted it was only to look after our mother, she actually stayed—or so Brigit confided into my ear—in hopes that Mr. Farquatt might appear in the guise of a miraculous angel of mercy.

When Brigit offered to look after me at court when Father would be led away by Mr. Tuckum, Mother was quite relieved to pass off the responsibility.

As we approached the court building, Father grew uncommonly nervous, giving me the impression that he was fearful of being observed at such a place. In fact, the courtyard was crowded with—as Mr. Tuckum cataloged them for us—lawyers, process servers, ushers, judges, constables, witnesses, defendants, solicitors, law clerks, plaintiffs, tipstaffs, sheriffs, barristers, beadles, prisoners, counselors, and bailiffs—though how he knew one from the other, much less their duties, was a marvel to me. All were men. Some were garbed in sumptuous robes and wore wigs—some powdered, some not. Others were without wigs or bore them in bags or boxes. Some were dressed in silk, or wool, or corduroy. All carried papers, parchments, portfolios, volumes, briefs, screeds, and evidence.

"It's England's old-fashioned way," Mr. Tuckum said, "to explain, bend, enhance, befuddle, defame, unravel, knot, or otherwise use the law for the benefit of freeborn citizens. Depending upon whose hand grasps that law, it's our mightiest tool, whether to build, bless, or bury."

It was all one long list to me.

Mr. Tuckum guided us through the legal mob, with many a "I beg your pardon . . . Excuse me, please . . . If you would be so good . . . Defendant in hand, my lord, prisoner in tow . . . Be so kind," and so forth. He seemed to be on familiar terms with many of these people.

We entered at the back of a large room with seats for spectators, of which there were many. Then Mr. Tuckum took Father off, calling back to us, "We shall meet on the street after the proceedings."

Brigit and I squeezed onto one of the benches at the rear of the room, a room well illuminated by gaslight. It was a motley, noisy assemblage, some people in finery, most rather tawdry, and a few in rags. If it were only men who made up the legal population, the spectators consisted in the main of women, children, and old people in numbers sufficient enough to set the balance right. But it was among these onlookers—four rows below us—that I spied Sergeant Muldspoon.

Though his back was toward me, I could have no doubt as to who it was. His stiff, military bearing set him quite apart from all the others. I hardly knew which I felt more—shock or shame—at seeing him, having little doubt he was there to lord it over my father. Or me. Why else would he absent himself from his school—an unheard-of dereliction of duty?

Feeling overwrought, I hastily faced the front of the room. There, beneath an ornate canopy, was an elaborate bas-relief of the great seal of the United Kingdom replete with lion and unicorn rampant on rear legs, like trick dogs at a circus. Before that was a row of four desks, at one of which sat a lord justice. He was a shriveled, wrinkled, pointy-nosed little rodent of a man garbed in a smooth silk robe and snow-white powdered wig with tail. His little hands were clasped before him, and I was quite certain he was twiddling his thumbs at a fairly steady rate.

One level below him was a long desk at which sat the court's scribes, not nearly so sumptuously robed, all writing, reading, or—in one case—cleaning an ear.

On the far right side of the room was a jury box in which waited the twelve true men who made up the jury. Some looked alert, some fidgeted, at least two appeared asleep: All were well dressed.

To the left were the unhappy defendants in *their* box, beadles close at hand. These defendants, of both sexes, were on the whole a sordid, glum-faced lot, slumped like wilted weeds. What shocked me most was not that my father be among them, but that he appeared as derelict as most others. Only one or two were gentlemen, and *they* sat as straight and bright as new tulips.

There was a high-railed box for the plaintiff. There was another for witnesses.

In the center of the room were three concentric rows of long, curved, and polished desks, at which sat the legal officers, lawyers and solicitors of the court, attorneys all, papers piled, legal volumes and law ledgers at hand, pens in fingers or behind ears. They were talking, sitting, standing, turning, walking—so that in their robes and wigs they looked very like an agitated flock of white-tufted crows confined to a cage. To my eyes, there was very little to see of the solemn majesty of the law so often touted by Mr. Tuckum. Solemnity was reserved for the prisoners.

Indeed, the room was full of chatter—lawyers to solicitors, scribes to lawyers, anyone to anyone. I saw as much snuff exchanged as sheaves of paper. Occasionally, someone laughed. Or sneezed.

Or asserted. Now and again the lord justice looked up and asked a question of someone about something regarding some other thing. Answers came, but from whom or to what purposes, I was never sure. Throughout, the judge steadily twiddled his thumbs.

Soon after we arrived, a man—a beadle, I believe—cried out, "Charlie Throcket!" Before I could tell just where he had come from, a boy was standing in the defendant's deck. He was at least as ragged as Sary the Sneak, though perhaps twice as dirty and barely tall enough to look over the railings to which he clung with both hands, as one might cling to the rails of a sinking ship.

With the constant hubbub and moving about by so many, I could not tell exactly what was happening, save that the boy—aged seven, the court was duly informed—was pronounced a "sneaksman," or pickpocket, by learned counsel representing Her August Majesty. The boy's numerous crimes were listed, which included being without home, parents, or Christian morals. Most recently, he had been arrested for stealing a coat. His excuse, or so the court was advised, was that he had been "a colt," which provoked much merriment.

With many a "whereas," the boy was portrayed—in lurid detail—as a singular menace to society, to the nation, and to the general advance of civilization. No one spoke for him. No one asked him anything. I rather thought I alone even looked at him. In perhaps seven minutes—one for each year of his life—the boy was found to be *very* guilty, sentenced to six months in Tothill Fields Prison, and whisked off, like so much chaff swept away by a huge broom.

Barely a moment later a court officer announced, "Writ of debt brought by Mr. Finnegan O'Doul against Wesley John Louis Huffam, Esquire."

I searched the court for Mr. O'Doul and discovered him in a far corner, leaning against a wall, eyes fixed on Father. I tried to imagine him in the guise of Inspector Copperfield. I rather thought he could be him, but I had to admit I *wanted* that to be the case, since it simplified matters. As for Sary's suggestion that O'Doul might be a woman, the evidence of my eyes made the notion a laughable fiction.

I turned back again to Old Moldy. Rigid as ever, he had not moved and therefore, presumably, had not seen me.

But then I watched—holding my breath—as Father, guided by Mr. Tuckum, climbed the few steps into the defendant's dock. I reached out and—I confess it—held on to Brigit's hand.

Father appeared anxious, leaning as he did on the rail before him. Next moment he seemed to recall himself and let go of the rail, as if to demonstrate that *he* needed no support but could stand on his own legs. He stood taller, straighter, chin up. It was his actor's stance, his gentleman's look. I could have sworn that—for a very small moment—he even puckered his lips as if to whistle his song. *He's acting a part*, I thought to myself, but I hardly knew whether to show pride or despair.

As for the lord justice, he had not moved, not a smidgen, save perhaps a flicker of an eye—and the unceasing revolve of his thumbs.

My father's case began with words bandied back and forth so quickly and with so many legal terms—English and Latin interspersed—that I hardly knew who spoke for or against him. *He* never asked anything, nor was he asked to speak.

Then, before I realized what was happening, the lord justice looked up, momentarily stilled his thumbs, and said, "Remanded to Whitecross Street Prison until a just settlement of this debt shall occur."

The trial—if trial it was—had ended, and the thumbs resumed their steady spin, the very engine of justice.

Father was helped down by Mr. Tuckum, then handed over to a beadle who led him away.

The next moment another beadle popped up before the court and cried out: "Lilly Scruchy!" With much difficulty, an old dame mounted the defendant's dock and stood there like a Judy puppet, but without a hand within to prop her up.

"We're done," said Brigit, and stood. With shaky legs and heavy heart, I, too, rose. Shame to say, what I wanted most to do was get away from Old Moldy before he saw me . . . or the tears on my cheeks.

Brigit cut our way through the milling crowd until we reached the courtyard and then the crowded street. Miserable, I hardly paid it any mind. Still, at one point I thought I saw—through my tears—the man in Lady Euphemia's hallway, the one I thought was the lawyer, Mr. Nottingham. He was gone before I could make certain. At that moment I truly didn't care.

Instead, I turned to Brigit, swallowed, and said, "What do we do now?"

"We'd best wait for Mr. Tuckum," she replied.

I stared down at the ground. "No," I said. "I mean, what should we do now that Father is in jail?"

"Master John, the bailiff will inform us."

"Brigit, there is *no* way he can raise that money. No matter what my employment might be. Besides, all our goods will no doubt be sold now."

At that moment my book, *The Tales of the Genii*, seemed the heaviest loss. Perhaps because it was my most precious possession.

"It's your father, not you, who must find some way," Brigit said—quite sternly, I thought.

I lifted my eyes and gazed up at her. Only then did I realize she was not looking at me, but turning this way and that in search of

someone. Suddenly, she stopped—as if she had found whom she was looking for. I followed her gaze. At the edge of the crowd stood Mr. O'Doul. Brigit was staring right at him. He was returning her stare.

"Brigit!" I whispered. "That's Mr. O'Doul!"

"Who? What?" she said, jerking around. "I was looking at a fine lady."

I gazed up at her, quite certain that now *she* was not speaking the truth.

⌬

CHAPTER 27

I Learn News of Mr. Farquatt

While I had expected to see Mr. O'Doul at court, I hardly thought a glance of recognition might pass between the man and Brigit. I was quite willing—wanting—to dismiss the exchange as fanciful on my part, still another coincidence. Next moment I chided myself for thinking of so many odd events as "accidents." Rather, I told myself I *must* discover their *connections* if I was to unravel the mystery that surrounded my father.

Disturbed by Brigit's conduct, I was glad to leave her and search for Mr. Tuckum. When I at last found him, he was in close conversation with another man. Much taller than the bailiff, this man was heavyset and broad-chested, with a florid, if smooth-shaven face. I had the distinct impression I had seen him before. Exactly when, I could not recall.

This man was all but leaning over the bailiff, talking into his face—not as if engaged in an argument, but with serious purpose. His left

hand held a top hat while his right hand—forefinger extended—tapped on the bailiff's chest as if to punch a mark on it.

"Heed my words, Mr. Tuckum, heed 'em," he said. "All is now ready. We're about to haul in our nets."

"I hope you're right, sir," Mr. Tuckum returned. "Old-fashioned as I am, my greatest fear is—" At that moment he caught sight of me standing there, looking on, listening. He immediately stopped talking.

The large man, following the bailiff's gaze, turned. I could feel his severe eyes appraising me.

Next instant Mr. Tuckum cried, "There you are, Master John! I've been looking everywhere for you." He hastened forward, took me by an arm, and determinedly guided me away from the man to whom he had been talking, making no introductions whatsoever. By then, however, I'd remembered who the man was: Chief Inspector Ratchet of Scotland Yard.

"Alas," said Mr. Tuckum, speaking rapidly as he led me off, "I'm afraid it went as we feared. A sad business, a sad business. As for me, I've grown quite fond of your father."

"Where is Father?" I asked, glancing over my shoulder at the inspector. He was looking after us.

"Placed in Her Majesty's police van. I don't know if he has already reached prison, but no doubt he will arrive there soon enough."

"What will happen then?" I said.

"Perhaps it would be best to return to the inn, where I can explain everything to your mother as well as to you." He had taken me around the corner, so the inspector was no longer in sight. "Was not your servant girl with you?"

"I left her by the curb."

"Then let us collect her and be on our way."

"Mr. Tuckum," I said, "I think I saw Mr. O'Doul at the court."

"The one who brought the writ of debt?"

"Yes, sir."

"Perfectly natural he should be there. All the same, *I* should have liked to observe him." To which he added, "Just my old-fashioned curiosity."

I said, "I do feel badly."

"Egad! An old-fashioned boy like you *should* feel distressed."

I was about to say that I felt badly because *he* was not being honest with me. Instead, I said, "I fear I won't be able to help my father."

"Now, now! Every day is a . . . hmm . . . new day, Master John. Quite new. Ah, here is your girl." He meant gray-haired Brigit.

United, we made our way back to the Halfmoon Inn in a Hansom cab, each of us in a silent, contemplative state of mind. But the moment we entered the inn, we were confronted by Clarissa, who, upon seeing us, sprang to her feet. "He's come back!" she cried, her face illuminated by a rare smile.

"Father?" I said. "Here?"

"Not Pa, silly," she exclaimed. "Mr. Farquatt!"

"Mr. Farquatt? Here?" cried Brigit.

"Himself!"

"Clarissa!" I said. "Don't you wish to hear what's happened to Father?"

"I know all—"

"Clarissa," admonished Brigit with a severity she did not often use with my sister, "you need to listen."

"Perhaps, my dear young lady," said the bailiff, "it would be best to fetch your mother so she, too, can hear our news and so may decide upon your next steps."

"I'll fetch her," said Brigit, and she went off. I sensed that, annoyed by Clarissa's self-centeredness, she wanted to leave.

I sat down on one of the benches to absorb such little warmth as the fire cast. Clarissa, quite irrepressible, took a place right next to me and took hold of my arm as if to make sure I, at any rate, would listen to her. "John," she said, "you don't seem to understand."

"Clarissa, Father is in prison."

"I know what happened," she said. "Mr. Farquatt was there in court and told me."

"He was?"

"Of course he was. And he saw it all. John, he told me that he was

so impressed, *so* moved by Pa's eloquence in making his defense."

Brigit returned.

"Indeed," Clarissa continued, "dear Mr. Farquatt—you *must* listen to me, Brigit!—was kind enough to say that Pa's spirit reminded him of *me*. As a result, despite what had happened between us before—you see how much he cares for me—he came directly here and once again asked for my hand in marriage. And, oh, John, I have accepted him!"

"You are quite sure he was moved by what Father *said*?" I asked, wanting to be certain I'd heard correctly. "And it was *that* which made him return to you?"

"Isn't that *wonderfully* romantic?" cried my sister, with nothing but joy. "I think Father will be pleased. Aren't *you* so pleased, Brigit?"

Brigit said nothing. If anything, she appeared quite glum.

I looked around. Mr. Tuckum was across the room, but I was sure he had been listening to this conversation. I turned back to Clarissa. "My congratulations, I'm sure," I said—rather flatly, I fear.

Clarissa was not to be denied. She clasped her hands and beamed. "Of course," she said, "before it is final, Mr. Farquatt will need to go to Father and ask his blessing and permission."

"He'll have to go to Whitecross Prison to do so," I said.

"John, I assure you, Jean cares so much for me, it will not matter."

"*Jean?*" I said.

"Mr. Farquatt's Christian name," said my sister. "You know, John, now that we are on intimate terms, it's altogether proper for us to use such names. Isn't that so, Brigit?"

"I would think so," Brigit replied, but with continued gloom.

"But I have even more news for all of you," my sister went on excitedly.

"Which is?" I asked.

"*My* happiness is quite secure. But Mr. Farquatt—Jean—is truly prepared to help Pa in his great difficulties."

"How?" demanded Brigit.

"Now that Pa shall be his father-in-law, Jean is willing to pay off his *entire* debt."

"That *is* wonderful news!" I cried, and looked around to share in the general delight.

Mr. Tuckum, however, was looking very solemn. As for Brigit, my sister's happy words caused the color to drain from her face.

None of this was what I would have expected.

৩৩৩

CHAPTER 28

I Confront More Riddles

It is difficult to describe my emotions as my mother, sister, and I—along with Brigit—gathered round to listen as Mr. Tuckum set forth our situation.

Had we not learned that my sister was to be married? Good news, surely.

Mother, for one, was very pleased.

Had it not been announced that Clarissa's husband-to-be—Mr. Farquatt—was to pay Father's debt?

Wonderful news in which my mother, my sister, and I rejoiced.

Then why was Brigit, who should have been equally joyful, so clearly *un*happy? The same for Mr. Tuckum.

The truth is, what filled that room gave me a sense of unease: an awareness that things were not quite what they should be, as if there were as many shadows in that room as people. And, whereas I could name all the people, I could not put names to the shadows.

Mr. Tuckum interrupted my thoughts. "The circumstances in which you now find yourselves," he began, "must be clearly understood. Mr. Huffam has been removed to Whitecross Street Prison. There he will reside until his debt has been certifiably paid or a settlement accepted and agreed upon by this Mr. O'Doul. Since the sum is so ... hmm ... large, the conditions of the Insolvent Debtors' Act shall not apply.

"The costs encumbered by Mr. Huffam in prison shall be four shillings a week. That is, of course, on the paupers' side. Mr. Huffam has the option of paying for a great variety of genteel comforts— lodging, food, drink, et cetera, et cetera, as set forth by the warden, Mr. Ambrose Makepeace, as fine a gentleman as this town or any town may see.

"Mr. Huffam's family—which is to say, you—have the option of living *with* Mr. Huffam in the prison, at such cost as Mr. Makepeace has established."

"I am *not* prepared to reside in prison," Mother snapped.

"Then where will we stay?" asked my sister.

The bailiff interjected: "Needless to say, Mrs. Huffam, Miss Huffam, Master Huffam—as well as you, Brigit—you retain your liberties and may come and go at the prison, within the rules, curfews, and such regulations as pertain."

"Can we not return to our home?" asked Mother.

"Mother," I reminded her, "the furniture is all gone."

"Quite true," said Mr. Tuckum. "And being the old-fashioned man that I am, I should remind you that the expense of living here, at the Halfmoon Inn, has already accumulated to the amount of two pounds, three shillings, and one pence. Many a debtor, cast into prison, finds it desirable—if merely from an economic point of view—to have his family reside with him."

Mother sighed.

"Perhaps we can stay with Aunt Euphemia," suggested my sister, a remark that brought forth one of Mother's most withering looks.

"In conclusion," continued Mr. Tuckum, "I can assure you that all of this falls well within the majestic traditions of English law and, as such, must surely bring a sense of well-being and comfort to you who have the good fortune to live in this . . . hmm . . . great nation. Any questions?"

"Sir," I asked, "may we visit my father so as to consult with him?"

"Excellent boy!" cried Mr. Tuckum. "I think that's just the thing to do."

"I'm sure," said my sister, "Mr. Farquatt would like to accompany us. Can he speak to Pa in private? He has specifically requested it."

"If he wishes," said Mr. Tuckum rather gravely.

"I have heard," said Clarissa, "that a marriage can be solemnized in prison. Is that true, Mr. Tuckum?"

"Clarissa!" cried Mother. "You cannot be married in prison! And I am sure Mr. Farquatt would not wish it either."

"I can only say," said the bailiff, "that there are distinguished clergy attached to all our prisons. Many a blessed marriage has been solemnized there."

"Very well," said Mother, "we shall go to the prison this afternoon and sort matters out." That said, she rose and went up to her room, none too happy, I could see.

After a moment my sister stood up. "Why is it that no one has congratulated *me* for securing Father's happiness and liberty? Is it because I, a young *woman*, have accomplished what no one else could do?"

When no one replied, she announced, "You are all beastly!" and hurried up the steps.

After a moment Brigit followed, murmuring, "I'd best be with her."

So it was that I remained alone with Mr. Tuckum.

The bailiff waited a moment, eyes on me, as if hoping I might speak. When I did not, he retrieved his installment of *David Copperfield* and settled down to read.

I gazed into the fire, sifting through what I knew and didn't know.

At length Mr. Tuckum put his reading down and pushed his eyeglasses up. "Master John, you do not appear in a contented state of mind."

"No, sir, I am not."

"Would you be willing to tell me *why*?"

I considered him. He was looking at me with a frank, open face,

his Piccadilly weepers framing a look of perfect benevolence. But then the inspector's phrase echoed in my head—*Then we must make sure to use 'im*—and I decided to put Mr. Tuckum to the test.

"That man," I said, "the one with whom you were talking outside the court, who was he?"

"Ah, well, yes. A . . . hmm . . . casual acquaintance."

"Does he have a name?"

"It . . . escapes me."

I had often—surely by my mother—been accused of having far too much fancy for my own good. But at that moment I was quite convinced that *no one* was telling me the truth!

So much for trust. But I went on, determined to use *him*. "Mr. Tuckum," I said, "you were in the room just now when my sister spoke of Mr. Farquatt's visit to her."

"I was."

"Did she not say that Mr. Farquatt was *at* the court and was so impressed by my father's eloquence in his defense that it made him return to her?"

"I do believe those were her words."

"As do I. Yet, I can't recall my father saying *anything* in court."

The bailiff nodded. "The law—in *its* eloquence—does not allow a defendant to speak on his own behalf."

"Then how," I asked, "do you explain Mr. Farquatt's report?"

"I fear I cannot."

"Nor can I." I turned away. "Forgive me," I said, "I'm in need of some air."

"Master John," Mr. Tuckum called after me.

I paused and turned.

"I believe your great-aunt has offered to find you a position?"

"She has."

"But your mother had unkind words to say about that possibility."

"She did."

"Master John, I would suggest—if I may be so . . . hmm . . . bold— that you don't put that offer aside."

"Why?"

"As you have heard me say many times, Master John, I'm an old-fashioned man. Ready employment should never be spurned out of hand. Not in difficult times."

"But Mr. Farquatt has offered to pay my father's debt."

The bailiff sighed. "Being old-fashioned, it remains to be seen if he will."

"Sir," I blurted out with anger, "I think you know far more than you are willing to say."

"Master John," the man returned with something akin to sadness, "I can say only what the law *allows* me to say."

"Or is it, what the law *told* you to say?"

When he made no reply, I went out the door and into the front court angrier, but more bewildered, than ever.

※

CHAPTER 29
I Have More Questions

My head was twisted with questions as confused as the London streets. To wit:

Why was Old Moldy at the court?

Why was Mr. Nottingham there?

Why—outside of court—did Brigit and Mr. O'Doul exchange a knowing look?

Why would Mr. Farquatt claim he was at the court when he had *not* been there?

Why should Brigit be unhappy regarding my sister's betrothal to Mr. Farquatt?

Why did Mr. Tuckum pretend *not* to know the large man with whom he had spoken, when it was Inspector Ratchet, the same person he had met at the inn in the middle of the night?

What business did Chief Inspector Ratchet of Scotland Yard have with any of this debt problem if debtors' prison was so common? Was he not required—as Mr. Tuckum claimed—"to investigate only the most serious crimes"?

And what did Inspector Ratchet mean by saying earlier, "We're about to haul in our nets"? Who—or what—was he about to catch?

Who was Inspector Copperfield?

And finally: Were these questions all connected?

As I mulled these riddles over, I wandered away from the inn, with no specific objective in mind save to get away. It was only as I turned onto Halfmoon Street that I looked up. Standing right in front of me was Sary the Sneak.

"You tried to trick me," she said by way of greeting.

"What are you talking about?"

"Yer Mr. Farquit."

"What about him?"

"You asked me to find out 'bout 'im, right?"

"I did."

"An' you said 'e was employed by a company goes by the name o' Cred Board-o, right?"

"That's where he told my sister he was employed."

"Then 'e were foolin' 'er."

"What do you mean?"

"Because in all o' London there ain't no such establishment, that's why."

"But—"

"Ain't no butter 'bout it. Yer Frenchy Farquit may work for someone at someplace, but you can be sure it ain't *that* place."

I stared at her.

Sary grinned. "Maybe now you can see the point o' 'avin' a sneak for a friend."

"I suppose I can," I admitted.

"Then 'ows 'bout you payin' me to follow this 'ere Farquit bloke the same as I followed you?"

I stood there wondering what game Mr. Farquatt might be playing, wondering too if Mr. Tuckum knew something about him he had not revealed. Why else should the bailiff question Mr. Farquatt's ability to pay my father's debt? In fact, a new question immediately loomed: Did Mr. Farquatt need to see my father because he wished to request marriage to Clarissa? *Or did he propose marriage so that he could go see my father?*

I was so mired in my thoughts that Sary tugged me on my sleeve. "What you thinkin' 'bout?" she asked.

"How much do you charge for your sneaking?" I asked her.

"Thrupence the day."

"I don't have any money," I said.

"Just tell me where I can find 'im an' I'll do the sneakin'," Sary assured me. "I'll mark you down for credit."

Recalling that Mr. Farquatt would presumably be joining us at the prison, I said, "Do you know where the debtors' prison is?" I asked.

"Course I do. Everybody does. It's on Whitecross Street."

"I must meet my father there."

" 'E in prison, right?"

"I fear so."

"Nothin' fearful about *that*," Sary replied. "Anyway, that prison is a lot closer than Australia, where me pa is, ain't it? Lots of chaps in prison for no reason I can see. Boy I knows, somethin' like five years old, 'e's been sent off six months for spinnin' a top where 'e wasn't allowed to. Another got five for fallin' asleep in Kensington Gardens."

I stared at her.

"It's true! Not that yer kind pay mind to such."

"I'm not doubting you," I hastened to say. "But will you meet me outside the Whitecross Prison at eight o'clock tonight? I should be able to point out Mr. Farquatt to you, or at least tell you where he lives. But make sure no one sees you."

Sary grinned. "Don't you worry none. I'll be there."

She started off.

"Wait!" I called.

She turned.

"How did you know my father was in prison?"

She grinned. "O'Doul told me 'e would most likely be."

As she went off, I was quite convinced she was the most unusual person I knew. That thought brought me against a harsh realization: Though I was trying to uncover the truth, my whole world—or so it seemed—was trying to keep it from me! But for all Sary the Sneak's oddness, she appeared to be the one person willing to speak truth to me.

తాలు

CHAPTER 30
I Visit Whitecross Street Prison

It was about five o'clock that afternoon when my mother, my sister, Brigit, and I, as well as Mr. Tuckum and Mr. Farquatt, alighted from the hackney coach that the Frenchman had kindly provided for transportation. As we cantered across the City, no one had spoken. I kept stealing glances at Mr. Farquatt, wondering where exactly he was employed, wondering too how I might discover where he lived so I could tell Sary. Unfortunately, no opportunity presented itself. He was too busy paying courtly attentions to my sister and my mother. To my eyes, the effort was rather forced. As for Brigit, he positively snubbed her, as she did him. I kept wondering why.

Once out of the carriage, Mr. Tuckum announced, "There she sits: Whitecross Debtors' Prison."

The dread building—already gloomy in the afternoon's dark—was a redbrick and gray stone structure four stories high with many a barred window. The central building had been expanded to the right and left. These wings sat behind high brick walls.

The main building had extensions reaching out to the street. Between these arms, somewhat recessed, was the main entryway, set behind a high, spiked iron fence.

A large arched window faced directly from the left arm of the prison building onto the sidewalk. Over this, window bars had been woven vertically and horizontally, with just enough space left between them so a man might reach out a begging hand. In the stone lintel, words had been chiseled:

PRAY REMEMBER POOR DEBTORS HAVING NO ALLOWANCE

Even as we approached the entryway, I observed a man behind these bars. Though I could not see his face clearly, he had reached through the grating with a small tin bucket in hand. He was trying to attract donations from passersby by rattling the bucket while endlessly repeating the phrase, "Remember poor debtors. Remember poor debtors."

Mr. Tuckum paid no heed but guided us toward the prison gate. "Built in 1815," he proclaimed, as if giving a guided tour. "Successor to Newgate Prison. Has accommodations for four hundred and ninety prisoners—exclusively debtors. Equally divided: Male paupers, male gentry, female paupers, female gentry. It gives me pleasure to inform you that each section has been named to commemorate previously existing—old-fashioned—prisons: Horsemonger, Fleet, Marshalsea, and the Clink. Shall we enter, please."

There was a uniformed guard posted before the main gate. Upon seeing Mr. Tuckum, he saluted, then he and the bailiff exchanged a few friendly words. Once done, the guard used a large brass key attached to his belt to open the gate. We went forward, only to be confronted by an ironbound door and yet another guard. Mr. Tuckum and this man also chatted briefly. Finally, that door was unlocked and swung back on heavy hinges.

We found ourselves in a poorly lit vestibule with yet another guard. He was seated next to a table upon which lay an open book, pen, and ink.

"Mr. Tuckum," the guard said in greeting. "Good afternoon, sir. Would you and your guests be so good as to sign in? Christian name, surname, please," he added.

"Of course," said Mr. Tuckum, and he bent over the ledger and signed with a flourish. Then, in order, my mother, my sister, myself, Mr. Farquatt, and finally Brigit did the same. Only after we all had autographed the book did the guard unlock the door that enabled us to proceed into the prison itself.

It was not what I expected. Here was a large, spacious courtyard in which perhaps seventy people—men, women, and children—were milling about in what appeared to be aimless fashion. It could have been a public London promenade. There were fair numbers of patently poor people, but there were others quite well dressed, including one or two gentlemen in top hats. People were sauntering alone or in groups, sitting, chatting, reading. At the far back wall—where there were no windows—a few men were even hitting a ball against the brick with small racquets. Among all these people—I presumed them to be prisoners—a number of guards mingled. One approached us. He recognized Mr. Tuckum and saluted. "May I help you, sir?"

"You have a new prisoner. Just delivered this morning. Mr. Wesley Huffam. His family wishes to visit."

"'E's a popular man," said the guard. "Been 'ere just a few hours and been visited already. This way, please."

As I speculated as to who might have visited Father, the guard led us to one side of the court, then down along a hallway. I presumed it was into one of the wings of the building I had seen from the outside. Facing this hallway was an array of doors, many of them open, leading into small rooms. Over all was a smell of decay. Nothing was very clean, and I observed many a pile of garbage left to rot.

I could see people inside the rooms. Some were alone, others in the company of two or three persons. In a few I saw what appeared to be whole families, including children.

"Here you are, sir."

We crowded into an undersized room, which contained a barred window, a low bed, a tiny table, and a stool. There was barely enough space for us to squeeze in. Father lay full length upon the bed, but as soon as we entered, he sat up and looked upon us with the eyes of a drubbed dog.

At first we just stood there, no one speaking, until Mother said: "Is there no food to be had here?"

It was the guard who spoke out, and he did so in such a brisk, clipped fashion, it was clearly a practiced response: "Breakfast: Eight ounces of bread, plus one pint of oatmeal, alternately seasoned with salt and molasses. Dinner: Four days a week, three ounces cooked meat, eight ounces of bread; three days a week, soup with three ounces of meat, plus vegetables. Supper: The same as breakfast."

"But, of course," interjected Mr. Tuckum, "that is the prison custom at four shillings a week. Considerably more may be purchased by arrangement with Mr. Makepeace."

Again there was silence. Father had yet to say a word. Clarissa went to him, sat by his side, and put an arm about his shoulders in a rare gesture of affection. "Pa," she said, "as you can see, Mr. Farquatt

has come with us. He has something particular to say to you. Something very good."

My father looked up. It was as if he had not noticed Mr. Farquatt. When he did, he frowned.

The little man stepped forward. "Mr. Huffam, sir," he said, making a brief bow. "I am so profoundly grieved to see you in such difficulties. But if I may speak to you—in private—perhaps I can return you to some joy."

My father gazed at him with little enthusiasm. "If you wish, sir," he said.

"And I, Mr. Huffam," put in Mother, "must talk to you as well."

"And, Father," I added, "I should like to speak to you too."

My father sighed. "Each in turn," he said without any visible eagerness.

"Oh, please," Clarissa begged, "let Mr. Farquatt speak first."

"As you wish," Father replied.

At which point we left the room and shut the door so that the two men might confer in private. But Mother, Clarissa, and a tense Brigit hovered just outside the door—twittering, it seemed to me. Not wishing to take part, I strolled back down the hallway. Mr. Tuckum and the guard came along behind me.

I returned to the courtyard, curious to observe more of the place. It was oddly calm, a world unto itself. And yet, as I looked further, there was barely a smile to be seen. Rather, a sullen gloom prevailed, an aimless mood that suggested not so much boredom as stagnation.

Around three sides of this courtyard were ranged balconies, with any number of doors leading out upon them. I was just strolling about when a movement above caught my eye. When I looked up, I saw someone I knew: Chief Inspector Ratchet.

Simultaneously, he must have seen me, for he immediately ducked

into a room, making it clear—to me, at any rate—that he did not wish to be noticed.

I spun about in search of Mr. Tuckum, but he, too, had gone. Not knowing where, but thinking he might have returned to my father, I hurried back down the hall, only to find my sister in tears, my mother consoling her, and Mr. Farquatt to one side, not looking like a man who was moving along the happy road to marriage. Brigit stood in shadows. I could not judge her emotions.

"What has happened?" I asked.

"Your foolish father," said Mother, "wishes to *consider* before agreeing to Mr. Farquatt's kind offers."

"You mean," I blurted out, "he doesn't approve of the marriage?"

"Nor," said my mother, "though it's impossible to understand, Mr. Farquatt's kindness in offering to pay his debt."

"But . . . why?" I asked.

"You had best speak to him yourself."

"But what did he say?"

"Master John," called Brigit from the shadows, "he wishes more time to think about it." It was as if she were defending Father.

"What is there to think about?" I asked.

"Master John," said Mr. Farquatt with his inevitable little bow, "*merci*. Now, *that* is a completely reasonable question. It is all quite insulting."

"It's awful," wailed Clarissa. "But I will marry on my own!"

"Now, now," said Mr. Farquatt, "I do believe it is right and necessary to have your father's blessing."

"I beg you," Mother said to me, "go and talk some sense into your father. He'll listen to you."

I hesitated, but since I did wish to speak to him, I went into the room.

༄

CHAPTER 31

I Learn the Truth

Father was sitting upon the bed, one hand covering his eyes in an attitude of much unhappiness.

I shut the door and sat down on the chair opposite.

He did not move.

"Have you," I finally said, "really withheld permission for Mr. Farquatt to marry Clarissa?"

"Mr. Farquatt requested no such thing."

I stared at him. "I beg your pardon, sir. Did you say Mr. Farquatt did *not* request Clarissa's hand in marriage?"

"That is correct."

"But you just met with him."

"So I did."

"Then . . . what did he say?"

"It is nothing I wish to speak to you about."

"Would you rather speak to Chief Inspector Ratchet?"

He looked up at me then, eyes full of wretchedness. "What do you mean?"

"Inspector Ratchet is in this prison. Now. He is, I believe, watching who comes to visit you. Have you had many visitors?"

My father covered his eyes again.

I summoned up my courage and said, "Father, it's time for you to tell me what this affair is all about."

As if pondering my request, he remained silent.

"The whole family is suffering," I pressed.

When he continued to say nothing, I determined to wait him out.

At last Father got up and began to pace. I watched in silence. Then, as if it took great effort, he paused and faced me. "Very well, John, you shall know all."

"But it must be the truth, Father," I said.

He had the grace to blush, then went back to the bed, sat down, rubbed his hands together, and started to tell his tale.

"You observed me gambling," he began.

"At the Red Lion," I said.

"That is but one such place I frequent," he admitted without looking at me. "There are others. Here, there." He sighed. "In truth, many places. But then, all London thrives upon gambling.

"Be that as it may," he continued, "it came to be that I owed money to a fairly large number of gentlemen. May I stress the word 'gentlemen.' But, John, I swear to you, in no case did my debt to any one man ever exceed ten pounds. And that includes Mr. O'Doul."

"But, Father—"

He held up a hand. "If you desire the truth, you must be patient."

"Yes, sir."

He continued. "In *total*, I will allow that the *sum* of my debts came to some three hundred pounds, but not—I repeat—to any *one* man. The law is clear: You cannot go to debtors' prison if your debt to anyone is merely twenty pounds or less.

"Therefore," he went on, "knowing the total, knowing how large it was, I sought a means by which to reduce it. Very well, then, I am employed by the Naval Ordinance Office. Do you know what I do there?"

I remembered what the clerk at the office had told me: "You copy ordinance specifications for the cannon manufacturers."

He glanced up at me. "I was not aware you knew. Yes, that's what I do. Do you know *how* a musket ball or cannonball works?"

Puzzled by his drift, I was nonetheless able to recall Sergeant Muldspoon's endless lessons. "A musket ball or cannonball is pushed into a smooth gun muzzle. A charge—the gunpowder—is set off. The force of the explosion throws out that shot with great energy."

"I am surprised you know. But, John, if you take that *round* shot and change its shape—make it oblong—*and* if the inner barrel of that musket or cannon has *spiraling* lines engraved in it, do you know what will happen?"

"No, sir."

"A round shot, without spiraling lines, might travel a hundred yards—and be inaccurate at that. But if those spiraling lines are in the musket or cannon barrel, an oblong shot will go *four* hundred yards and *be* accurate!

"The spiraling is called 'rifling.' An extraordinary invention. It has been known for some time. But we *British* have perfected it," he said with some pride. "Rifling will change warfare forever. Once introduced, the Royal Navy will gain an enormous advantage over our enemies. The same for our infantry. Think of it, John—no more close battles. Britain shall attack and defend from a safe distance, an *untouchable* distance. We shall be invincible. I assure you, such will be our superiority, all wars will cease. Peace—enforced by noble Britain—shall come to mankind."

"Father," I said, for I was losing patience, "I'm very glad to know all this, but ... but what has this to do with your debt?"

"Everything. You see, it was *I* who copied out the specifications of our rifling invention. Memorization—be it the lines of a play or anything else—is easy for me. Which is to say, the complete specifications for rifling—for this amazing advance—are in my head."

"But still—"

"John, listen! Now then, it occurred to me that there might be other nations interested in this invention. I thought: If I could provide the information, they would pay me enough money to wipe away our debts."

"But, Father," I cried, "*that* would be treason!"

He smiled weakly. "Not if I gave them *false* information. John, I am an actor. Unlike that asinine Nottingham, I am a good one. I assure you, I can play a part to perfection."

I looked at him, astonished.

"Very well, then. In various gambling establishments I let word out that I had this information. That it might be purchased for . . . three hundred pounds. Unfortunately, as it happened, the Home Office got wind of this. Chief Inspector Ratchet—"

"What about him?"

"—came to me. He informed me the government had learned of my . . . game. I assume we have our own spies."

"Who, Father?"

"I have no idea who told him. What difference does it make? In any case, Ratchet warned me that he knew what I was planning. Well, yes, the word 'treason' was mentioned . . . in passing. But I gave the inspector my word as a gentleman that no such thing was ever intended. In turn, though *he* is just the son of a Chelsea publican, he promised that the government would not press charges *if* . . ."

"If what?" I managed to say through my dismay.

"If I played a part for them. That is, by *appearing* to be a traitor, the government might discover what spies approached me. Those spies would be apprehended, and the secret of rifling would remain a British secret."

"What . . . what did you do?"

"What choice did I have? Besides, John, I realized it would be my greatest acting role. So *of course* I agreed to work with them. But . . ."

"But what?"

"Now then, John, I did not owe any *one* person three hundred pounds. I told you, I could manage small amounts. Five pounds here, seven pounds there. But, suddenly, *all* my debts were gathered into one sum. Someone purchased them *all.*"

"Mr. O'Doul?"

"Perhaps. But where O'Doul got such an enormous sum of money is quite the mystery. When I asked him where he got it, he refused to say. Still, there is no question he is after the secret."

"For whom?"

"He's an Irish rebel," Father stated.

After a moment he continued: "In short, I am being offered freedom from that debt in exchange for the rifling secret. Blackmail. Ratchet is waiting to see who comes to make me an offer. He believes there will be more than one. And he will arrest them all."

"Does this mean that as soon as Inspector Ratchet apprehends these spies, you will be freed?"

"Alas, the inspector promises only that when—and if—they arrest the spies, I will not be charged with treason. I still have a debt to pay—to someone."

"Mr. O'Doul?"

"Surely his name is on the writ. You said you saw me with him at the Red Lion. That's when he made me an offer: If I give *him* the secret, he would release me from the debt. But if I did provide him with the secret, would he *truly* release me? Is he a man to be trusted?

"Moreover, Inspector Ratchet suspects that someone is using him—perhaps without his even knowing. Now do you see, John, why I sent you to my great-aunt? Ratchet may catch his spies, but . . . my debt could well remain."

"Do *you*," I asked, "have any idea who is behind it all?"

"Of course not."

"Has anyone else besides Mr. O'Doul made an offer for the secret?"

"Mr. Farquatt. *That's* what he just spoke to me about."

"Mr. Farquatt! For what country?"

"France. Does it matter?"

"What did he offer?"

"Three hundred pounds."

"Do you expect *more* offers?"

"Ratchet thinks so. As I said, he does not believe either O'Doul or Farquatt has the money to buy the secret. He's quite convinced there is someone else behind them—a supreme spy, if you will."

"The *same*—behind *both* of them?"

"Whoever put up the money does not care how he obtains the secret as long as he obtains it."

"Do you know," I asked, "about an Inspector Copperfield?"

"Never heard the name. Someone working with Ratchet, I assume."

Not about to explain, I said, "Does Mr. Tuckum know about all this?"

"He is working with Inspector Ratchet."

"What will happen next?"

"The government has promised that my salary from the Naval

Ordinance Office shall continue. Our home goods have not been sold. All this will allow me—and our family—to remain here in relative comfort."

"Why here?"

"It's theater, John, grand theater! Creating the illusion that I am helpless."

I wanted to suggest that he *was* helpless, but I could not find the tongue to say it. Instead, I said, "Father, what if they cannot find the chief man?"

"Well you might ask. They intend to hold me here until they *do* find him. I am," Father said with some pride, "the gate through which all these spies and traitors must pass. A dramatic image, to be sure, but, yes, one might say that."

"Do you wish to be?"

"Need I repeat the words of that song, 'Money Is Your Friend'?"

I stared at him, hardly believing all that he had told me.

"But . . . but what can I do?" I stammered.

"My dear John, it's *you* who must discover the primary individual who is behind it all. It's *you* who must find three hundred pounds. As soon as you do, we shall be truly free of all constraints."

"Why me?"

"Then I won't be at the mercy of Ratchet."

"How could I do it?"

"Has not my great-aunt Euphemia promised to find you a position?"

"She has, but——"

"Then by all means, take it."

"Father——"

"John, let us hope that she intends to do more for you. You *are* the last Huffam. I repeat, that's worth much. Of course, your mother and sister must remain here, in prison with me. It will be safest. But employment will enable you to live *outside. You* will be free to go about. *You* will be able to uncover the one behind this."

"Isn't that Inspector Ratchet's task?"

"But I am not sure how far to trust him. He *has* used me, John, most cruelly. I don't doubt he will use me again. And . . . there is still the debt."

"Does Mother know all this?"

He shook his head. "John, I beg you, speak *nothing* of it to her or your sister. Or Brigit, I might add. You know how the women talk amongst themselves."

He reached into his inner jacket pocket and took out a folded sheet of paper. "Here it is."

"Here is *what?*"

"The plan for rifling. The true plan, not a false one." He unfolded it and laid it out for me to see. There, in his meticulous drawing and writing hand, were a series of numbers, equations, drawings of spiraling lines.

"Why are you showing this to me?"

"I am not showing you; I am giving it to you."

I recoiled. "Father, I'm sure I should not—"

"John, if something happens to me—now that you know all—you must have it for safekeeping. It will ensure that the family is treated properly. But be careful: If it is known you have it, it might place you in grave jeopardy."

I stared at him. When he first began to speak, he had rarely looked at me. As his story unfolded, his gestures grew bold, his eyes brightened. Truly, he was relishing this role—as he said, his greatest acting challenge.

Gingerly, I took the paper, folded it, refolded it, and placed it in my pocket.

"I repeat," he said, "tell *no one* you have it. It's you and you alone I trust." For the first time that day he smiled genuinely.

"What about your gambling?"

The smile vanished. He placed a hand on his heart. And in his actor's voice he proclaimed, "From this day forward—I swear to you—I shall never do so again."

As if in a play, from somewhere in the prison, a bell began to toll, as if for a funeral.

"What's that?" I asked.

"It means that those who are not required to stay here must leave in an hour. They call it the stranger's bell."

In truth: Never did I feel more a stranger to my father than at that moment.

CHAPTER 32

I Look Beneath the Stone

When I left Father, I was not quite sure how to behave with my mother, sister, Brigit, or Mr. Farquatt. Perhaps they had not changed, but I had. I knew so much more than they.

"What could have possibly taken so long?" Mother demanded.

"Did you get Pa to accept Mr. Farquatt?" asked my sister.

And from Brigit: "Did Mr. Huffam tell you what he intends to do?"

I looked at them as if they had spoken a foreign language. I might have tried to explain all Father had said, but there was his strong caution *not* to speak to them about *any* of it. So I kept my silence. Besides, Mr. Farquatt was standing right next to Clarissa, intently gazing at me with his bland, childlike face.

"Mother," I said, "he wishes you to reside here. With him."

"Here?" she cried.

"Here?" my sister joined the cry. "In prison?"

"That's what he said."

"That's unacceptable!" said Mother, and she flung open the door to my father's cell and rushed in. My sister and Brigit followed.

That left me alone with Mr. Farquatt. We looked at each other, wondering, no doubt, what the other knew.

He made his little bow. "Is there any hope for me?" he asked.

I do not know how he *meant* the question, realizing, as I did, that it could be taken in any number of ways. In truth, it was unnerving just to look upon a man whose features revealed so very little. Was he my sister's suitor, my future brother-in-law, or merely a French spy bent on stealing England's greatest military secret?

The best I could say was, "I'll need to talk to my father again. If . . . if you can tell me where you reside, I'll be more than happy to keep you informed."

He considered this suggestion, allowed himself a tiny smile, and made his customary little bow. "Master John, I do so appreciate your every kindness. It's for your sister, I'm sure. Better than have you troubled by coming to me, I shall make certain I remain in constant contact with dear Mademoiselle Huffam. You can reach me that way. Now, I must bid her adieu."

Adieu. With that French word, he joined the family in the prison cell.

From that moment on—though no hostile words had been exchanged—I was sure we understood each other: We were enemies.

Left alone, I longed to think through all I had been told by my father. All the same, I remembered asking Sary to wait for me beyond the gates of the prison. It occurred to me that she might be a great help in doing what I needed to do, though in just what fashion, I was unsure.

I went back to the main courtyard. Even as I did, the City church bells began to chime, proclaiming the eight o'clock hour. I was certain Sary would be waiting.

Not seeing Mr. Tuckum handy, I approached one of the guards. "I beg your pardon, sir. My father, Mr. Wesley Huffam, is a prisoner here. Am I free to come and go?"

"You may go, but know you must be back—if you are staying here—by nine o'clock. The gates are locked for the night then."

He escorted me to the first door, called through it, and it was opened. I stepped forward, the door shut behind me, and I found myself in the dim vestibule.

"You'll be good enough to sign out or make your mark," the guard said to me, gesturing toward the table.

I picked up the pen and searched for my name. I found it with the other family names. There was a row of them, mine preceding Brigit's, as she was the last to sign. I gasped. There indeed was Brigit's name, her *whole* name:

Brigit O'Doul

O'Doul!

I stared at it for such a long time, the guard asked, "Is something the matter, boy?"

"No, sir," I managed to say. I scribbled my name and then, eyes averted, stood trembling before the next door, which was opened for me.

In moments I was standing outside the prison, trying to still my pounding heart.

Brigit *O'Doul*.

What could it mean? I immediately recalled the exchanged look outside the court between Brigit and Mr. O'Doul. In my mind's eye I saw his face. I saw hers.

Brother and sister!

Then I remembered two things she had said. First, when speaking of Ireland and the famine: *To live, a people will do whatever they need to do.* And at another time: *Know that for things held dear to the heart, all kinds of sacrifices must be made.*

I then recalled how often she had urged that it be Father, and he alone, who should solve the problem of the debt. I recalled how conflicted she was about Mr. Farquatt. *Of course!* The Frenchman was her brother's rival!

And how tense she was about my visit to Lady Euphemia! As well she might be: If my great-aunt gave us money, her brother's hold upon my father would disappear and he would not get the secret!

" 'Ere, what's the matter?"

I looked around. It was Sary. "You're lookin' like you just swallowed a live fish an' it's flappin' round yer belly. Is that what it is?"

"I think I am ill," I replied.

" 'Ow come?"

"I've ... discovered too many things."

"Like what?"

"Just ... things," I replied, hardly knowing where to begin.

"Did you find out where that Frenchy Farquit lives?"

I looked at Sary. She was staring at me as if she truly wished to know my thoughts—a friend.

"Can I trust you?" I said.

Sary's gap-toothed grin bloomed. "Sary the Sneak 'as a reputation for bein' as true as the Queen 'erself. Maybe more."

"How more?"

"I don't think, livin' as she does, rich an' all, with all them lords an' ladies, she knows much 'bout the world like I do."

I remembered something. "When I asked you who it was that hired you to follow me, you admitted it was a person named O'Doul. But you said, 'Don't be so sure he's a man!'"

"What if I did?"

"It *was* a woman, wasn't it?"

Sary did a little jig of glee. "Fooled you, didn't I? What's it 'bout boys an' men? You either 'ates the girls or loves 'em, but you never *knows* 'em."

"It was our servant, Brigit, who hired you, wasn't it?"

"You can think so," she said, taking obvious delight in my distress.

When I was very much younger, Brigit had often taken me to play at a tiny grass park not far from where we lived. At that park, by the side of the path, sat a stone. Many a time I'd passed it with indifference. After all, it was only a gray, dull, and lifeless stone. One day—for no reason I can recall—I decided to turn that stone over.

To my astonishment, beneath that stone lived a whole colony of ants. Thus exposed, the ants raced about in a confusing, teeming panic. I found it fascinating . . . but disturbing.

I dropped the stone where it had been and made certain never to turn it over again. *But*, from then on, whenever I passed that stone, I had only to glance at it to know that *beneath* it lay a frightful, disturbing world.

The series of discoveries I had just made—my father's secret life, Mr. Farquatt's French connection, Brigit's duplicity—caused me to feel much the same. It was as if I had looked beneath the world I knew only to uncover a whole *new* world. Indeed, the whole experience—from

my father's arrest to my recent discoveries—had made my old sense of the world, ordered and set, obsolete. It was now changing, different, and . . . terrifying.

I looked at Sary. By contrast, her old clothes, her crooked-toothed grin seemed honest, open. I wanted to trust her. Needed to trust her. And why not? Mr. Tuckum's old-fashioned world had failed me. My father's world had failed me. It was all gammon and spinage. I must turn to something new. "Do you truly know the world?" I asked.

"Go 'head an' try me."

"If I tell you many things—private things—can I trust you to keep them to yourself?"

She placed her dirty cap over her heart, tossed her head so her tangled hair fell free, and grinned. "On me 'onor as a sneak."

I will not deny I was smitten. What I said was, "And can we work together to solve this puzzle?"

"What puzzle is that?"

"I'll tell you," I said. "But we need a place to talk. A private place."

"Follow me," she said. "I'll take you to a world you never seen before."

And she did.

⸙

CHAPTER 33

I Visit the Rookery of St. Giles

The darkness was compounded by an eddying haze of thick brown fog, so that even if I had wanted to, I'd hardly have noticed where we were going. In fact, I was completely caught up in relating to Sary all that concerned my father. Now and again she'd ask a question: "When did this 'ere Frenchy, this Farquit, come round to court yer sister?" Or, "Tell me again what Inspector Ratchet said? What's riflin'? When did that other inspector, the one called Copperfield, show 'imself?"

It was such a relief to share it all, I held nothing back and answered as best I could—even what I understood about rifling. Not to tell her would make a confusion of all the rest.

She listened attentively.

I hasten to add, I did *not* reveal that I carried the plan for the rifling in my pocket. I needed to keep my father's secret as a sacred bond—*one* last thing I could believe in that existed between father and son.

When I'd finished my tale and looked up and around, I had no idea where we were. "What is this place?" I asked.

"Welcome to me loverly neighbor'ood," said Sary. "The Rookery of St. Giles."

I halted. "Why's it called the rookery?"

"Know all them flocks o' blackbirds that fly 'bout—masses of 'em? Ugly, scruffy, screechy birds they are, without much song for singin'? Always peckin' 'bout for bits o' food? They got to roost somewhere, don't they? In a rookery, then. Well, it's the same for ugly, scruffy, scratchy folk like us. We got to roost somewhere too, don't we?" There was a bitterness in her voice I'd not heard before. "Well then, 'ere we are."

I peered about. The deep fog and lack of illumination made all indistinct. What I did see was a shadowy, uninviting place, a confused maze of narrow, stifling streets, alleys, and byways. Buildings were crowded together like so many heaps of bricks and sticks, nothing straight, nothing sorted, everything in a state of decomposition, collapse, and disarray. Nothing whole, nothing uncluttered, nothing clean, nothing new, but everything tossed everywhere, abandoned, left to molder away like the wreckage, or so I imagined, that lay beneath the seas.

Though it was November, and raw, only the odd window was closed. In many a place there was simply a square (or *almost* a square) hole that might have once been a proper window. Other holes were crudely boarded up, some with paper coverings or with ragged laundry hanging out. Doors, if they survived, hung on broken hinges, locks being, apparently, a lost—or stolen—art.

Such light as existed came from hanging lamps or from broken candles here and there, revealing a jumble of barely readable signs: LODGING FOR TRAVELERS. DRY ROOMS. MILLER'S GIN. CHEAP CLOTHING. USED GOODS. OLD RAGS. LADIES' LACE MADE HERE. PAPER FLOWERS. LOANS. LONDON MISSIONARY SOUP SOCIETY.

The air was foul, thick with the nose-stopping stench of rotting garbage and putrid waste. Single privies—if one existed—served entire houses. Single water-spigots—with brown, evil-smelling water trickling out—provided for whole blocks of homes. Oh, evil to him whom evil drinks!

People clogged our path: all dirty, all ill clothed, all poorly shod, if shod at all. They were sitting, drinking, staggering, limping,

stumbling along, sleeping, clinging to one another, or falling down. Some sang hymns. Others sang vulgar songs. They talked to others or themselves. Mothers clutched naked children to their breasts, while other children, barefooted, followed as best they could. For despite the hour, there was many a hollow-cheeked child upon the street, playing with bits of crockery or oyster shells. Indeed, among the throngs there were more children than adults, yet plenty of old folk, too, in every stage of decrepitude—hands or feet bandaged, many on makeshift crutches. What young and old had in common were bleary-eyed looks of hunger and an air of hopeless neglect and abject misery. Many continually wept, as though their reservoirs of grief were infinite.

Was there nothing healthy? I did see numbers of dogs and cats and rats—the rats, actually, looked fat and sleek.

It was as if all London were a stone, and here was what lay beneath.

"Come on," said Sary, giving me a yank on the sleeve, for I had been just standing there, agape. She seemed not in the least taken aback.

In a daze I followed as she made a sharp turn down an alley so disgusting and narrow that I might have touched the walls if I'd spread out my arms, which I was loath to do. As it was, I stumbled twice in the dark—but did not want to know over what. Sary kept me moving. I would have been lost otherwise. More than lost: swallowed whole.

"Steps down," she cautioned.

We entered a low room at basement level: Dirt floor—lit by one small, smoky lamp. If I had been any taller, I'd have had to stoop. The air was dank, smelling of too many bodies pressed into too small a space, of tobacco, of filth. I counted some twenty people, appearing no different from those on the streets: a thoroughly wretched lot of old and young, men, women, and children.

A few looked up with glazed eyes.

"Brought me friend John!" Sary announced. "John, this is me family."

"Pleased . . . ," I managed to say, though I wasn't, "to meet you."

No response. No greeting. Whether they were not pleased or, more likely, not caring, I didn't know.

Sary took up the lamp with her free hand and, pulling me along by my jacket, guided us over many a body. At the far side of the room we entered an alcove, which had a ragged curtain drawn across its front.

" 'Ere we are," Sary said, "me 'ome sweet 'ome."

A cubicle, hardly more than four feet by four, with something like a shelf against an oozing back wall. In one corner a bunched coverlet. A bed, I guessed. Nothing else.

"Pretty good," said Sary, "ain't it?"

"Is this where you . . . live?" I asked.

"I only pays sixpence a week for it," she said, "so it's all mine 'cause I make the most money in this place."

"Does someone own it?"

"Some say it's Lord Silverbridge. Might be Prince Albert for all I care. I pays it to an agent who comes regular as the full moon, 'cept there are plenty o' times I can't see the moon—but I always sees 'im."

"Sary, are those people out there truly your family?"

"Naw. Just call 'em that. They likes me well enough, an' it's better to feel near *somebody*, I suppose. Go on," she said, "sit down."

I did. She sat next to me and blew out the lamp.

"Why did you do that?"

"Saves the odd penny," she said, "an' most pennies I get are odd."

Settling into the dark, she drew the coverlet round both our shoulders. Snug then, she said, "All right, we got to make a plan 'bout what to do."

"I need to know something first."

"What's that?"

"Are you still working for Brigit O'Doul?"

"Nope."

"Even if she asks you to?"

"Least not till this 'ere business is done with. I'm sneakin' just for you now. You're me bloke. And you don't even 'ave to marry me." It was dark, but I was sure she was grinning.

"I don't know how I can repay you."

"Didn't yer lady aunt say she'd get you work?"

"Yes."

"All right, then. Don't sniff at it. First thing tomorrow mornin', go to it. From the sound o' things, you're bound to make a bit. We can share, right?"

"Of course. And you?"

"I'll go back to Whitecross Prison so as to keep me eye on that Brigit of yers. If she come out, I'll sneak after 'er. See where she goes."

"Is that the one you think is behind this all?"

"She or maybe 'er brother."

"My father didn't think so."

"Who'd 'e think?"

"He didn't know."

"Don't matter," said Sary. "After we done our day, we'll meet up an' see what t'other 'as found. What we'll be is our own inspector detectives."

"I suppose I should go back to the prison," I said. "They're expecting me. I don't want them to worry."

"You're free to go," said Sary, "but it's a long way."

I thought of what I'd have to go through to reach the prison. "I'll stay," I said.

"Then be comfy."

We talked more, she asking me what a school was like. What I did there. And very curious about Old Moldy she was too. But somehow I came round to telling her about *The Tales of the Genii*, and I told her my favorite story from it, "Ali Baba and the Forty Thieves."

Sary adored it. "That slave girl, Morgiana, she's me!" she cried when I was done. "I love the way she outwits all o' them fellas an' goes on livin' 'appy. That's me for sure! That were the best story I *ever* 'eard."

We slept back-to-back.

☙❦❧

CHAPTER 34

I Meet Mr. Nottingham

The first thing Sary said when we woke in the morning was, "I kept dreamin' of yer Ali Baba world, me bein' that Morgiana."

Teeth chattering, we emerged from Sary's alcove into the basement. It was not quite as full of people as the night before, but it was crowded enough. I wondered if they would go anywhere that day.

But the scene on the street was much the same as the night before. Countless people milling about, almost shuffling, but this time moving away from the rookery. I presumed it was toward gainful labor, or at least the hope of employment.

Sary found a hot tea seller and paid a penny for a pint along with two slices of bread. Sharing, we consumed the fare on the spot.

Then she led the way back out of the maze that was the rookery.

The night before, when I'd told her all I knew, she had only asked questions to help her understand my bewilderment. Now, clearly having thought more, she raised others.

"I think we best find out more about that Inspector Copperfield, shouldn't we?" she said.

"But you said you didn't have anything to do with him."

"I didn't, but 'e still is *someone*, ain't 'e? You thought 'e was that Mr. O'Doul, tryin' to scare you."

"I did think so, at first."

She caught the indecision in my voice. "Not now?"

"I don't know," I admitted. "I'm still puzzled about what this Inspector Copperfield knew and didn't know."

"What didn't 'e know?"

"About Mr. Farquatt," I said. "Because Brigit knows all about Farquatt. Doesn't that mean O'Doul should have known? So perhaps Copperfield isn't O'Doul but . . . someone else."

"Who?"

I shrugged.

"But you're sure 'e's after the riflin' secret too?"

"Ratchet thinks him a spy. But then, everyone seems to be."

"Me?" she asked, grinning.

"Of course not."

"I thanks you for that!"

Things were rushing forward so, I was reminded of one of those railroad trains. Though I had yet to ride one, a friend had. He said it went fearfully fast—fifteen miles to the hour! I imagined the sensation as something like what I was experiencing.

When we reached a parting point, I suddenly found myself anxious. For the first time ever I had spent the night away from my parents without their knowing my whereabouts. Now there loomed a day during which I was to find out what work had been secured for me.

I said, "I'll meet you . . . at the prison . . . as close to six or seven as I can. I need to tell my family I'm all right."

"I'd like to do that for me pa," said Sary. "But 'e's too far off, ain't 'e? Australia. I do always wonder 'ow 'e be. Thinkin' o' me, 'is lovin' daughter, I 'ope. Don't know if 'e even knows Ma died." There was sadness on her face. Next moment, with a shake of her head, she returned to her normal, cheerful grin. "Anyways, I'll be keepin' eyes on yer Brigit, then waitin' at the prison for you 'less somethin' else 'appens."

Pleased to be her friend, I watched her go.

I went the opposite direction. By listening to the bells and noticing clocks as I walked, I arrived at Great Winchester Street close to my appointed time of seven thirty. When I knocked, William/Wilkie opened the door promptly.

"Good morning, Wilkie," I said.

"Good morning, sir," he returned quite civilly, his eyebrow suggesting that this time I was truly welcome. "And while I appreciate your use of my Christian name, Master John, I beg to remind you *not* to use it in madam's presence."

"I'm sorry," I said. "I promise. Will I be seeing her?"

"Madam is not well."

"Is she dying?"

William/Wilkie's lifted eyebrow seemed to say, *Are we not all tending that way?* "If you please, sir," he said, opening a door into one of the rooms off the main hall, "just follow me."

"Whom will I be seeing?"

"Mr. Nottingham."

My father's enemy!

We entered a small room, the walls covered as elsewhere with flowery-patterned silk. Otherwise, it was furnished sparsely: A table behind which sat a chair and another chair facing the table. A very low coal fire glowed in the fireplace, providing barely enough warmth to make the room bearable.

"Please be seated," said William/Wilkie, indicating the chair facing the table. "Have you breakfasted?"

"Yes, sir," I said, not wishing to say where I'd been. "Thank you."

"Mr. Nottingham shall be with you shortly." The butler bowed and started out only to hesitate at the door. "Master John, a word of advice: Mr. Nottingham can be . . . somewhat *dramatic*, what might be called 'theatrical.' He creates a performance where others do not." His eyebrow seemed to say much more, but I could not decipher it.

Left alone, I sat down, wondering how I would deal with Mr.

Nottingham when there was so much mutual dislike between him and my father. I was consoling myself with the thought that the solicitor could hardly be worse than Lady Euphemia when the door burst open and a man, top hat in hand, rushed in.

I jumped to my feet.

This man, tall, thin, and angular, all but sprang to the table, flung his hat upon it, set himself down in the chair, and clasped large hands before him. But his arms, legs, and fingers were in constant motion, like an erratic windmill. His face was long, high-cheeked, and sallow, with a large nose, thin lips, and eyes that fairly glowed with hostility. His jaws, moreover, were clamped tightly together, making an angry line of his mouth. Indeed, he leaned toward me, nose and jaw jutting forward, a posture that suggested that not only was he prepared to argue, he was prepared to *win* the argument. After glaring at me for a while as if to intimidate me—which he assuredly did—he jumped up, fairly danced around the table, then began to pace right and left before me. For my part, I could do nothing but remain where I was and watch him, absorbed by the oddness of his behavior.

"The defendant may stand at the bar!" he abruptly commanded.

Since there was no one else in the room, I gathered that *I* was the defendant. I stood stock-still.

"Are you aware," he cried, pointing an accusatory finger at me, "that I am Lady Euphemia Huffam's solicitor?"

Though taken aback by his peculiar question, I said, "Yes, sir, I am."

"That my name is Connop Nottingham?"

"If you say so, sir," I said, but I recalled my father's jibe, "noncompoop."

He paced some more only to suddenly swing around to confront me again. "Now then, are you then *willing* to admit to being John Horatio Huffam?"

"Yes, sir, I am."

"Are you *capable* of confessing that you are the son of Wesley John Louis Huffam?"

"It's not a confession, sir," I said. "It's the simple truth."

"The defendant will just answer the question," he said. I began to grasp that his use of the word "defendant" suggested that he was *playing* at being a trial lawyer. The more so when I recalled William/ Wilkie's words: *Mr. Nottingham can be ... somewhat dramatic. ... He creates a performance where others do not.* That grasped, I relaxed somewhat.

"Is it within your *limited* powers, John Huffam," he went on relentlessly, "to perceive that I am not in this room *because* of my own desires?"

"I thought as much, sir."

"John Horatio Huffam, are you further prepared to *acknowledge* that your father, the aforesaid Wesley John Louis Huffam, is a man of poor judgment?"

"He *is* my father, sir."

Mr. Nottingham gripped the lapels of his jacket. "The court

requires explanations, boy, not excuses! So will you, John Huffam, finally *admit* that your father's actions, as suggested by his current predicament, are not beyond reproach?"

"No, sir, I don't wish to say that."

He frowned. "But you *are* willing, are you not, to admit that, as Lady Euphemia has informed me, he is in *dire* straits?"

"He is that, sir."

"In, I believe, a *shameful* debtors' prison?"

"Yes, sir."

"Are you not—the truth now!—John Huffam, residing *in prison* with him?"

I hesitated, wanting to say I was not in the prison, yet uncomfortable with admitting I had slept in St. Giles Rookery. "No, sir."

"Ah! At the Halfmoon Inn. A notorious sponging house, then?"

"Yes, sir," I said, that being the easiest to say.

"My lord," he said to a nonexistent judge, "we approach the sordid evidence! You have heard the defendant admit to much. One can only hope he has told the truth." He swung round and glared at me. "The penalty for perjury *is* severe.

"I shall proceed," he said. "Now then, John Huffam, you are, are you not, the *last* of the Huffam line? You even *look* like the infamous Wesley John Louis Huffam."

"It appears so, sir."

"Given all that, are you, John Huffam, aware of the fact that I, Connop Nottingham, am here because—and *only* because—Lady Euphemia ordered me to be so?"

"I didn't believe you'd want to help me out of kindness, sir."

His face reddened. "The defendant will just answer the question! Do you, John Huffam, know that she *insisted* I do something for you?"

"She's most considerate, sir."

"You may have every reason to think *her* considerate, but that has nothing to do with the case." He turned from me. "Let the court know that *I* think my lady is wrong to aid the boy and have advised her accordingly. In truth, she has chosen to *ignore* my sage advice and has commanded me to act otherwise. Therefore, I have done so." He turned back to me. "Did you know all that?"

"Yes, sir."

From his jacket pocket Mr. Nottingham extracted a piece of paper. "Then I can inform the court that I *have* secured employment for John Huffam at a church. You are expected there—at this address—in one hour, at nine o'clock sharp. Be late at your peril. It is my hope—not my expectation—that the church may do you some good, spiritually and morally. When you arrive there"—he pointed to the paper that he had placed upon the table—"you will ask for Mr. Jeremiah Snugsbe. You will present my compliments to Mr. Snugsbe. If you do as he bids, you will be paid accordingly. Such is the wish of my lady. Can you accept all that?"

"Willingly, sir."

"Now then, John Huffam, be advised that I shall do *everything* in my power—have already done all in my power—to *dissuade* Lady Euphemia from providing you or your family any further assistance. Is that perfectly clear?"

"Yes, sir."

"Furthermore, if you *fail* to meet your obligations at this place of employment, I shall learn of it. Indeed, I shall investigate frequently and will inform Lady Euphemia of any dereliction of your duties. All your hopes shall be dashed then—as they should be."

"Yes, sir."

"Therefore, my lord," intoned Mr. Nottingham, turning back to the imaginary judge, "since the defendant agrees with *me* in all particulars, I rest my case. There is nothing left for me to say except good day. I trust the jury will find this Huffam boy guilty—*exceedingly* guilty."

With that, Mr. Nottingham snatched up his top hat and set it upon his head—accentuating his great height—and bounded out of the room. I stood there for a moment, partly bewildered, partly bemused, then looked at the address on the paper:

CHURCH OF ALL HALLOWS BY THE TOWER OF LONDON

I was still standing there wondering what possible employment I might find in a church and why Mr. Nottingham had sought to place me there when William/Wilkie slipped into the room.

"Master John," he said, "I gather your meeting is over."

"I believe so," I replied.

"Was it satisfactory?" asked the butler, indicating with his extended hand that I was to exit the room. "Mr. Nottingham rushed from the house without saying a word."

"He certainly doesn't like me," I said. "Or my family. He acted as if I were on trial."

"As I tried to suggest, sir, Mr. Nottingham is a man of feverish— not to say, *theatrical* tendencies."

"He said he told Lady Euphemia not to help me."

"I have no doubt."

"Why did she not listen to him?"

"I advised her otherwise, sir."

I looked at William/Wilkie in surprise. "Do you have more power over her than her solicitor?" I asked.

"My lady is not without some heart."

Having reached the front door, I looked up at him. "Thank you, Wilkie," I said. "Mr. Nottingham did secure some employment for me. At the Church of All Hallows—"

"By the Tower, yes."

"Do you know why?" I asked.

"I believe," said William/Wilkie, "he has a good friend there. A Mr. Snugsbe. Mr. Nottingham no doubt considers that man a collaborator." His lifted eyebrow indicated: *Be forewarned!* "Here are three pennies for the omnibus," he said, offering the coins. "You will need to be there soon. I wish you well."

"Thank you," I said, taking the coins and realizing—for him to mention the hour—that he must have been listening to the whole conversation from behind the door. "Should I come back?" I asked from the threshold.

"Only if summoned, sir," he said, and if I translated his eyebrow correctly *that* time, there was no indication as to when that time might be—if ever.

ოდოდა

CHAPTER 35

I Go to the Church of All Hallows by the Tower

I did what William/Wilkie had suggested: found an omnibus heading in the general direction of the Tower. It would get me close to All Hallows.

After paying my three pennies, I climbed into the horse-pulled carriage. Though it was crowded, I managed to squeeze myself onto one of the two facing benches between two portly gentlemen who were not pleased to have me take up any space at all. In fact, I received so many jabs from their elbows—under the pretense of turning the pages of their *Morning Herald* and *Times*—that I finally got up and stood by the entrance, where the conductor was standing.

"Never mind the nobs," he said, nodding to the two gentlemen who had forced me out. "They aren't much for sharin'. Where you 'eadin'?" he asked in a friendly fashion.

"To the Tower," I said, that being nearly next to the church.

"Then you best 'old *on* to yer 'ead, lest they cut it off," he said, chortling loudly at what he apparently believed was an original joke.

When I got off, I still had a few streets to walk. Of course I could not help but see the Tower of London, surrounded as it was by its thick walls and moat. In the dove gray of morning, its ancient turrets presented a ghostly image of hard stone and roiling river mist that quite satisfied its grim reputation. As I gazed upon it, one of its infamous ravens appeared atop the wall, leaned toward me, opened its black beak, and screeched. It was as if it were giving me a warning, which led me to recall the conductor's words in a more somber light.

Nonetheless, I turned away and went toward the church. Its name, All Hallows, suggested how truly ancient it was—"hallow" being the

Old English way of saying "holy." Some claimed a church had been there since Saxon, even Roman, times. I knew nothing of that, though I'd heard say it was the oldest church in London. What I saw was a large, bulky stone structure, with a square tower steeple of brick and some stained-glass windows.

I went round to the entryway on Seething Lane. There, the church had two old wooden doors beneath a large clock, but both doors were firmly closed. I found, however, a small side door left ajar. I slipped in quietly.

I entered a small vestibule, went down a few steps into another larger chamber, walked forward—there was nowhere else to go—past steps that I suspected led up to the steeple, then stepped into the church itself.

A grand nave loomed before me, lofty and still. A double row of pale yellow limestone columns supported a flat ceiling. The raised pulpit was at the far end of the church, to one side. Opposite from where I stood was the chancel altar with its cross. Between the back of the church and the altar were many rows of wooden pews, the old wood here and there impressed with what looked to be ghostly—in fact, dusty—handprints.

Curious as it was, I reminded myself that my immediate task was to find Mr. Jeremiah Snugsbe.

At first glance the church seemed to be empty of any living humans. That is to say, it appeared not only hallowed, but hollow. But as I grew accustomed to the gloom—the light was muted, speckled with multihued dust motes—I gradually realized someone was sitting in the very first pew to the far side. What I could see of him was his back, but his posture suggested he was slumped over, asleep.

I walked down the nave toward him, my footfalls echoing loudly—deliberately—on the flagstones and memorial brasses, in hopes the man might wake. But when I reached the pew, the man still slept.

Moreover, he was encased within a very large black greatcoat, closed up by more buttons than I could count in a glance. The bottom hem of the coat reached the floor and hid his feet, while at the top all that appeared was a crest of curly white hair—reminiscent of cauliflower. Of flesh, I saw naught.

Since the person—I assumed it was a man—had not stirred as I approached, I could only stand by his side, shifting uneasily from foot to foot, uncertain what to do. Was he part of the church staff or a weary parishioner?

In time, my presence seemed to disturb the fellow. Like a tortoise emerging from his shell, his head—on a scrawny but fleshy neck— rose up out of his coat. Whereas the coat he wore was quite outsized, *he* was quite small, with the raddled face of a newborn babe. His nose was a stub, his cheeks round, his mouth small, with a small dimpled chin. Not quite in harmony were two beady black eyes, which fastened on me while rapidly blinking—as if unused to light.

"Who," he asked, "are you?" His voice was gargled, soft-spoken, and hesitant—as if unsure whether he should speak or not.

"I'm looking for Mr. Jeremiah Snugsbe, sir."

The man studied me silently, blinking. "And if you found Mr. Snugsbe," he inquired, "what would you . . . *do* with him?"

"Do, sir? Nothing. I've been sent to him by Mr. Nottingham."

"Is that the Mr. Nottingham," murmured the man, "in the employ of Lady Euphemia Huffam?"

"Yes, sir. Her solicitor."

"*She* contributes money to this church. I don't know why. She never *comes* here."

"I don't think she goes anywhere, sir," I said. "She's ill."

"You might think *that* would encourage her to attend church more often. But giving money as she does enables her to make demands of this venerable establishment. What is your name?"

"John Huffam, sir."

"Ah, yes," he said, eyes continually blinking. "It's Mr. Snugsbe's understanding that she requests *you* be employed here." That said, his head lowered back into his coat as if taking refuge.

"Are *you* Mr. Snugsbe, sir?" I asked, causing him to reemerge.

"An interesting question, that," he whispered. "I don't greatly desire to *be* Mr. Snugsbe. There's not much advantage—that I can determine—in *being* Mr. Snugsbe."

"Why is that, sir?"

"Consider: What *could* Mr. Snugsbe have done with his life? Very *much*. What *has* Mr. Snugsbe done with his life? Very *little*. Offered preferment, Mr. Snugsbe could have gone into the church and risen high. What did Mr. Snugsbe do? Went into financial speculation and fell low. How low? Mr. Snugsbe cleans the church. He *dusts* God's holy name. Mr. Snugsbe would like to believe there's glory in that. He suspects not. But being here has allowed Mr. Snugsbe to stitch together a theory."

"A theory, sir?"

"Of coats."

"Coats?"

"Exactly, a *theory of coats*. Mr. Snugsbe's theory is this: God gives each of us a coat to wear. Here is Mr. Snugsbe's coat," he said, plucking at his own black one with doll-like fingers. "Sometimes a man fills his coat, or overflows it. Sometimes he shrinks within. The Mr.

Snugsbe *you* are looking at is very much.... reduced. One button for each year of his life."

"I'm sorry to hear it, sir. But if you are Mr. Snugsbe, Mr. Nottingham sends you his compliments and begs to remind you that he has secured employment for me here."

Mr. Snugsbe said, "Nottingham and Snugsbe share an interest in failure. Which is to say, they both wear the same coat. Is there not as much bonding in failure as in success? Perhaps more, since failure is in fashion for most of mankind. Why should Mr. Nottingham help you? Have *you* failed?"

"I hope not, sir. Besides, it's not he who's helping me, sir. It's my great-great-aunt, Lady Euphemia."

"Do you *need* help?"

"I fear so, sir."

"Then *that* is the coat *you* must wear," said Mr. Snugsbe, and he lapsed into silence, even as he shrank down below the collar line. I stood there, not knowing what to say, when he rose up. "Five shillings a week is the offered compensation." That said, he sank anew.

I immediately noted that such a sum would cover the weekly expenses of my family's prison keep. "I am very much obliged, sir. But ... what shall I do to earn it?"

Mr. Snugsbe craned his neck to gaze at me with his hard, blinking eyes. "Mr. Nottingham made a singular point of saying *he* didn't care. 'My lady,' says Nottingham to Snugsbe, 'wishes to give the boy John Huffam *something* so as to try him out for a "part."' Nottingham says 'part.' I say 'coat.' 'Let him play it,' says Nottingham, 'as he chooses. If he does well, say nothing. If he receives poor reviews, forgoes his cues, misses entrances and exits, or fails in any fashion, report to me immediately and I shall inform my lady so she shall cancel the performance.' In other words—in Mr. Snugsbe's words—give the boy cloth and see what kind of coat he makes for himself."

"Am I here to establish my character, then?" I asked.

"As Snugsbe says, every man tailors his own coat."

Once again the little man retreated into the black folds of his own coat until only his blinking eyes were peeking over the collar at me.

"Shall I . . . dust the pews?" I offered.

"Lady Euphemia will receive no ill report from Mr. Snugsbe if you do that," the little man whispered, withdrawing farther only to pop up saying, "There's a bag of rags behind the vestry door."

All that morning I dusted pews. Upon two occasions the minister duly and dully appeared to offer the regular morning prayers. He did so to a handful of men and women who came and went quietly. Now and again I saw Mr. Snugsbe moving about the nave of the church, slowly performing I hardly knew what tasks.

After midday prayers he led me to a small chamber in the undercroft, an ancient Saxon crypt—or so he claimed it to be—and offered me a lunch of crusty bread, a piece of cold mutton, and tepid coffee, which I was more than happy to consume.

"Is the coat fitting?" he asked, which I took to mean was I getting along with my work.

"Yes, sir."

"Mr. Snugsbe approves."

"Excuse me, sir, why do you refer to Mr. Snugsbe as, well, another person?"

He was thoughtful for a while and then whispered, "I'm not fond of Mr. Snugsbe. *He's* a failure. What's to admire in failure? Speaking of him as I do allows me to keep my distance."

Afterward Mr. Snugsbe led me to a loft where I worked polishing brass memorial plaques. Here, I was able to see the pews I'd just cleaned.

It was while gazing about that I suddenly realized I was looking down at none other than Sergeant Muldspoon. He was sitting off to one side of the main aisle, stiff and erect as ever. His hands were resting on the top of the pew before him, in an attitude of prayer. But I knew him well: His posture was *only* an attitude. His head was cocked slightly to one side, his signal that he was waiting for a response. For what response—and from whom—I could hardly guess.

The answer came shortly.

Into the church, down the nave, and taking a seat right next to Old Moldy was someone I recognized: Mr. Farquatt.

From my perch in the loft I could not hear any of the conversation that passed between them. It was enough to know that they met and talked. Was not Mr. Farquatt representing the sergeant's ancient enemy, the French? Who was Old Moldy representing?

When Mr. Farquatt shook the sergeant's hand, bobbed a bow, and

left with no blows exchanged, I was tempted to follow my sister's suitor and see where he went. But sticking, shall I say, to the coat I wore, I dared not. As for Old Moldy, when he left—which he soon did—I had no doubt he would be returning to school, ready to attack his slate in his best military fashion.

It was while thinking of Old Moldy that I had a startling recognition: The day previous my father had asked me if I knew how a gun worked. I had replied correctly because my teacher had given many a lesson about firearms. *Was he not an artillery man?* In fact, during my last day at school he had inscribed the following on his slate: WAR, RIFLE, GUN, DEAD, HURT, HARD

Rifle!

In other words, if there was one man who would know the value of rifling as my father had explained it to me, that man was Sergeant Muldspoon.

Yet, how could he—patriotic Englishman whom he endlessly affirmed himself to be—how could *he* be a spy?

I could not wait to talk to Sary.

こめのめ

CHAPTER 36
I Return to Whitecross Street Prison

It was perhaps seven o'clock—I had been in the church almost ten hours—when Mr. Snugsbe found me sweeping the steps to the crypt.

He told me I was free to go, but he said I should be back in the morning no later than eight.

"Is the coat fitting?" I asked.

"It is indeed," said the odd man. To which he amended in a whispery voice, "Just be sure you keep it buttoned up so Mr. Snugsbe shall have no call for requesting a tailor."

The last sight I had of Mr. Snugsbe was of him settling into an out-of-the-way pew and retreating into his coat.

The evening outside was oppressive, the air heavy, as if about to rain. I went as fast as I could, not wanting to miss Sary. But even as I approached the prison gates, she appeared.

"There you are," she said. "I was gettin' worried."

"I couldn't leave my employment any sooner," I explained, glad to see her.

"What work is it?"

"In a church. Cleaning."

"Well now," she said, "you're lucky it's inside. All this nasty weather with winter comin'. An' not likely to get into any trouble there. Did you preach a sermon?"

"Dusted things. And you?" I asked.

"Been sneakin' after Miss O'Doul. Got lots to tell."

"So do I," I said. "But I need to tell my father and mother that I'm here. Mother is sure to be vexed with me. Will you wait?"

"Sarah Waitin' is my true name."

"Is it really?"

She laughed. "Not likely."

I went through the gates and signed in. As I did, I paused to note that Brigit had also gone out and returned. This time, however, she signed only *Brigit*. When I turned the page and looked for her previous signature, her last name, *O'Doul*, had been blotted out. I had little doubt she had corrected her blunder.

I went right to Father's cell. There, I found things somewhat altered. Crowded though it was, two more beds had been added.

Moreover, a table was laden with a full dinner. Father sat on one bed like a host at the end of the table. Mother and Clarissa—both looking miserable—sat on the other bed, but the dimensions of the cell being exceedingly tight, they sat at the table too. Mr. Tuckum occupied the chair, a napkin tied round his neck.

Brigit was serving.

"John!" cried Mother. If she'd room enough, no doubt she would have leaped up. "We've been frantic with worry. Where have you been? We thought you'd gone to the Halfmoon Inn for the night, but Mr. Tuckum reported otherwise."

Wishing to avoid the question, I said, "I spent the day at the employment Great-Aunt Euphemia found for me."

"And where might that be?" asked Brigit.

"All Hallows Church."

"How convenient," said my father. "Right near my work. You will be able to collect my salary."

"But near the Tower," put in Mr. Tuckum, which I understood to be a word of warning.

"What do you do there?" asked my sister.

"Clean," I replied.

"Clean!" exclaimed my mother, altogether distracted from her question about my night's lodging. "Mr. Huffam, do you see how your poor judgment has brought your son down?"

"Now, now," suggested Mr. Tuckum, "it is perhaps old-fashioned to express it, but a boy can't move up until he *is* first down."

My sister sniffled. "If Mr. Farquatt visits this evening, I beg you all, do *not* speak of John's employment. It's too degrading."

"But I will earn five shillings a week," I announced.

"Well done, John!" enthused Father. "You see, money *is* our best friend!"

Refusing to engage with him on *that* subject, I only said, "And you, sir, how did you pass the day?"

"Most agreeably. There are appealing people here with considerable talent. I think I may even be able to set up a dramatic society. What more could a theatrical producer want? There is, so to speak, a captive audience, abundant time, and little competition by way of entertainment."

"Mr. Huffam," scolded Mother, "what you have in this place is a house of martyred saints. There's not *one* person here, not one soul that I spoke to, who will admit to having *any* fault that could have tumbled them. Every man, woman, and child insist they have been brought to debtors' prison because of someone *else's* folly, cruelty, or spite. The words 'I am responsible' are not spoken here."

I looked at Father, but all he did was wink at me.

"Where *were* you last night?" my sister suddenly demanded.

"I met with a friend, who invited me to stay."

"A friend from school?" asked Mother.

"Just so," I replied.

"I fear there is not much room here," said my father, "but of course ..."

"You *are* welcome to return to the Halfmoon Inn with me," said Mr. Tuckum. "We are all . . . hmm . . . family now. I assure you, Master John, I shall charge no fee."

I studied his face, wondering if he merely wished to make some use of me. No, I had no desire to stay there but would go with Sary.

"If you will excuse me, sir," I said, "I have already accepted a second night's invitation with my friend."

"And food?" asked Mother.

"That, too," I said, turning to the door. "I'll be back tomorrow evening."

"Master John," said Brigit, "may I walk with you to the gates?"

"It's not necessary," I said—rather coldly, I fear.

"I should like to," she returned, sufficiently firm that it amounted to a command.

But no sooner did we leave the cell, the door shut behind us, than Mr. Farquatt appeared before us in the passageway.

"Good evening, Master John," he said to me. "Mademoiselle Brigit," he added with a curt nod.

Brigit drew herself up to her full height, towering over the man. "Mr. Farquatt," she said, "will you be pushing your marriage proposal upon Mr. Huffam again?"

I was aware that their words meant quite another thing—though neither dared speak plainly—and the question hung in the air.

Mr. Farquatt offered up a faint smile. "I assure you I shall not renounce Mademoiselle Huffam in these difficult times," he said with a little bow. "And any comfort I can bring to the Huffam family is my privilege. Master John, your sister informed me that your aunt will be providing for you after some fashion. I wish you well."

Before I could say anything, Brigit said, "She has provided: He's cleaning the Church of All Hallows."

Mr. Farquatt started. "Near the Tower?"

"Yes, sir."

"Have you begun?" he asked me, suddenly tense.

Not wishing the man to know I'd seen him there, I said, "Tomorrow."

His anxiety eased. "Ah! I'm pleased to know that. Now, you must excuse me," he said, and he crowded into the cell.

"You told him you did not begin your work," said Brigit. "Why?"

"Brigit," I said, continuing down the hallway, "I was only respecting Clarissa's request that we say nothing about my employment."

"Master John," Brigit said after a moment, "I should tell you, I don't believe Mr. Farquatt *is* a good match for your sister. My advice—and I told your parents: The marriage should be forbidden. It's this offer he's made to your father. Sure, it's as if he's buying your sister, as they say the heathens do."

"What did my father say to your advice?"

"He would give no opinion." Suddenly, she stopped, turned me about, and with as much force as she could muster, leaned over and said into my face, "Master John, you *must* tell Mr. Huffam that only he can solve this problem." She seemed distraught.

"But how can he?"

"If he put his mind to it," she said in a sulky voice, "he surely can."

Not wishing to debate the point, I started off again toward the gates. "Master John," said Brigit, "I presume you saw your aunt this morning. Will she be doing *anything* for your poor father?"

Having no doubt Brigit's insistence came from wanting my father to sell his secret to her brother, I shook my head. "I fear it's no different than before."

When we reached the gates, I bid her a good night.

"John," she said, holding me back, "what friend will you be staying with tonight? Surely he has a name?"

I could not resist. "It's not so much a friend," I said, "as it is my teacher: Sergeant Muldspoon."

"The sergeant!" she exclaimed, and bit her lip as if to keep from speaking out.

"I didn't wish to tell Father," I added. "The two don't care for each other."

"But you've always said how much you hate the man."

"I chanced to meet him and told him of our plight. He was unexpectedly kind," I said over my shoulder.

As I went out of the prison, I could positively feel Brigit's fierce eyes upon my back, and I wondered if I had done a foolish—or even a dangerous—thing.

∾⦿⦿∾

CHAPTER 37

I Hear Sary's Astonishing Story

Sary was waiting on the pavement, her back against the prison walls, sitting on her cap. "Me bum gets cold sittin' on the stone," she explained. "That's why I've got a big cap." No, I had never known a girl like her.

"Are we goin' back to the rookery?" she asked. It was beginning to drizzle lightly.

"Wait," I said, thinking over what had just occurred with Brigit. "Something's happened."

"What's that?"

"Just now I was coming to the gates—to meet you. Brigit wished to talk to me, so she followed along. She was pressuring me to tell my father to solve his problem. And she wanted to know where I was staying tonight."

"What for?"

"Don't know."

"You didn't tell 'er nothin' 'bout me, did you?"

I shook my head. "And since I didn't want to say, I told her I would be with Sergeant Muldspoon."

She stared at me, leaning forward.

"I thought you remembered everything," I teased. "I told you about him. Sergeant Moldy. Remember? My schoolteacher."

That time she nodded.

Then I explained what I had neglected to tell her before, that I had seen Old Moldy at the Red Lion in conversation with O'Doul.

"Brigit's brother?" said Sary.

"Right. And Old Moldy was at the court too, when my father's case came up. And, Sary, just today I saw him in conversation with . . . Mr. Farquatt."

"You did? The Frenchy? Where?"

"In the church."

"Where you were workin'?"

I nodded.

"And they weren't prayin'?"

"Not at all."

"They see you?"

"I'm sure they didn't."

She thought for a moment and then said, "Seems like this 'ere teacher of yers knows everyone an' is everywhere," she said.

"Sary, when I told Brigit I'd be stopping with the sergeant, she became very upset."

" 'Ow come?"

"Don't know. But there's more," I said.

"Let's 'ear it."

"If there's anyone who can appreciate and understand the importance of rifling, it's Old Moldy."

" 'Ow so?"

I told her about my teacher's military history and his love of guns.

Sary drew up her knees and hugged them. "All right, then: What's this bloke look like?"

"Tall, stiff, gray-haired, dressed all in black, and with one wooden leg."

Sary grinned.

"What is it?" I asked.

"I'm guessin' you'd like to know the doin's I done."

"I would, yes."

"Almost as good as yer Ali Baba story."

"Tell me!"

"Want to get away from the rain?"

"Just tell me what you did!"

"All right," she said, laughing. "Listen 'ard. Now then, like we agreed, I waited round, to see if yer Brigit would come out."

"I saw her name in the sign-out book."

Sary nodded. "She came out with a shoppin' basket under 'er arm."

"There's nothing special about marketing, is there?"

"As may be, but she only did it after she done other things."

"Such as . . . ?"

"Shhh! Now, out she comes. I was over there—keepin' me distance, you understan'. Yer Brigit just stood 'ere, afore the gates. As if she were tryin' to make up 'er mind. An' she didn't look none too 'appy, either. Anyways, she must 'ave made up 'er mind 'cause she started goin', but slow, like somethin' 'eavy was on 'er back. See, you can tell what folks got in their 'eads by watchin' their feet. Mind, she only 'ad 'er basket, an' as much as I knew, it were empty.

"Well, I keep meself behind, sneakin' the way I do. Never a thought she were bein' followed. Leastways, she never looked one way t'other, save the way she was goin'.

"Down she goes, 'long King William Street. Then it comes to me"—Sary paused dramatically—"she's 'eadin' for the bridge. Now, one o' the tricks o' me trade is this: If you knows where yer man— only in this case it's a woman—is goin', you skip 'head an' watch 'em come. That way you see things different. The face mostly. So that's what I done, goin' fast, but not too fast, 'cause I'm a girl an' people gets suspicious seein' girls trottin'." She edged forward and glanced at me as if to see if I was taking it all in. "Us maids," she explained, "always 'ave to find our own ways of doin'.

"Well then, I gets in front of yer Brigit, an' I can see 'er face. An', blimey, weren't she the sad one. Cryin'. Wipin' tears away."

"But why?" I said.

" 'Old on. Comin' to that. Well, now she's on the bridge, walkin' slow as drippin' ice in January. An' I'm still sneakin'. She gets to the bridge middle. River there somethin' fierce, all churnin', tumblin', an' foamin'. She's leanin' over the wall there. Suddenly, I understand . . ."

"Understand what?" I cried.

"Yer Brigit is 'bout to end 'er life."

"Kill herself?" I cried.

"Nothin' special there. Lots o' ladies do," said Sary. "I've known four 'as done it meself. Things get terrible 'ard, you get down, or with child, and nothin' is goin' to 'elp you, *nothin*'."

"But why should Brigit think that?"

"Don't know. But I'm watchin' 'er an' I just know what's in 'er 'ead. 'What if she goes for it?' I asks meself. 'What does I do? Keep 'er from leapin'?'"

"Did you?"

"Didn't 'ave to. She changes 'er mind. Turns back to the City. Down she goes this way an' that, but I'm keepin' close till she gets where she's goin'."

"Where's that?"

"Some coffee-servin' place. By the customhouse. And who do you think she sets down with?"

"Her brother?"

"Can't be certain it was 'er brother 'cause I don't think I've ever seen 'im, right? But I'm willin' to say, an' I *am* sayin', they looked like brother an' sister, though she bein' the much older one."

"It makes sense she would see him," I said.

"But, you see," she said with a grin, "there was a second man there."

"Who?"

"The same as you just described . . . yer teacher."

"Sergeant Muldspoon?" I cried, astounded. "But why?"

"Couldn't get close enough to 'ear 'em talk. But puttin' it together, that one sure keeps sittin' in the middle o' things. Fact, the two men gets into some argument. Brigit jumps up an' runs off. Upset. Wipin' tears. I kept sneakin' after 'er. She goes to Covent Garden for eatin' stuff. Then back she goes to the prison."

"But what does it all mean?" I said.

"Don't know. But if you were askin' me if there were one bloke behind all the doin', an' if I were doin' the answerin', I'd likely say it were none other than that darlin' teacher o' yers—what you call him?—Old Moldy."

⤜◉⤛

CHAPTER 38

I Receive an Invitation from Mr. Tuckum

Old Moldy! I was so taken by Sary's notion that—despite the dark and the cold rain, not to mention my hunger—I leaned back against the prison wall trying to put my thoughts together.

Mr. Farquatt: Mr. Farquatt was French, our ancient enemy. There was, I supposed, reason then for him to act as he had, which I could comprehend.

Mr. O'Doul: I knew little of Ireland, save what Brigit had told me, though I was aware in a hazy sort of way that there was always trouble in Ireland. No doubt Mr. O'Doul could play a part in that.

And I remembered Brigit's fierce remark: *For things held dear to the heart, all kinds of sacrifices must be made.*

But Sergeant Muldspoon! In school, if he proclaimed his patriotism once, he did so twenty times a day, forever denouncing the red revolutionaries in other places—in Paris, Rome, and Berlin—as well as the "English Mob," as he called them, who would, he foretold, tumble the monarchy. Why should he desire the secret of rifling? What need had he? Was he about to shoot his students?

I shared my thoughts with Sary, whose only comment was, "I know nothin' 'bout the world beyond—'cept Australia. Never been out of the City, save once when I was *on* the river. Never even crossed it."

Though the City bells rang for nine o'clock, we continued talking. Shortly thereafter I heard the prison gates open and close. People emerged—visitors, I assumed. One of them was Mr. Tuckum. The bailiff fairly waddled out across the pavement to stand by the curb. From the way he looked up and down, I was sure he was seeking a Hansom cab.

Sary, who knew nothing of Tuckum, paid him no mind. But I could not help but observe. Draped over his squat frame, his faded red greatcoat seemed drab, his Piccadilly weepers quaint. No smiles and bows. In truth, at that moment he looked less old-fashioned than just beyond his time. And troubled, too. I wondered if I was seeing the real man.

Then, as he looked about, he spied us—or I should say me, for he knew naught of Sary. On the instant he was all smiles again, nothing but familiar amiability.

"Master John," he cried, "you're still here!" He extended his hand.

I got to my feet.

"You said you were stopping with a friend," he said. I saw his eyes shift to Sary.

"I *am* with a friend," I replied. "This is Sary," I said, not quite willing to say *Sary the Sneak*, or *Sarah Waiting*.

"A pleasure to meet you," he said, bowing in his way but looking upon her in puzzled fashion, as if he could not quite fathom my acquaintance with such a ragged girl.

Sary only grinned, saying, "Pleased to meet you."

"You told your parents," said the bailiff, turning back to me, "that you were staying with a friend from school. Is this . . . ?" He hardly knew what to say, but his eyes appraised Sary again.

"Mr. Tuckum," I said, "be assured, I have no better friend than Sary."

"Where does she . . . hmm . . . reside?"

"St. Giles Rookery," said Sary, bold as polished brass.

"Indeed," said the bailiff, at a momentary loss for words. "Well then, as you say. But I'm glad to see you, Master John. Very glad. And glad to have been visiting your father. A most amiable man."

Perhaps it was my brief glimpse of Mr. Tuckum beyond his buoyant good nature that made me take a chance.

"Mr. Tuckum," I said, "I suspect I know what brings you to him."

"I hope friendship, Master John, is above suspicion."

"And not, in any sense," I said, "at the request of Chief Inspector Ratchet?"

Mr. Tuckum inhaled deeply, then pursed his lips as if to let that same breath out. He scratched one side of his Piccadilly weepers. "Well . . . hmm. . . . yes," he fairly stammered, "if you know about that."

Then he seemed to make the same decision I had made. "See here, Master John, I am, as you know, a most old-fashioned man. That being the case, there are those below me. To the same degree, there are those *above* me. It's the nature of our well-established order that those above can and do give me orders. How much . . . how much of this . . . hmm . . . matter concerning your father do you know?"

"Sir, you once asked me if my father had confided in me. At the time he had not. Since then he has."

"Ah!"

"So I've discovered a great deal. And I beg to tell you, sir, between my friend Sary and me, we know even more . . . now."

Mr. Tuckum's eyes shifted to Sary, then back again to me. "More than . . . Inspector Ratchet knows?" he asked.

"With all due respect, sir, I think so," I said.

He paused to consider. "Master John," he said, "would you do me the honor of returning with me to the Halfmoon Inn? We might best talk there. Share some food. The weather, in its old-fashioned way, is wretched tonight and probably will get worse. At the moment I have no other . . . hmm . . . guests."

"I'd be happy to," I said, "but only if my partner comes with us."

"*Partner*, Master John?"

"We're detectives," Sary blurted out, her face a yard of grin.

"Are you?" cried Mr. Tuckum. He allowed himself a smile. "Then by all means, the two of you *must* come along. I should like to hear what you have detected."

He hailed a Hansom cab, and the three of us climbed in and drew the cab blanket up to our chins. A good thing, too, for the cold rain began to come down hard, making the streets glisten and pedestrians fairly run.

During the brief, jolting journey to the inn we did not talk at all about my father's circumstance. Instead, Mr. Tuckum enlightened us with the latest developments—as he had read them—of his beloved serial novel, *David Copperfield.*

"It's quite a remarkable tale," he insisted. "Do you know what I like about it the most?"

"No, sir, I don't."

"It's not as if I were *reading* what transpires. No, I fear I'm no longer fond of reading. My eyes are—"

"Old-fashioned," I suggested.

"Perhaps merely *old.* The nature of my duties, Master John, has me reading mostly *facts.* But to read facts is to read only of *other* souls. Read Mr. Dickens, and it's as if I were living life with my *own* soul."

He went on from there to tell the story in some detail—all that he had "seen." While Sary seemed very interested, I confess the story only put me in mind to think again about Inspector Copperfield. In all our reckoning we had ignored him. But who *was* he? How did he fit in?

All too soon, however, we clattered onto Halfmoon Alley. When we stepped out, it was evident from the Hansom standing before the inn that Mr. Tuckum had a visitor.

"Ah," said the bailiff, "Chief Inspector Ratchet has already arrived."

࿊

CHAPTER 39
I Make More Discoveries

"Ratchet?" I demanded. "Why is he here?"

"He's my superior."

"'E's not mine!" exclaimed Sary with surprising vehemence. "Don't want nothin' to do with that man!" She started out of the carriage.

"Please," I said, holding her back. "I need you to stay."

"What for?" she said, gazing at me.

"We must solve the mystery," I said. "And I can't do it alone."

She considered.

"And you're the only one I trust," I whispered.

"That true?"

"It is."

"All right, then. I'll come."

The inn's main room looked dingier than ever, illuminated as it was by a hearth fire far brighter and warmer than I ever saw Mr. Tuckum burn. And Chief Inspector Ratchet was indeed within, as big and burly a man as I had recollected.

The inspector had taken a chair and pulled it close to the grate with his booted feet extended to the side hob, his fingers interlaced over his ample stomach. His oilskin cloak hung about his shoulders, touching the floor. It gave him a massive, brooding appearance. He appeared to be deep in thought.

"Is that you, Tuckum?" he said in a voice heavy with authority, made even more powerful by the fact that he did not turn about when we entered. He seemed to assume.

"It is, sir," replied the bailiff, "with company."

The inspector turned. "Ah, Master 'Uffam," he said with a quick nod. Then he looked toward my friend. "And Sary the Sneak," he added dryly. "Always 'appy to see *you*."

Astonished that he knew her, I turned. She was grinning.

It was for Mr. Tuckum to say, "Do you know the girl, then, sir?"

"I know 'er very well indeed," returned the chief inspector. "A clever young lady, if I do say so myself. Smart 'ead with smart eyes and ears. Though at times too smart a mouth."

"Why didn't you tell me you knew the inspector?" I demanded of her.

"You never eggsactly asked me, now did you?" she said. "'Sides, I've got me own business to consider. Sneakin' don't want to be too public."

"Then you've worked with him?" I asked, not knowing if I should be angry.

"It's what I told you—when we first talked. Peelers are some of me best customers."

"The only thing wrong with this girl is 'er father," Ratchet interjected. "Transported to Australia . . . for felonious assault upon 'is employer."

"Get off that!" cried Sary, throwing her hat down, her smile replaced with a look of such absolute ferocity, it startled me. "The man insulted Pa. Called 'im lazy when 'is back was 'urtin' that bad. So me pa bopped 'im one in the nose, an' what did you do? You sent 'im off—for what?

Seven years—to the other side o' the world. God blin' me," she cried,
"if that's yer justice, there it sits!" That said, Sary spat upon the floor
and stamped the spot with her foot.

"Now, now, Sary," Ratchet said, "I only arrested 'im. Wasn't me that
sent 'im off. Magistrate did that."

"Call yerself 'uman, but you don't care one speck what 'appens to
them you arrest, do you?"

I had never seen her so angry before.

"My dear girl," began Tuckum, "the majesty of the law——"

Ratchet cut the bailiff off by saying: "Sary, you are adept at
changin' the subject, aren't you? But I should like to hear: Are you
caught up in this business?"

"Don't act all innocent! You knows right well I am. Wasn't it *me*
who brought you to it all in the first place? But I'm not so sure if I
should be in it—you sayin' like you did."

"You're right. I shouldn't have spoken that way. I beg your pardon.
I'm prepared to apologize."

"Right, then," said Sary, and she picked up her hat and pulled it
down over her head.

"But," added Ratchet, "I gather you have somethin' to say to me."

"*Somethin'?*" she said, her face erupting into a laugh as quick as it
had turned to fury. "I suspect my friend an' I"—she indicated me—
"knows a *lot* more than you do."

"Don't doubt it for a moment," said the inspector.

I had listened to this exchange with considerable amazement, as had Mr. Tuckum. "I beg your pardon, sir," I felt compelled to say to Ratchet. "Do you mean to say you have been working on this matter for a . . . long time?" I turned to Sary. "And you *began* it?"

"'Deed I did," she said, all grins. "What was it, Ratchet? Some time last summer?"

"Last summer!" I cried.

"Late July," said Ratchet.

Sary put a hand over her mouth to restrain her laughter.

"But—"

"'Ere now," said the inspector. "Debatin' who and when it began is a waste of time. I propose we sit down and share what we've all come up with. As it is, I'm gettin' considerable pressure from my superiors to conclude this matter."

"If you please, sir," I said to him, "I had thought Sary and I knew a great deal that was new. But now"—I shot an unfriendly glance at her—"I am not so certain."

"Come, come, Master John," said Ratchet. "We're all friends 'ere. I've no doubt Sary the Sneak knows more about the business than all of us together. Well then, we need to 'ear it. But first, Mr. Tuckum, sir, you must play the publican and provide warmin' food and drink all round. From the looks of these 'ere infants, that wouldn't be amiss. Make no mistake, it's a foul night beyond, but in 'ere we should make best cheer."

"Now you're talkin'!" said Sary.

"My pleasure," said Mr. Tuckum, who was apparently only a little less bewildered by the previous conversation than I was myself. "My great pleasure." And off he went.

It was not long before the four of us were sitting round the fire, stomachs full of bread and toasted cheese and a glass of something warm in hand. The talk, while we ate, had all come from Ratchet, who entertained us with facts relating to the dreadful Manning case and how the police force had tracked down the killers—Mrs. Manning in particular—with the use of an amazing device called the "telegraph." It was as horrible as it was enthralling.

But at length Ratchet—for it was he, clearly, who was in charge of things—said, "All right, then, let's get to the singular matter of Wesley John Louis 'Uffam."

"My father," I said.

"The wery one. And with all due respect, Master John, 'owever amiable the man is—"

"He truly is, sir," put in Mr. Tuckum.

"—'e 'as acted," continued Ratchet, "the part of a fool. Mind, I'm aware 'e fancies 'imself the actor, but the Lord Chamberlain never offered 'im a license to put what 'e's done on any *legitimate* stage. The *ill*egitimate one, per'aps, but surely not the legal one.

"All right," he went on without allowing me a rejoinder, "sometime last summer Sary 'ere comes to me and says—what did you say, Sary?"

"'There's somethin' goin' round the gamblin' dens that you might want to know.' 'What's that?' you says. An' I told you, 'Someone's talkin' 'bout sellin' navy secrets.'"

"Well, of course I thank 'er wery kindly," Ratchet picked back up, "give 'er the usual shilling reward for useful information, and tells the major inspector. Major inspector tells the 'ome secretary, who consults the First Lord of the Admiralty. Quick as blazes, word comes tumblin' down the other way, and the meaning is: 'Urgent! Ratchet, you are ordered to see what can be uncovered!'"

"And what you discovered," I put in, "is that my father was offering to sell a secret to cover a very large gambling debt."

"Can't take credit for discoverin' that fact, either," said Ratchet. "Sary was the one."

Astonished, I looked at the girl in wonder. She was grinning so hard, I thought her dirty face would break in two.

"The world is always sayin'," Ratchet went on, "that women talk too much. That's as may be. An old saw will cut. All *I* can say is that it's *my* experience it's *men* who do most of the *loose* talkin', while the women do the *best* listenin'. Like Sary 'ere.

"Never mind," he continued. "We decided—and by 'we' I'm sayin' the government—that we'd use yer father as a gate, if you will, to see who might be spying out secrets. That's to say, the thing about spies is that they prowl aimlessly about, but if there's a useful gate *open* to them, they'll pass on through. Fact is, I even 'elped one of them—that O'Doul fellow, who's with the Irish rebels—by sending 'im to Mr. 'Uffam. Lord 'elp me, I even spoke to 'im one night in the middle of the river."

"Not even knowin'," said Sary to me, "'e 'ad a sister workin' for yer father."

"I admit to that," said Ratchet with a shake of his head.

"God works in His old-fashioned ways," suggested Mr. Tuckum.

"He does indeed," agreed Ratchet. "Anyway, after a while I inform your father we know what he's up to. In fact, we threaten him. He don't have much choice but to help us."

"Then Mr. Farquatt comes along," I said, "to court my sister."

"Right, the Frenchman," said Ratchet. "Doesn't matter they've changed their governments. They're *always* changin' governments, but they're still our old enemy. Very good, then, Farquatt's a spy. O'Doul's a spy. But we believe there's someone lurkin' behind. And why? Because someone bought up *all* your father's debts. That took pots o' money. O'Doul may be a gambler, but he don't have that much. His sister surely don't 'ave it either, bein' on servant's wages, and I'd wager she don't get paid too often."

I said, "But Mr. Farquatt offered to pay the debt."

"But if *he* owned the debt," said Ratchet, "why would Mr. O'Doul's name be on the writ that sent yer father to prison? Yes, Farquatt wants the secret. And to get it, he's *willing* to pay down the debt. But we don't believe he has the money either. Someone is backing him, too. So then, where *is* the money coming from?"

The inspector turned to Mr. Tuckum. "Mr. Tuckum 'as been my deputy of late. Anyone else come visit Mr. 'Uffam in prison?"

"No one."

"So I repeat," the inspector continued, "who's the bloke—what's the nation—who 'as money enough to buy up the debt? Who's puttin' O'Doul (brother and sister) and Farquatt forward? That's why I'd like to know what you've got, Sary."

But she said, "Let John tell you. 'E's got the best idea."

Gratified by her remark, I sat up.

"All right, then, lad," Ratchet said to me, "what have you found?"

I felt fairly self-satisfied saying, "I think Sary and I have found the person you're looking for, the one behind it all."

CHAPTER 40

I Decide Upon a Plan of Action

"Have you now?" cried Inspector Ratchet.

"We think so," I said.

"All right, then. Begin," he commanded. "I'm nothin' but ears."

"I'm not sure," I said, "how much you know of my family affairs. How my father directed me to his great-aunt Euphemia—"

"*Lady* Euphemia 'Uffam," Ratchet interjected.

"Do you know her?" I asked.

"Quite well."

"Does she have anything to do with the matter of the secret?" I suddenly asked.

"Not in the slightest," Ratchet said with finality.

"As I say," I continued, "I went to my great-great-aunt to get help with Father's debt. While she rejected his plea, she did arrange for me to find employment at All Hallows Church—"

"On Tower Hill," Ratchet interjected again, making me wonder if he was the kind of man who insisted he knew everything. Seeing me pause, he said, "Forgive me," he said. "Please go on."

"My employment," I said, "began today. Mid-afternoon I was work-ing in the loft when I chanced to look down and saw Mr. Farquatt talking to a man I know."

"Who was that?"

"Sergeant Anthony Muldspoon."

"An army man?"

"Retired. He owns Muldspoon's Militantly Motivated Academy. It's the school I've been attending."

Ratchet thought for a moment. "That's a man I *don't* know. What's 'is connection to all this?"

I turned to Sary. "Go on, tell him what you saw when you followed after Brigit."

"Brigit O'Doul?"

Sary nodded, and then she related—word for word—what she had told me about Brigit's doings that day, including her meeting with her brother and Sergeant Muldspoon.

When she was finished, Mr. Tuckum asked: "But how and why should this Sergeant Muldspoon be connected to all of this?"

"My question exactly," said Inspector Ratchet.

"I'll tell you, sir," I said. Then I described my teacher's artillery background, his constant lectures about guns and cannons. I mentioned his animosity toward my father and toward me. But I did not neglect his oft-spoken love of England and his patriotic fervor.

"As for that," said Mr. Tuckum, "it's perhaps old-fashioned to mention Samuel Johnson—'Dictionary Johnson,' we used to call him—who was born almost one hundred and fifty years ago. To him is attributed the memorable phrase 'Patriotism is the last refuge of a scoundrel.'"

Our eyes shifted back to Chief Inspector Ratchet. Chin tucked down, he was deep in thought.

"There may well be a connection 'ere," he said. "And it seems to

be one I missed. 'Ate to admit to it, but there it is." He turned to Mr. Tuckum. "Well, sir, you said the boy was bright. You appear to be on the mark."

The bailiff beamed at me, his Piccadilly weepers almost radiant.

"All right," said Sary, pushing the conversation forward, "what 'bout doin' what you said? You said, speakin' of spies, if there be an open gate, a spy will pass on through. Why don't we open a gate to this 'ere sergeant an' see what 'e does?"

"Excellent idea!" cried Mr. Tuckum.

Ratchet fell into private musings again. But at last he turned to Mr. Tuckum and said, "One problem. Can you guess what it is, sir?"

The bailiff nodded. "Evidence. Habeas corpus."

"Exactly," said Ratchet.

"What's hocus-pocus?" asked Sary.

"Habeas corpus," said Ratchet. "Let's say that this 'ere Sergeant Muldspoon passes—as Sary says—through the gate. That'll prove to *us* that it's 'e who's workin' to get the secret. But unless we arrest 'im *with* the secret in 'is 'and, no court will convict 'im. The same for the others. No evidence, no conviction."

"It's England's old-fashioned way," agreed Mr. Tuckum.

"So what we need," said Ratchet, "is to get 'im to pass through our wery own traitors' gate *with* proof that 'e's a traitor."

Silence came upon us all until I said, "Please, sir, I could manage it."

"How so?"

"I could put the secret in his hand."

They stared at me.

"What do you mean?" asked the chief inspector.

I said, "I have a copy of it. My father drew it and gave it to me. For safekeeping."

"Did he?" cried Ratchet. "Where is it?"

I was certain I could feel the plans in my pocket. But all I said was, "I hid it. . . . But I can get it."

I felt Sary's eyes on me. She was clearly enjoying this.

But the chief inspector frowned. "Are you aware, boy, that you should *not* 'ave it?"

"Yes, sir."

"That just havin' it makes you a traitor?"

"I'm not, sir."

"Then exactly *what* are you suggestin'?"

"You gentlemen don't know Sergeant Muldspoon. If *you* were to approach him, he might become suspicious. Particularly you, sir," I said to Ratchet. "If Sary tried, I'm sure he would be dismissive and pay no heed."

Sary nodded.

"But," I continued, "what if *I* approached him tomorrow and said my father was willing to sell him the secret? What if I tell him I'll give him the secret plan—tell him my father drew it out—and that for three hundred pounds he can have it. He'll need to come to All Hallows Church."

"Why there?" asked Ratchet.

"As I said, I'm employed there. I must report to work tomorrow morning by eight o'clock. I'll be there all day. I don't wish to threaten my arrangement with my great-great-aunt. There's a good deal at stake. But I should be able to take time from my lunch to see the sergeant. I'll offer to meet with him there. Later. It seems to be empty then."

"Right!" said Sary. "Tell 'im to be there at the strikin' of the bells at eight o'clock tomorrow night."

"If Sergeant Muldspoon doesn't walk through the gate," I said, "nothing's lost. But if he *is* the man, I'm certain he won't think my father or I can do him any harm. He has mocked us—both of us—often."

Ratchet took all this in silently.

It was Mr. Tuckum who said, "You described him as a stern ex-military man. Is he . . . hmm . . . violent?"

Remembering how Old Moldy used his cane, I could only say, "Yes, sir, to some degree."

"So what you're proposing may be dangerous," said Mr. Tuckum.

"I can be there to protect 'im," Sary offered.

Again Ratchet pondered. At last he said, "And if yer man comes through the gate and you 'and 'im the plan, then you need only give a rattle and we'll be there to nab 'im."

"A rattle, sir?"

He held up a policeman's rattle—the kind they used to call their comrades for help. It was L-shaped, the handle being the longer leg, the rattle itself a rectangle with a wooden tongue, so that when one twirled the handle, it gave off a loud clacking sound audible for some four hundred yards.

"Use it," said Ratchet, "and we'll come quickly."

"Yes, sir."

Ratchet gazed hard at me. "Master John, are you truly prepared to risk takin' that plan to the church and, if this man asks for it, givin' it to 'im?"

"Yes, sir."

"Because if you are, and 'e 'as that plan in 'is 'and, we can arrest 'im—for treason."

"And the charge would stick," Mr. Tuckum added.

"And 'e would 'ang," said Ratchet.

"In the Tower?" I asked.

"Per'aps," said Ratchet.

All looked at me as I made up my mind. But it took little effort. "I'm willing," I said.

At which point Mr. Tuckum sat up and clapped his hands with glee. "'Barkis is willin'!'" he cried. "'Barkis is willin'!'"

Ratchet swung around. "What are you talkin' 'bout?"

"It's something that's said in *David Copperfield*."

"Ah, yes." Ratchet nodded. "The serial story so many are readin'."

Which put me in mind to ask, "Sir, is there an Inspector Copperfield on your force?"

"Tuckum asked me the same question," said the inspector. "I assure you, there's no such inspector." He took a deep breath. "Wery well, Master John 'Uffam, I'll go along with it."

"Yes, sir."

"Then we have a plan," said Tuckum.

Sary clapped her hands.

With everything agreed upon, Inspector Ratchet said his farewells, climbed into his Hansom cab, and went off into the cold, rainy night.

"Now, Master John," said Mr. Tuckum once the chief inspector had departed, "you may have your former room. Mistress Sary, Master John can show you where his mother and sister slept. Take up candles. You'll not be charged for your accommodation. Not tonight. I admire you both. You're doing a good deed—in the bravest, most old-fashioned way. Sleep well."

With that, he went off to his rooms—wherever they were— leaving Sary and me alone.

At first we were silent, watching the fire dwindle down.

"Did you 'ear that? That Mr. Tuckum, 'e called me 'mistress.' Never 'eard that afore."

I said to her, "I had no idea you knew so much. Do you have any more secrets?"

As always, she grinned. "I'm a professional sneak, ain't I? Got plenty o' secrets. But if you think I'm tellin' you, you best 'ave other thoughts. Anyways, you've got yer own secret—the plan. Goin' to tell me where it is?"

It was only what I expected her to say. I shook my head and laughed. Then I grew serious. "But . . . I'm nervous about this. Did you mean it when you said you'd help protect me?"

"On me 'eart an' 'onor as a sneak!"

I led her to her room. "It's as good as the Queen's palace," she announced when she looked it over. "Where's the privy?"

"Out back," I told her.

"Outside?"

"Afraid so."

"No complaint. Bed, room, food in the belly. It's 'eaven. Or maybe"—with a sly look at me—"Ali Baba land."

Leaving Sary bouncing on the bed, I went to my room, blew out the candle, and lay back.

As I rested, I heard someone walk along the balcony. Sary, I assumed. I decided to keep awake until I heard her return: Me protecting *her*.

Then I suddenly recalled a question we had not answered: Who *was* Inspector Copperfield?

Thinking about that, I fell asleep.

And did not hear Sary return.

ഹൈ

CHAPTER 41
I Discover the Real Traitor

Awaking in the morning darkness, I immediately put my mind to Old Moldy: Could he truly be the man behind my father's misfortunes? For having already come to hate the schoolmaster, I made myself admit it was pleasing to contemplate a greater reason to do so.

Then, recalling my mother's words about responsibility, I checked myself. Whatever Sergeant Muldspoon was, he had not *caused* my father's tribulations. Father—with his gambling—did that for himself. Old Moldy's crime was to take cruel advantage of my father's predicament.

Indeed, even when we solved this problem of spies, there would still remain—Father said so himself—the three hundred pounds he owed. Though his troubles had become connected, the resolution of each was separate. The only possible help I could provide remained with Great-Aunt Euphemia. I must—in the words of Mr. Snugsbe— fit within the coat that had been cut for me.

I took the rifling plan from my jacket pocket, unfolded it, and gazed at it. Even though I was aware it was of great value to many, its maze of swirling lines and arithmetic equations remained incomprehensible to me. I refolded the sheet of paper, pressed it flat, and returned it to an inner jacket pocket, over my heart.

I got up, used the privy, and then stepped out of the inn's front door to gauge the day's weather. The air was the color of iron and just as cold. While it was no longer raining, courtyard puddles were veneered with ice. The morning light grew apace, but the omnipresent and dreary fog was thick enough to make the solitary gas lamp near Halfmoon Alley appear nothing more than a smudge.

I'm not sure how long it took me to notice that a man, perhaps twenty yards away, was standing in wait—indeed, looking right at me. Staring at me. It took a further moment for me to realize he was none other than the tall man with the low-brimmed hat and false beard, the man who called himself Inspector Copperfield.

Even as I grasped who was there, he pointed his umbrella right at me and shouted, "Be warned!" Then he turned about and immediately dashed away.

I ran after him only to slip on the pavement ice. It was hardly more than a stumble, but I needed a moment to right myself. When I reached the end of the court, I looked both ways along Halfmoon

Street. I saw people in the fog, but only vaguely, and no one I could identify as the man I sought.

Discouraged, angry at myself that I'd faltered, I made my way back toward the inn only to abruptly stop halfway. How, I asked myself, had this Inspector Copperfield even known I was at the inn? Someone must have told him. But if someone had told him, the next question was obvious: Who? Who knew I was going to stop there for the night?

Thoughts rushed upon me.

The evening before, at the debtors' prison, I had been evasive about where I intended to stay because, at the time, I thought it would be at the rookery. Indeed, Mr. Tuckum had invited me to stay at the inn, but I had *declined*—publicly. That meant neither my family nor Mr. Farquatt knew where I would eventually stay. As for Brigit, I told her I'd be with Sergeant Muldspoon. In fact, as I now recalled, I'd decided to stop at the inn only *after* I'd left the prison. In other words, the only ones who knew I was there were Inspector Ratchet, Mr. Tuckum, and . . . Sary.

Sary!

Suddenly feeling sick, I entered the inn, took a seat before the cold fire, and gave myself over to hard thinking.

Mind, at that point I was suspicious of *everyone*, even Inspector Ratchet. Had he not ensnared my father in this nasty business? Yet it was beyond even my imagination to think the inspector had anything to do with this false Inspector Copperfield.

For his part, Mr. Tuckum was a trusted colleague of Ratchet's. As for *being* Inspector Copperfield, the roly-poly bailiff could not possibly disguise himself as the tall, thin man who had accosted me. So he, too, was an unlikely suspect.

That left only Sary. Not that *she* was Copperfield, but—

I could feel myself trembling. It was as if a small hole had been made in a dam, and the escaping water, first trickling, quickly grew forceful enough to smash the dam itself. So it was with my suspicions. For—as I had recently discovered—it was *Sary* who had *begun* this whole affair by alerting the police to what my foolish father was attempting: the selling of the rifling plan.

It was *Sary* who had hidden from me—from the beginning—that she worked with Ratchet. In so doing, not only had she brought the chief inspector to my father, but that policeman had aimed O'Doul at Father too.

It was *Sary* who had sneaked after me, leading me to believe—at first—that it was *Mr.* O'Doul rather than Brigit who had hired her to do so.

It was *Sary* who had instigated our friendship by offering to sneak for me.

And it was *Sary* who said she had seen the O'Douls with Sergeant Muldspoon. But—I now realized as well—I had only her word for that.

Then too it was *Sary* who had pushed my suspicions to Old Moldy.

And it was *Sary* who said there was no such place as the Credit

Bordeaux, where Mr. Farquatt was employed. Was that true? Had she lied?

Just the night before when I asked her if she had any more secrets, what did she say? *I'm a professional sneak, ain't I? Got plenty o' secrets. But if you think I'm tellin' you, you best 'ave other thoughts.*

And it was *Sary* who said *she* would *protect* me!

She could hardly want the secret for herself. But, I thought, what if there really was someone else—maybe this Inspector Copperfield —behind it all? Did not Ratchet say he was likely a spy? What if *Sary* was working with *him*, if all she'd done was meant to turn me from the real culprit? Indeed, as I thought upon it, I realized that Copperfield was the one person Sary had *not* accused! Was not that, all things considered, reason enough for suspicion?

Had I not heard her leave her room the night before? Might not she have met with Copperfield and told him where I was? Told him of the plan so that he could be forewarned?

If all of this was true, then *Sary*—as far as I was concerned—was the real traitor.

The chill I felt—the chill of realizing such betrayal—had nothing to do with the inclement weather or the cold hearth.

In my rising anger I determined upon a course of action: Yes, I would go to Sergeant Muldspoon. Yes, I would tell him my father was willing to sell him the plan. Then, when he refused to take the bait, as I was now certain he would refuse, I'd have proof that all Sary had said was *untrue*. With *that* knowledge, I'd go straight to Inspector Ratchet and inform him that he, too, had been deceived by Sary the Sneak.

Except at that moment Sary herself appeared on the steps.

"Good mornin' to you," she called in her usual cheerful voice.

Not able to even look at her, I offered a curt "Good morning."

"I never slept so fine afore," she said.

I made no answer and thereby must have revealed some of my mood.

She paused on the lower step. "'As somethin' 'appened?"

"No," I said, trying to act as if nothing had. I stood up. "I need to go to work."

"To the church?"

"Yes."

After a moment she said, "When do you go to yer old teacher?"

"When I can," I replied, forcing myself to face her.

She gazed at me. There was no grin now. "An' when," she asked, "an' where are we two goin' to meet up with yer news about what yer teacher says?"

"You heard what we agreed," I said. "I'll offer to make the secret available to Sergeant Muldspoon at eight o'clock tonight at All Hallows."

"An' me?"

My anger overwhelmed me. "As it happens," I blurted out, "I've no need for you at all." Avoiding her questioning eyes, I rushed off without any further words.

I made my way in haste. Having no pennies for the omnibus, I had to walk and run. At some point along Fleet Street—I'm not even sure where—I happened to look up. What I saw was a building to which was affixed a sign:

Mr. Farquatt's place of work!

Did I need any more proof that Sary had lied to me? I think not. But as I went on, whether the wetness on my face was from braving the fog or from tears, I could hardly tell.

CHAPTER 42

I Meet with Sergeant Muldspoon

I was very glad to reach All Hallows Church. The rain had begun to fall again, a steady drizzle that left me clammy and cold without. I was wretched enough within.

The early-morning service had just been concluded. Wanting to report to Mr. Snugsbe as soon as possible—so that he would know I'd come on time—I wandered among the pews. I found him in the south side, or, at least, I found his greatcoat. It was the shock of curly white hair that crested the coat's collar that encouraged me to believe the rest of him was inside.

Feeling less bashful than previously, I took the liberty of pulling at his sleeve. "Mr. Snugsbe, sir," I said. "It's me, John Huffam."

I had to jostle him a number of times before his head rose slowly up on his scrawny neck, his face as red and wrinkled as that of an organ-grinder's street monkey. He looked round, fastened his beady, blinking eyes on me. "Ah, it's you," he whispered. "Once again you have uncovered Mr. Snugsbe. What do you intend to do with him today?"

"I'm reporting for work, sir."

"Staying within *your* coat," he said.

"Yes, sir. I'm trying to."

"A good thing too."

"Why is that, sir?"

"Last evening, shortly after you left, Mr. Nottingham came round to see Mr. Snugsbe. He wanted to know the everything of anything you did ill."

"What did you tell him?"

"That your coat has been designed, cut, stitched, and fits perfectly. There is—as yet—nothing askew."

"And what was his response?"

"Disappointment."

"Mr. Snugsbe," I said, feeling much pent-up exasperation, "do you know *why* Mr. Nottingham is so set against *me*? Is it merely because of what my father wrote about him?"

Mr. Snugsbe shook his head. "The man is jealous."

"Of what?"

"You."

"Me! But why?"

"Mr. Nottingham has long sought promotion by your relation, Lady Euphemia Huffam. To achieve that, he believes he must push your father aside. He did. Then you appear—I'm told you look much like your father—so he worries *you* will engage her affections. Which is to say, he worries Lady Huffam will alter *his* coat."

Recalling how my great-great-aunt had abused my father, I said, "I assure you, sir, she made it very clear that she has no intention of helping me and that Mr. Nottingham is very strong with her."

"But she *has* helped you," he whispered.

I thought of William/Wilkie.

He went on: "In his long and mostly useless life Mr. Snugsbe has discovered that the easiest way to know a man's weakness is to know his fears. Mr. Nottingham fears rejection. *I* fear being outside my coat." To prove his point, he retreated into it.

"Mr. Snugsbe!" I called.

"Mr. Snugsbe is attentive," came a voice from within the coat.

"Have you ever heard of an establishment called the Credit Bordeaux?"

"It's a large French banking establishment in the City. Off Fleet Street."

By then—for I had discovered that myself—it was not a revelation. But hearing it confirmed brought such deep pain that, given the choice, I would have vanished into *my* own coat.

When, out of necessity, I summoned Mr. Snugsbe up again, he set me to cleaning the pulpit with a small bottle of oil—oil he took pains to assure me was *not* of a sacred nature, but derived solely from barley seed.

So it was, with rag in hand, that I worked with a will all that morning, wanting—more than anything—to obliterate my sadness with effort. Gradually, my clothing dried. My chill eased. At midmorning Mr. Snugsbe was kind enough to bring me bread, butter, and some hot tea.

Even as I brooded over what that curious gentleman had said about Mr. Nottingham, I forced myself to, one, *not* think about Sary and, two, *to* think about Sergeant Muldspoon. I had to decide at what point I might suggest to Mr. Snugsbe that I'd an errand to run, then what I'd say to the harsh schoolmaster.

By then I was quite convinced that he would dismiss me with sarcasm and contempt, if not a caning. That would be painful enough. But that dismissal would leave me with no other course of action than to go to Inspector Ratchet and denounce Sary. Though convinced of her treachery, it was the revelation I dreaded.

Although desiring *not* to think about Sary, I did conjure up a possible motive for her vile actions: Perhaps she *wanted* to be caught, charged, found guilty, so as to be transported to Australia. It was not uncommon for imprisoned children to be sent there. By such means, she could rejoin her father. I'd witnessed her fury about the matter with Ratchet. And once again I recalled Brigit's words: *Master John, to live, a people will do whatever they need to do.* Sary might well have substituted the word "love" for "live."

Yet, while understanding Sary's feelings of loss about her father, I could not condone her way of addressing them. As far as I was concerned, *she* was the villain in the case, a traitor to me.

When Mr. Snugsbe suggested that the time for lunch had arrived, I asked, "Please, sir, I have an errand to do on behalf of my father. Might I attend to that instead of lunch?"

"How long will it require?"

"Not long."

"It will be fine, but Mr. Snugsbe gives warning: It's more than likely that Mr. Nottingham will come here again, so as to determine if you've slipped out of your coat. Therefore, Mr. Snugsbe suggests you complete your errand quickly and return."

"Yes, sir, you may be sure I will."

In fact, I waited till mid-afternoon, when I was certain the sergeant would be back in the classroom. Then, alerting Mr. Snugsbe that I was going, I headed off, running all the way.

Happily, the rain had eased and the air felt somewhat warmer, so

I had no worries about slipping on ice. I was soon panting beneath the school sign: MULDSPOON'S MILITANTLY MOTIVATED ACADEMY. I could even hear the boys chanting within:

"B-A-T-T-L-E spells 'battle'!"

I took a deep breath and pushed the door open. It was, as usual, extremely gloomy in the classroom, with only the oil lamp on the master's desk to provide some feeble glow, thereby leaving the students as unenlightened as ever.

Sergeant Muldspoon was also the same, standing perfectly balanced, stiff and upright, on his one flesh leg and his wooden one next to the gray slate, his twitching cane in hand.

The moment I walked in, a hush—a hush deeper than normally filled that room—descended. My classmates—with a flagrant disregard for the conduct of Old Moldy's educational war—turned as one to look at me.

So did Sergeant Muldspoon.

I gazed at him. He gazed at me. For some reason I focused my eyes on his reddish nose—perhaps because I could not abide the ferocity of his cruel eyes. If the truth be known, only then did I fully realize how much he frightened me. I recalled Mr. Tuckum's question as to his violent nature. I had no doubt then, looking at him, that he *was* a violent man, like a charge of gunpowder ready to explode. That red nose of his, which I had thought of as a garden strawberry, I now thought of as a burning fuse.

"Please . . . sir . . . ," I began.

"What have we here?" he snapped, cutting me off as if he had taken a rapier to my words and sliced them up like a carrot. "I do believe it is Master Huffam. Young *gentleman* Master Huffam. Master Huffam who is a *deserter* in his war against ignorance!"

"Please, sir . . . ," I tried again.

"Have you come back to beg for pardon?" he went on, the cane a-tremble in his hand. "To reenlist? Have you returned to *your* obligation, *your* duty, to satisfy *your* country's need for intellect? If the latter, you are too late. You have proven *your* stupidity."

"Please, sir," I blurted out, "I have a message for you from my father."

That caused him to halt.

"Your *father?*" he said, his voice curiously uncertain.

"Yes, sir."

What he did next, I could hardly believe.

༺◌◌◌༻

CHAPTER 43
I Am Amazed

Sergeant Muldspoon smiled.

He even nodded agreeably. The next moment, as if he'd caught himself out, the smile turned to a frown. His rigidity returned. "Now then," he said, eyes sharp upon me. "Be quick. The class is waiting. What possible message," he sneered, "might *I* want from your *gentleman* father?"

"The . . . one . . . ," I stammered, "that he thought you . . . might want."

"That he is in prison?" he said.

There was an audible gasp from the students.

Taken by surprise, I hardly knew what to say.

The sergeant glared at me intensely. "Do you wish to speak to me now, here, or in some . . . private place?"

Through my agony, I sensed his intent. "Private," I managed to say.

"Very well, then. Step outside. March!"

I retreated in haste, hardly listening as he provided instruction to the class as to their behavior during his momentary retreat. Meanwhile, I waited for him just outside the door, uncomfortable and unsure. Did he or did he not want the secret?

Before I could think further, he came clumping out of the room.

"Now then, John Huffam," he said, making sure he shut the door securely behind him, "why is your father even sending me a message? Has it something to do with your absence from school?"

"He is . . . as you know, in prison, sir," I said.

"And deserves to be."

"Did . . . did Brigit O'Doul tell you that?" I dared.

His belligerent mode seemed to falter slightly. There was, I thought,

a sudden flicker of nervousness in his eyes. What he said was, "I do not know the woman."

"She's our family servant. It was she who fetched me from school."

"I do not associate with servants."

"What about her brother?"

He started.

"And Mr. Farquatt. Do you know him?" I pressed.

Again that flicker of unease as he considered my question. "A French gentleman," he said. "Only yesterday he asked that I meet with him in private. When I did, *he* informed me that your father was in prison. He also told me that he was marrying your sister and that, by so doing, he, henceforward, was to be considered the head of your family, and that all business should be channeled through him."

I tried to grasp his meaning.

Not waiting for me to reply, he said, "Master Huffam, *why* is your father in prison?"

"Debt, sir."

"Has he found a way to repay it?" he said, clearly challenging *me* to respond. I felt as if we were dueling.

"Sergeant Muldspoon, sir," I lunged, "if you want my father's secret, he will sell it to you for three hundred pounds."

Sergeant Muldspoon took a fair time to reply, as if crafting a suitable answer. His eyes shifted, as if looking to see if anyone else was about—watching, listening.

"Master Huffam," he parried, "I am not aware of *any* secret your father might have that would be of the slightest interest to *me*. Surely nothing worth three hundred pounds."

"He's copied it all out," I said. "I shall have the plan with me this evening. At All Hallows Church—by the Tower of London—when the bells strike eight."

He remained silent, though continuing to gaze at me with hard eyes. I could have sworn another smile flickered upon his lips, though this time it was a smile he would not allow himself to fully show. All he said was: "Dismissed!"

"*Will* you come?" I said.

Instead of answering, Old Moldy turned about and clumped back into the classroom.

Left behind, I could not truly say if he had revealed anything as to whether he would appear at the church and thus pass through our traitors' gate. On the face of it, he surely did not say yes; but then again, he most certainly did not say no.

I waited until I heard his cane striking the slate. The next moment the boys chanted, "V-I-C-T-O-R-Y spells 'victory'!"

I admit, I wanted that singular choice of word to mean he *would* come, but I knew that—at best—it was but the choice of my desire.

Dejected, I headed back toward All Hallows. Uppermost among my emotions was a feeling of grief—no longer believing that Old Moldy was the villain of the piece, but that, by my own logic, Sary was.

And I would have to report her to Inspector Ratchet.

Except . . . I was not *absolutely* certain. Was Sergeant Muldspoon being extra cautious? Might he in fact appear? What had that extraordinary smile truly meant? What "victory" was in his mind?

The truth was, I did not know.

CHAPTER 44
I Am Alone

Thoroughly frustrated, I returned to the church and for the rest of a very long afternoon resumed my work. Mr. Snugsbe had sent me down to the crypt, where I polished various silver plates and goblets. Monotonous work, indeed, but my mind seethed.

There seemed little choice: I must find my way to Scotland Yard, ask for Inspector Ratchet, and tell him what I'd learned. Let him deal with it all. I needed to put all my efforts toward freeing Father from prison.

Yet, as evening drew in, I gradually came to another plan. Perhaps, after all, Sergeant Muldspoon had been merely playing with me. Perhaps he *would* come at the appointed hour. Should I not wait and see? For if Old Moldy did appear, it would mark *him* as the culprit. And my heart would be the lighter.

In truth, I *wanted* him to show up, *wanted* him to be a traitor. Even as I wanted Sary to be innocent. Had I become like my father, full of theatrical fantasy? Was I wishing, as Sary spoke of it, for an Ali Baba world?

I had barely come to this conclusion when Mr. Snugsbe appeared— it must have been about five o'clock of the evening—and allowed there was someone above who wished to speak with me.

Taken by surprise, I said, "Who is it?"

"Mr. Snugsbe doesn't know him. Nor would he give a name. He no doubt correctly surmised that Jeremiah Snugsbe's coat is of no significance."

"Does he have a wooden leg?"

"No."

Puzzled, I climbed the stone steps into the nave. A moment's glance and I saw that the man desiring to speak to me was none other than Chief Inspector Ratchet. As I saw him, I knew I should reveal—perhaps was *obliged* to reveal—my knowledge about Sary.

I darted a quick look over my shoulder to see if Mr. Snugsbe had followed me. He had not. Even so, in that same moment I made up my mind to wait and see—for myself—who, if anyone, might appear at eight o'clock that night.

I approached Chief Inspector Ratchet with caution. "Did you wish to see me, sir?"

He considered me for such a long moment, I had the impression he was trying to read my mind. All he said, however, was, "I'm here to inquire whether anyone walked through the gate."

I knew perfectly well what his cryptic question meant: Did Sergeant Muldspoon indicate he was the chief traitor?

But I said simply, "I delivered the message."

"And the response?"

Perhaps if he had pushed me, I might have given a different answer. As it was, I replied, "It was not clear."

"Ah! Then what do you think we should do?"

"Nothing," I burst out. "In fact, I don't think there's any need for you to be here."

He studied me, then held out a police rattle. "Just in case."

I shook my head. "I won't need it."

"In case," he insisted, all but forcing it upon me.

Not given a choice, I took the rattle and was rude enough to turn my back upon the inspector and descend into the crypt. Such was my frustration that I dumped that rattle into an empty urn at the bottom

of the steps. It spoke too much of what I'd have to do if Old Moldy did *not* come.

I returned to my polishing chores.

I had been working some eleven hours when the city bells must have tolled seven. I say "must have" because I didn't hear them deep in the crypt, where I was polishing silver, spending much time on a large Communion plate. When Mr. Snugsbe appeared, the lamp that lit my work was burning low.

"The bells have struck, Master John," he confided. "You are free to go."

I set down the plate. "Is my coat still fitting?" I asked, feeling a deep weariness.

Mr. Snugsbe extended an arm, picked up the plate, and scrutinized my work. "Mr. Snugsbe has rarely seen a coat fit so well," he informed me. "In contrast to the coat *he* wears, which is always too big for him."

"Has Mr. Snugsbe considered going to a tailor?" I said, referring to him as another person in deference to the way he spoke of himself. "His coat could be taken in."

"For the coat to be taken *in*, Mr. Snugsbe would have to be taken *out*," he said, his face suggesting great pain.

"The result might be a better fit."

"Mr. Snugsbe doesn't know if that would work. A boot or a glove: Such articles come on and off with ease. A coat requires massive unbuttoning. According to Mr. Snugsbe's general theory of coats, once a person achieves his majority—say, twenty-one years, or twenty-one buttons, if he has a coat—he will fit *it* rather than the coat fit *him*. He is, as it were, an oyster in his shell, which may be pried apart only at the peril of life itself."

I did consider telling him I expected to meet someone at eight o'clock in the church, but I decided against it. It would, I suspected, provoke much talk of coats. At the moment my mood was ill suited for that.

"Then I hope to see Mr. Snugsbe in the morning," I said, and after bidding that singular gentleman a pleasant evening, I left him in the crypt. Believing, as I did, that he slept there, I wondered if he did so in his coat. Surely, upon his death, he would be buried in it.

On the way to the upper level I passed the urn where I'd left the rattle. On reflection, I put the rifling plan in with the rattle, my thought being that I should take no chance of losing it—or having it filched from my pocket. That such an action suggests the contradictory state of my mind, I readily admit.

The evening services having been concluded, the nave was perfectly empty, perfectly still. The building's great age, dimness, and quietude made me feel too young, too vulnerable to meet the challenge that lay ahead.

Unsure if I should simply wait out the hour in the church, I chose to seek some air. I had been underground for most of the day, and the truth is, I was finding it hard to breathe, hard to deal with the passing time, hard to stay calm. An image came to mind of the slow ticking clock in Great-Aunt Euphemia's vestibule. Like time on that clock, I was being dragged forward. Toward what, I hardly knew.

Outside, the lamps around the Tower punctuated the heavy fog,

which was creeping slowly up the hill like an unrolling blanket. The air, however, was no colder than it had been in the morning. I found it bracing.

Among the buildings visible over the Tower walls, I could see a few twinkling lights, reminding me that the fortress was not completely deserted. The White Tower of 1078 stood as strong and implacable as ever, like a historic ghost. While I did not believe in ghosts, *I* was haunted with thoughts of traitors.

Restless, I strolled down the hill past the outer gatehouse. When I passed the lone Beefeater on guard, I began to regret telling the police to keep away.

But then as I thought about it, why should I trust them, either? Virtually everyone—Mr. Tuckum, Sary, Inspectors Ratchet and Copperfield, Brigit—*all* had been trying to use me, trying to bring pressure on Father. Even Father was trying to use me! I suppose I could say I was angry, but the closer truth is that I felt miserable.

I continued on along the long wharf that fronted the Tower. Here, the river fog was thickest. I could just make out an assortment of boats, mostly at anchor or tied up. Then I saw a small steam launch nosing out of the mist toward the riverbank. It must have been screw driven, for I saw neither sails nor paddle wheels. I observed what looked to be a furnace mid-ship—red sparks drifting from its funnel—and even a few men, at least one at the bow, one at the rudder. Then I heard the splash of what I presumed to be an anchor. The launch ceased moving. But sparks still flew, suggesting it did not intend to stay for long. So deep was my sense of isolation that just the sight of the little boat with its small crew provided some comfort. It allowed me to think I was *not* entirely alone.

I gazed down at the Traitors' Gate, the tide lapping with cat licks against its weighty portcullis. The next moment I felt a sudden chill as it occurred to me how close I was to meddling in treason. How glad I was then that the rifling plan was not in my pocket!

Determined to remain steadfast, I made my way back to All Hallows certain that I'd wasted enough time—that it now had to be close to eight o'clock.

Using the small side door, I entered the church and stood at the head of the nave. A few flickering candles in widely spaced wall sconces provided some little light, creating long, shifting shadows that poked about the ancient structure like softly prying fingers. The double row of pale yellow columns reached into high obscurity while the lead tracings of stained-glass windows, as if to challenge the evening gloom, managed some small winking radiance of their own. The church was not merely quiet, but utterly devoid of sound—as if life itself had passed into the solemn sleep of unmeasured time. I saw no one. Still, I had to admit someone *could* be there, lying on a pew, invisible to my eyes. I lacked the desire—and courage—to check.

Instead, after some thought, I chose to sit and wait in the farthest back pew, at the far side of the south aisle. By so doing, I would be *behind* anyone who entered through the vestibule. It seemed likely that a newcomer would look down the nave, toward the altar, not toward the back or side, where I would be waiting and watching.

So it was that I hunched down, resolved to stay until it was beyond time for anyone to appear. I knew whom I wished to come: Sergeant Muldspoon. How curious, I thought, that I wanted my enemy to appear!

But what, I asked myself, would I *do* if Old Moldy *did* appear? I'd have to confront him *alone.* How? Simply show myself? Try to hold him? Surrender the plan? Oh, why had I told Ratchet I did not need the police? Foolish boy! For what if the schoolmaster did prove violent? I considered fetching the rattle, but I feared it was too late to budge.

The truth was—and I finally was willing to acknowledge it—I did *not* know what I should do in any instance, and I was also very frightened.

But about then the City bells chimed the hour of eight.

ೋ◉◍ು

CHAPTER 45
I Make an Astounding Discovery

As always, there was a cacophonic swelling, a metallic clanging and sounding of bells, arching into a deafening crescendo, only to gradually diminish to less, to nothing, to none, until the ensuing silence encased the solemn soul of stillness itself. Hardly daring to breathe, remaining where I was, I kept my eyes fastened to the door.

How much time passed, I am not sure, but quite suddenly, I was sure I heard footsteps in the outer entry. I listened harder. I could have no doubt: Someone was approaching.

I stared, wide-eyed, as the door swung open. A figure stepped into the nave. My heart pounded.

I could see nothing of the person's face, though I sensed it was a man . . . a tall man at that, with a top hat. He appeared to be all in black, but the view was so steeped in shadow, I could not tell for sure.

Whoever he was, he hesitated at the inner door as if searching for someone. When no one else appeared, he walked down the central aisle. I listened for Old Moldy's distinctive *clump*. I could not hear it. At the same time I spied something in this person's hand that looked very much like a sword.

Halfway to the altar the man stopped and turned. Doing so, his face was caught in a flicker of candlelight.

I gasped. The man was bearded.

It was Copperfield—which is to say, it was the man *pretending* to be a police inspector.

Though dumbfounded, I had not the slightest doubt that he was looking for me and that he was there to lay hands upon the rifling secret.

Oh, how I then regretted my telling Inspector Ratchet to keep away! But because I had done exactly that, I knew it was my responsibility to confront this man.

I'm not sure how long I watched him, trying to determine his identity. I failed at that. There being no choice, I gripped the pew before me with both hands and stood up.

"Were you looking for me?" I called out, my voice echoing down the nave.

Taken by surprise, the man leaned sharply in my direction, staring into the shadows, his patently false beard dangling from his chin.

"Who's that?" he cried.

I could not identify the voice.

"You know perfectly well who I am," I returned. I could see now—and was greatly relieved—that what he held in his hand was not a sword, but an umbrella.

He leaned forward again, squinting. "Oh, it's *you*," he said, straightening up. "Why are *you* here?"

His question struck me as odd. "This is my place of work," I replied. "Why are *you* here?"

He considered my remark and me momentarily, then shouted: "Impertinent boy! Who are *you* to question *me*? It's not as if I haven't warned you! You may be quite sure you shall pay the consequences!" Finally, as if dismissing me, he called out, "Snugsbe! I must see you."

That he should call for Mr. Snugsbe was a further bewilderment to me. None of this was making sense. Emboldened, I thought to

slip out of the pew and move down the aisle, making sure I remained between the man and the entryway.

"You are not a police inspector," I said as I advanced. "Tell me who you are and why you've come."

He did not deign to answer my demand. Instead, he moved down the aisle away from me, toward the altar.

"You've come for the secret, haven't you?" I said, my rising anger giving me strength.

He continued to ignore me.

"Didn't you?" This time I shouted.

"Mr. Snugsbe!" was his only return. "Come forward! I must see you!"

With growing frustration, I yelled, "Who are you?"

At this he halted and pointed his umbrella right at me. "Boy," he cried, "you shall keep away from me!" Then, again disdainfully, he turned his back on me.

I was not to be denied. I darted forward and snatched at the sleeve of his cutaway jacket. "Tell me who you are!" I shouted. "And why you have come!"

He whirled about, lifted his umbrella, and brought it down hard upon my shoulder. Though it hurt, the blow was not enough to keep me from making a grab for his false beard. As if sensing what I intended, he struck out again, this time smiting me on the chest. I reeled from the sharp blow, but I was now so infuriated that I dove at him, wrapping my arms about his lower legs. He tottered and fell hard upon the stone floor.

Though we were both thrashing about, he was able to pull one leg free and kick me on the side of the head, hard. Momentarily dazed, I rolled away onto my back. He twisted around so that I was looking up at him. As I did, he staggered onto his knees, lifted his umbrella, and prepared to strike again.

I lifted my arm to protect myself.

Suddenly, someone appeared from behind him, grabbing his arm with such surprise and strength that the man dropped his weapon.

It was Sary.

There was no time to be astonished. The man was now struggling with the girl, trying to pull free. Small though she was, Sary more than held her own as I leaped up and flung myself onto the man's back, reached over his shoulder, grabbed his beard, and yanked it away. It came with ease.

"Sary!" I cried. "Let him go!"

She backed away. In a fury the man swung around toward me. That was when I saw his face.

Mr. Nottingham!

The two of us stared at each other.

"Insolent boy!" he cried out. "Ham-fisted clod! How dare you assault me?"

"You lifted your umbrella to strike *me!*" I cried, panting with the strain of it all. "You told me you were a police inspector. Inspector Copperfield, which you aren't! You were warning me, scaring me about I know not what!"

Mr. Nottingham glared at me with utter contempt. Then he took time to regain his dignity by dusting his jacket and straightening his waistcoat and neckcloth. "You are talking complete nonsense," he said once he'd adjusted himself. "I've come here lawfully to receive an accounting of your work that I might report to Lady Huffam. Now, of course, it shall be my very *great* pleasure to inform her that whereas your father attacked me verbally, you have done so physically."

He smiled coldly. "You may be quite certain, *young* Huffam, that from this point forward Lady Huffam shall have *nothing* to do with you—nothing in the slightest!"

"My goodness," intruded a soft, gargled voice. "What is happening here?"

It was Mr. Snugsbe, looking quite bewildered as he turned from me, to Mr. Nottingham, to Sary, then back again to Mr. Nottingham.

"Snugsbe!" the man cried. "I call upon you as a witness. This boy attacked me!"

"Mr. Snugsbe," I said, "it was *he* who attacked me."

"I am afraid," the churchman said softly, "that Mr. Snugsbe saw nothing. But then, being within his coat, he fails to see a great deal. Perhaps it's a loss. But when Mr. Snugsbe considers the modern world, he doesn't think so. The more one sees, the more one is forced to do. Mr. Snugsbe *doesn't* do. Perhaps someone might explain what has happened."

"This man came to purchase my father's secret," I said, pointing to Mr. Nottingham.

"Your father's *secret*!" Nottingham exclaimed with scorn. "Your *father* has absolutely no secrets that I should *ever* want. I came here to see Mr. Snugsbe that I might have a report about you. Well, no need for him to issue *any* report now. None. I'm quite prepared to issue my own. Mr. Snugsbe, dismiss this boy forthwith. That is an order. I speak for Lady Huffam."

I could see Mr. Snugsbe wanted to retreat into his coat as he looked at me, then at Mr. Nottingham. "Mr. Snugsbe," he said, "without removing his coat, requests the cause."

"I told you," said the solicitor, "he attacked me."

"Mr. Snugsbe merely inquires: Did you give him reason?"

"Of course not!"

Mr. Snugsbe looked at me . . . not, I thought, without some compassion. All the same, he said, "Alas, Master John, I fear your coat has become unbuttoned. You stand quite naked to a hostile world, and for that Mr. Snugsbe offers his deepest sympathy. He can provide no garment of his own. Mr. Snugsbe has but one coat. And that coat does not even have pockets. Only buttons."

"Good," said Mr. Nottingham. "That's done!" He pointed at me with his retrieved umbrella. "I warn you not to waste a moment of time appealing to Lady Huffam. You may be quite sure she will not see you. *Ever!*"

That said, he turned to Mr. Snugsbe, said, "Good evening, sir," and clutching his umbrella, he marched directly out of the church.

After a moment Mr. Snugsbe sighed. "It's only what Mr. Snugsbe was suggesting might happen," he said. "Sometimes Mr. Snugsbe believes Mr. Snugsbe is not as resolute in his life as he might be. Perhaps it's *because* of his coat. People speak of an old shoe's comfort: It's nothing to an old coat's."

"But why," I asked, "did he wear a disguise to come here?"

"Mr. Snugsbe tried to explain: Mr. Nottingham is one of those men who has been fated to wear a *wrong* coat. The result? He's forever seeking to make alterations, an actor who does most of his acting *off* the stage."

He turned to Sary. "Mr. Snugsbe extends his compliments and asks: Who are you?"

"Name is Sary, Sary the Sneak. I was 'ere lookin' after 'im," she said, nodding in my direction.

"Do you know this . . . person?" Mr. Snugsbe asked me.

"Yes, sir," I said. "She's my friend."

"Indeed. . . . But insofar," he said to me, "as your employment here has been terminated, there is very little that Mr. Snugsbe can say or do. As you know, Mr. Snugsbe does very little, *ever.* At best he can wish you a well-dressed evening—indeed, a well-dressed *life.* Of course, you are always free to partake in this tranquil and sacred house, a closet, so to speak, for souls *and* coats. Farewell."

He turned and with small, slow steps, descended down the dark stairs toward the crypt.

I watched him until he was gone and only then turned to Sary. Feeling full of relief, I had to smile. "You were sneaking after me."

"A good thing too," she said, all grins. She pointed to the pews down front. "I was lyin' low in a pew. Was that yer Inspector Copperfield?"

I nodded. "He's connected to my aunt. Nothing to do with wanting the secret. Nothing."

"I'm glad for that," she said.

"I need to sit for a moment," I said, taking a place in one of the pews. I was content to regain my breath, thinking all the same that I must go and retrieve the plan before I left.

Sary slipped into the pew just in front of me and knelt over its back so she could look down at me. "Where's that strange fella gone— the one bein' swallowed by 'is coat?"

"Mr. Snugsbe? He works here. He went back to his crypt. Where he sleeps, I think. He'll not bother us again."

Sary looked at me. "You went off this mornin' in such a 'uff," she said, "I didn't know what to know."

"I was upset."

"'Bout what?"

"That man—Mr. Nottingham—came to me early this morning at the inn. Pretending to be the inspector again. Warning me. I . . . I thought it was you who told him I was there."

She looked at me, her eyes all but laughing. "Why should I do that?"

Not wanting to say what I had thought of her, I shook my head to dismiss the question. "I see now it was the only place he knew I might be staying. In fact, I now remember: It was *I* who told him I was there. He was just trying to goad me into doing something ill so he could report it to my great-great-aunt. And he's succeeded. There shall be no more help from her."

"And 'e's got nothin' to do with the spyin'?"

I shook my head.

She said, "I've been sneakin' after you all day. So I knows you went to that teacher o' yers. Watched you talkin' to 'im. But I couldn't get close enough to 'ear what 'e said to you."

"He said . . . nothing."

"Nothin'?"

"Nothing to suggest he was *not* interested. Nothing to say he *was*. So . . . I told the police not to come here."

"You did?" She laughed. "'Ow come?"

"Because I didn't think he would come."

She gazed at me. "Who do you think *will* come for that plan?"

"No one . . . now."

She grinned. "That's where you're all wrong, John 'Uffam. 'Cause, you see, I 'ave come."

‎⸎⸑⸎‎

CHAPTER 46
I Follow the Traitor Through the Gate

"Of course you did," I said, sitting back with relief. "I see that. And . . . Sary, I'm truly thankful you did."

"Then I guess you can repay me."

"How? I'm afraid—you heard it—I've just been dismissed. I wasn't even paid for my two days' work."

"It ain't money I wants," she said.

I looked at her. "I don't understand."

She grinned. "You can give *me* that secret plan."

"What . . . what do you mean?"

"I need it," she said, looking very serious.

"*You?*"

She nodded.

"Why . . . why would . . . you want it?"

"'Ow else am I goin' to get to Australia an' to me pa?"

I stared at her.

The silence in that church seemed as heavy as lead. For then I knew that all those things I had thought about her—those things I did *not* want to think—were, in their way, true. I looked at her face and, even in the shadowy gloom, saw the fierce cockiness I first had observed in her. I felt sick—sick at heart.

"See," she said, "when I began knowin' 'ow many folk were after the secret an' the way Inspector Ratchet was 'avin' the fits over it, I could sniff pots o' money to be 'ad. Tremendous pots."

"But those others? O'Doul, Farquatt, Muldspoon . . . ?"

"Oh, sure," she said, grinning widely. "Them blokes want the plan too. But looky 'ere—just like that Morgiana in yer Ali Baba story with all them thieves, guess *I'm* the only one who played the game right."

"But what would you . . . do with it?"

"Just said. Sell it for 'eaps o' money."

"But . . . that would make you a . . . traitor!"

"Traitor to what? You think the Queen's world is my world? What's the Queen to me? Not a mite! I'm just a girl sellin' watercress on the street. Only I guess I got somethin' better to sell than that, didn't I?"

I stared at her. "You can't possibly get anywhere with it."

"Course I can. Didn't you just tell me you sent the police away? Along with that Nottingham? An' that coat fella? An' ain't there a boat waitin' for me just down the hill? They'll take me right off an' away."

I remembered the little launch.

"Sergeant Muldspoon might come."

She shook her head. "I told you, I *was* close when you went an' spoke to 'im. Not that *you* noticed. Yer type don't notice much. Folk like me, we're all too low for yer high eyes. I waited till you left an' then walked right into 'is school—fancy that, first time I ever was in a school—an' told 'im 'e'd best keep off. Said it in front o' all them boys, too. Don't think 'e liked that. Told 'im it were a trap if 'e came." She grinned again. "A traitors' gate."

"Was he the one who bought up my father's notes?"

"'E was," she went on, tickled with all she knew and had done. "Just usin' the others to get the plan."

"For whom?"

"The Roosians. Or somethin' like. Who cares? No more than anybody cares for the likes of me. You takes care of yerself an' yer family. Well, I better do for mine, too. Don't 'ave no rich great-aunts."

"Who do you intend to sell the secret to?"

"Don't know. Don't care. They talk funny, not like me, that's all I know, savin' they promised they'd get me to Australia."

I just gazed at her.

She held out her hand. "So, Master 'Uffam, you best give over the plan. I know you 'ave it. You said you did. I'll say this for you: You're 'onest."

"They'll catch you."

"If they do, they'll put me in prison. Do you know what 'appens there? Give me a number. Put a 'ood over me face. Say I can't talk to anyone. *Anyone.* Preach at me. Make me work like a slave. Walk a treadmill to nowhere all day. Or turn a crank to shift a ton o' sand. You know about all that?"

I shook my head.

"That's me point. Sweep us off the street. Yer kind don't care to know, do you? I'd sooner die than 'ave all that 'appen to me. I'd rather do what Brigit was too feeble to do. So don't you worry, John 'Uffam—they won't catch me alive. Anyways, I'm goin' to find me pa. Australia can't be 'alf so bad as 'ere. Least we'll 'ave each other."

I looked at her and—eyes full of tears—whispered, "I don't want you to."

"Awful sorry," she said, "for playin' with you. John 'Uffam, you're as good a bloke as I've ever liked to meet. You been fair. An' you tells the best stories. I'll tell you what: Why don't you come to Australia with me? Be me best pal? I like you. Fairer to me than I to you, I admits. Only first off you need give me that paper." She held out a dirty hand.

"I don't have it."

She started. "Where is it?"

"I hid it below. In the crypt."

There was no grinning now.

"I could thrash you," she said, "if I want. I'm small, but I'm strong."

"It's . . . it's unwomanly."

That brought back her grin. "But I'm not a woman, see. Not yet. Bein' a girl, I can still do what I wants."

I decided she was right. All the same, I thought I should stall for time in hopes it might help in some way. "I'll show you where the paper is," I said.

"You do that. An' no dodges." She lifted a fist and held it before my face. "I'm powerful set on gettin' it. I'm on me way to me pa, so I'll not likely stop now."

"I'm sure. This way," I said, edging out of the pew and making for the crypt. She came along with me, staying close.

At the foot of the stone steps a single candle burned. I had to stop and peer about, trying to find the urn in which I'd put the plans. "Over there," I said, finally seeing it.

"Fetch it," she said.

I went forward. She remained close.

When I came up to the urn, I put my hand in, to feel both the rattle and the paper. The rattle, I knew, would be useless down here.

Sary saw me hesitate. "Get it!" she snapped.

I pulled out the paper. She held out her hand. Hesitating for a moment, I gave it to her. She unfolded the paper and stared. "This it? I can't read."

"It's what my father wrote and drew."

She folded the paper and tucked it in her right sleeve. "'Ope my new friends can read. Now then," she said, "I'll be goin'."

"Sary," I pleaded, "you mustn't. It's treason."

"John 'Uffam," she said, "I tol' you I like you well enough, but if I 'ave to, I'll go *through* you."

I stood there. I think I even lifted my fists.

Sary grimaced, balled up her hands, lowered her head, and charged. She struck me hard in the chest, and I, not ready for such an attack, was thrown back. She darted past me, or at least tried to, but I reached out and grabbed hold of one arm of her jacket. She swung round and brought down her fist so hard upon my hand, I was forced to let go. She dashed for the steps.

I leaped back for the urn and snatched out the police rattle, then ran after her. She was ahead of me, of course, almost at the steps, when I saw Mr. Snugsbe rise up before her. Exactly where he'd come from, I don't know. Perhaps his place of sleep. What mattered was, he was there.

"Mr. Snugsbe," he said, "has no desire—"

Sary crashed right into him, almost bounced off his greatcoat, and stopped. In the instant I made another grab at her jacket. This time a sleeve tore off in my hands.

Free of my grasp, she darted past a bewildered Snugsbe and raced up the steps. I threw what I had of her jacket at Mr. Snugsbe and charged after her.

By the time I reached the nave, she was bolting down the south aisle toward the entry doors. She reached them before I did and was out of the church in moments.

I kept right after her and saw her race down Tower Hill. She was heading for the river where the fog was thickest. To the little steam launch, I was sure.

As soon I reached the top of the hill—with no stopping for breath—I began to twirl the rattle furiously. Its clacking shattered the foggy silence—*cak–cak–cak.* . . .

As I ran, I saw the shadows of men appear from all sides of the hill and Tower, but the mist was so thick, it was hard to know who they were and where they were heading. I didn't care: I was certain I knew where Sary was going—the wharf by the Traitors' Gate. It would allow her to reach that boat.

I heard more rattles, which told me that it was the police who were following. Thank heavens! Chief Inspector Ratchet had not heeded my request.

Stopping on the wharf, the Traitors' Gate to my left, I stared out into the water. I was just in time to see that little steam launch pulling away out into the River Thames, spewing sparks like hot confetti. I'm not certain I saw Sary, but I know I heard her voice.

For no one else would have cried out, "'Ey, John! Don't forget me. This girl 'as a 'eart too!"

CHAPTER 47
I See an End to It . . . Almost

I was still hearing her words when Chief Inspector Ratchet caught up with me, bull's-eye lamp in hand. He aimed the light into my face, its brightness making me shut my eyes.

"Who was it?" was the first thing he asked.

"Sary," I said.

"*Sary!*" he cried, and swore. "I should 'ave known," he said. "Who was she workin' for?"

"I don't know."

"Don't you?" he demanded.

"No, sir."

He sighed. "Did she get the secret?"

"I don't know that, either," I said. "Maybe not. We need to go back to the church. She left part of her jacket."

"Come on, then," to which he added: "A good thing we ignored you."

I had nothing to say.

When we arrived at All Hallows, we found Mr. Snugsbe in conversation with Mr. Tuckum.

"'Ave you the girl's jacket?" demanded the chief inspector without ceremony.

Mr. Snugsbe held up the sleeve. "A man's—or woman's—coat," he said, "*is* his destiny."

I plunged my hand down.

And came up with the plan.

I handed it to Chief Inspector Ratchet. He unfolded it, glanced at it, nodded toward Mr. Tuckum, and left the church without another word.

My first thought was that he was angry with me. But when I thought about it, I realized he was angry at himself. Sary had fooled him—and everybody.

Most of all, she had fooled me.

လ⊚⊚ယ

Of course, there *was* more.

Next day Mr. Tuckum informed me that Brigit's brother was gone from London. Did he go to Ireland or America? By his own leave or forced? I never learned.

For her part, two days later Brigit herself took me aside. Weeping, she begged me—without confessing what she had done—to forgive her sins. She was not sure they were sins, she explained. She was only wanting to help her family, her *two* families, as well as her oppressed land.

For my part, I was willing to forgive and forget.

Sergeant Muldspoon closed down his school and left the country quickly too. Again it was Mr. Tuckum who told me. The word was that Old Moldy was engaged by the Imperial Russian Army as an artillery instructor.

Mr. Snugsbe? He and Mr. Tuckum became good comrades, talking no doubt of old-fashioned coats.

Mr. Nottingham? I suppose he went on as before, playing various roles of his own creation before unsuspecting audiences, never winning much applause. I never—knowingly—saw him again. Who knows on what stage he performs?

As for my father, his circumstance was odd. Though it was clear to authorities just who Mr. O'Doul was, the law being the law—as Mr. Tuckum eloquently explained—there could still be no release from the writ of debt. Apparently, Mr. O'Doul had to withdraw it himself or the repayment had to be at least offered to the court. If the money was not claimed, the writ would go forfeit, yet it first *had* to be paid.

But since O'Doul was gone, my penniless father remained in prison. There things stood.

A week after the events that led to Sary's escape, I was at the prison when I learned *I* had a visitor.

Surprised, I went to see who it was and found William/Wilkie. My great-great-aunt, he said, wished me to visit her.

"For good or ill?" I asked, reluctant to attend another abusive scolding.

He only looked at me, replying, "You shall see." I could read no more in his otherwise eloquent eyebrow.

So it was that I found myself once again in my great-great-aunt's presence. She was as huge as ever, surrounded by her medicines, waited upon by her maid.

"You sent for me, my lady," I said, my head already bowed to take on her attack.

She inhaled deeply. "You have acted well," she said.

That, coming as a surprise, made me look up.

"Have I?"

"So I have been told by my friend."

"Mr. Nottingham?" I asked.

"Chief Inspector Ratchet. He informed me you were a hero and urged me to reward you suitably. You will receive a gift of three hundred pounds. From me."

"My lady, you are more than kind," I somehow managed to say through my astonishment.

"I am exactly that," she said. "I am. It's the least I can do for the last Huffam."

As I was leaving, I turned to William/Wilkie at the front door. "She proved generous after all," I said.

"Not so," he whispered. "It was Inspector Ratchet's doing. He knows my lady. I know him too, and he told me much. It appears the government wished to reward you for saving that secret—about which I know nothing—from our enemies. But the authorities did not desire to make the circumstances of your reward public. The government therefore gave the money to Lady Huffam, with specific instructions that she give it all over to you—in her name."

"Truly?" I cried.

William/Wilkie looked at me and lifted his eyebrow, which I understood to mean: *You may believe it.*

I gave the money to my father and insisted he present it to the court. This he did, but only after much pressure from Mother and me. Since there was no Mr. O'Doul to claim it, the money was refunded back to him and he was set free, of both prison and debt.

Truth to tell, he resumed his life: clerk, amateur actor, husband, and father—in his own fashion—and richer by three hundred pounds.

As for my sister, she did marry Mr. Farquatt. No doubt he was a spy, but he *had* worked for the Credit Bordeaux. And since he didn't actually *commit* any crime, he was only asked to leave England. Which he did. With my sister. Even spies—as I saw—can fall in love, marry, and prove good husbands. He and Clarissa live in the little town of Surlot. Letters are exchanged. Mother has visited, but she is unhappy with my sister's French ways and her grandchildren's French language. Letters and visits grow fewer.

I, too, resumed my life—at a different school, to be sure, but otherwise much as before—excepting I am always wondering at what lies beneath stones . . . and at the life that's all about me.

I must admit that from time to time I think about these events and, most often, about Sary.

I wonder if she ever reached Australia. If she ever reached her pa. And if I might not go out someday and find her.

But where would I begin? I didn't even know her full name.

In that regard I had wanted to ask Inspector Ratchet, but since he was completely out of my life, I turned to Mr. Tuckum—who had become a kind of uncle to me—to see if he knew Sary's surname. She had only told me in jest once that it was "Waitin'."

"I don't exactly remember," he said. "Sagwitch. Magwitch. Lagwitch. Something like. Why did you need to know?"

I was not about to tell him.

Thus the days and months and years pass. Sometimes that melody my father used to whistle, "Money Is Your Friend," comes to my mind. It seems to mock me. But mostly when I think of all that happened, I think about Sary. For while she *had* fooled us all, she did *not* get the secret. I had saved her from becoming a traitor. What, I wondered, had she done and thought to do once she discovered that fact?

And . . . would she come back?

Most of all, I often think of Sary's last words: *This girl 'as a 'eart too!*

I can only hope.

For *I*, at least, will not be a traitor. Not to her.

ᥕᥩᥰᥫ

AUTHOR'S NOTE

The full name of Charles Dickens, the extraordinary Victorian novelist, was Charles John Huffam Dickens. Not only was the name of my hero of this book taken from the writer, one of the key incidents of the writer's life—his father's imprisonment for debt—lies at the heart of this story. That said, there is little in the imprisonment of Dickens's father that truly resembles the events of this novel, although Dickens's father did work for the navy establishment and his aunt did provide sufficient financial help to enable him to get out of prison.

Other aspects of Dickens's life have been used here. The year 1849—when this story takes place—marked the publication of *David Copperfield*, the author's famous autobiographical novel.

Police Inspector Ratchet is based on a real person, Police Inspector Field of Scotland Yard, one of Dickens's good friends.

The Tales of the Genii, by Charles Morell, was an eighteenth-century rendition of the work we know as *The Arabian Nights*. It was a favorite of the young Charles Dickens and is mentioned in some of his work, including *A Christmas Carol* and *David Copperfield*.

Sary's last name, Magwitch, derives from Abel Magwitch, the

formidable transported felon and benefactor of Pip from Dickens's novel *Great Expectations*. But Sary's world of poverty was very real indeed. Consider: Even in 1873, four fifths of Britain's land was owned by just seven thousand individuals.

London street names and locations are based on contemporaneous maps. But both the City and the Church of All Hallows Barking (to give its full, proper name) were different in 1849 than they are today insofar as the area was severely bombed during World War Two and since then much rebuilt.

Of course, the city of London itself—so central to Dickens's life, work, and art—is, in its way, a central character here too. Having read much about London—in fact and fiction—having often visited, having lived there, and having had one of my sons born there, the city holds much allure for me. One recalls Samuel Johnson's much-quoted remark: "When a man is tired of London, he is tired of life; for there is in London all that life can afford."

It has been my great desire to bring some of that life to these pages.